Dancing with the Monkeys

John Samson

TSL Publications

The monkeys danced as the humans made love, their questioning faces peered through the branches, while their small bodies swayed gently in time to the rhythm of the people below. Curious eyes at odds with the wry smiles that touched their lips.

It was not the first time the humans had come to this spot, and it was not the first time that they had mated on the rocks under this tree. Speckled sunlight found a way through the leaves and bounced off the lily-white skin of the male's buttocks creating a shimmering tea doily effect. This fascinated the baby of the troupe to the point where it wanted to go and investigate, only to be pulled back by its mother, a protest noise being swallowed in the face of its parent's warning glare.

The grunts and groans of the couple mixed with the snuffles, shrieks, whoops, trumpets, whistles, tweets, cries and calls that littered the African bush.

The landscape rolled away for miles beyond the tree that protected the couple from the harsh sun and in which the monkeys danced. Scrub and ugly squat thorn trees tinged the wan-brown dust with grey-green tones while, on a far horizon, clouds began to build. A storm was brewing, the earth's natural response to the heat that built up during the day.

The rhythm of the bodies picked up pace, almost as if they sensed the impending storm, the volume of their sounds increased as they urged each other on.

One monkey nodded knowingly to another and soon the couple began to shudder and moments later exuded a groan of satisfaction. The second primate nodded back, an acknowledgement that the humans were nearly done and that the troupe could start to move around freely again, no longer trapped by the hypnotic antics of those creatures below.

James Aitken slid off the body of his lover, a layer of sweat had made their skin slick. He wanted to revel in the afterglow. He wanted to enjoy these moments as he slowly climbed down from his stimulation high. But his thoughts, freed from the needs of lust, were bombarded with feelings of guilt. He knew that his parents would never approve of this union. They would never understand, their concerns would be for their standing in the community.

He sighed inwardly, angry at his inability to enjoy the moment. But then he caught her eyes looking at him, milky black yet shining with love. Her rich brown skin catching the glow of the smile on her lips.

He touched her cheek gently, his anger evaporating to a fine mist which now only slightly blurred the outline of the feelings of love that returned. 'Miriam,' he whispered her name.

Away on the horizon lightning flashed and a muted rumble stretched lazily across the sky. He looked up.

'We'd better get back,' he said, and she nodded sadly. Going back meant separation. Going back meant him going into the opulent farmhouse to sit at the large dining room table where fine china and crystal glasses rubbed shoulders with sparkling silver cutlery and a stiff upper lip attitude. Going back meant she would don her servant's demeanour and, alongside her mother, would serve dinner, the colour of her skin demanding subservience, demanding apartness.

They stood and dressed slowly, unaware of the consequences of their recent actions, unaware of the life that these stolen moments had created.

The monkeys watched them leave, hearing the creak of the wagon wheels as it carried the couple off along the dusty road. Once they were sure the humans had gone, they emerged from the trees, moving quickly, arms darting out to grab at leaves and berries in a feeding frenzy before they had to retreat into the depths of the trees again when the storm broke.

James Aitken was born three years after his parents moved from England to British East Africa in the latter part of the 19th century. His father, Richmond, was not a particularly adventurous man, but like his future son, he could not wait for the marriage vows before satisfying his carnal urges. He found it easy to seduce women and have his way with them. However, an encounter with a young woman called Agnes Kenilworth resulted in a pregnancy which would produce James' older sister. In order to avoid a scandal, Richmond and Agnes had hastily married before clambering on the first boat out to the colonies, their mumbled 'I do's – said before an almost sympathetic vicar – sounding more like an apology to God and to each other for their indiscretion than vows of commitment.

Freed from the eyes of those they knew, Agnes' belly could grow in peace amongst the strangers on the boat to whom they lied with ease about the marriage date. But the unborn did not want to know the peace that Richmond and Agnes sought. It kicked and squirmed in the womb, angry at the upheaval and sea-sick from the constant rocking of the ship. It felt to

Agnes that there was a note of resistance to its future in the kicking, as if the unborn feared this far off land that they were heading to.

A few months after arriving in Mombasa, Agnes experienced a difficult birth in a sweltering land, surrounded by strange sounds and foreign smells. She struggled to expel the additional cargo they had smuggled across the sea, and it took five hours before her exhausted adult cries gave way to the lung-filling squeal of a newborn. Rosemary-Jane was given her grandmother's names as a kind of atonement for the hurt and shame Agnes felt she had caused.

The weary midwife was too tired to notice the reluctance with which Agnes took the baby while Agnes herself was wracked with guilt at her inability to embrace her child with the love due to a first born. But this creature that curled, unfurled and re-curled had become a physical manifestation of the reason for her exile and she could not shake this association. As she fell into a deep and exhausted sleep following the birth, she folded herself into a blanket of depression.

Richmond smoked the requisite cigars with the men in the Mombasa Club. Most were still strangers to him as he began to feel his way in this bewildering land. His money – an early instalment of his inheritance – allowed him access to the club and, more importantly, to the contacts he could make there. It was a place where the established settlers met to laud their local knowledge over those 'just off the ship'. But they did so in a reserved way, secretly hoping that this newcomer would become a friend. Kindred spirits were scarce this far from the motherland and newcomers of good breeding were few and far between.

'Have you considered coffee farming?' Edward Sinclair asked as they stood around sipping a celebratory brandy. He was one who had been 'in country' on for years.

'Coffee farming?' Richmond welcomed the change in direction of the conversation having quickly tired of pretending to be excited about becoming a father.

'There is some good land near Kilimanjaro down south, close to the border with German East Africa. Very fertile. I can put you in touch with someone if you are interested.'

Richmond was interested and, while Rosemary-Jane settled down for her first night unprotected by the womb, her fate was sealed over cigars, brandy and a cup of coffee ordered late in the proceedings to mark her father's decision.

The weeks that followed Rosemary-Jane's arrival were difficult ones. Agnes hardly left her bed, her mood rarely lifting enough for her body to follow. She felt hollow, the loss of the recent inhabitant inside her became a metaphor for the loss she felt having been wrenched from her family and life in England. A moment of madness and everything had all but ended. She didn't even know if she loved Richmond. Yes, he was handsome, a dashing character who commanded attention at dances but, despite what was said in the romance novels that she hungrily consumed, love was something more than a physical attraction. The bitterness she now felt, thousands of miles away from the idyllic settings of these novels, was sharp but not without a degree of self-reproach.

She hated Richmond, the way he had seduced her, his arrogant charm and the self-confident manner in which he had taken her. Despite this, she could not help believing that she should have done more to resist. Even back then, she knew that she did not love him, but her mind had fought weakly against his advances and her body, blindly driven by some unseen force, had capitulated to curiosity and a shaking anticipation that she had never known before. Even now, as she fought with the sheets of the bed, she still could not understand how that physical closeness to a man and his touch on her naked skin, had so powerfully and completely switched off her brain.

She felt alone in a foreign land. Her confinement prevented her from meeting the ladies of Mombasa and Richmond was never there. He was always off somewhere organising the purchase of this wretched coffee farm that he kept talking about. But even if she had felt the urge to leave her bed, she did not want to meet the women here. 'They would know,' she said to herself. 'Nothing will be said, but they would know that my being here does not stem from a sense of adventure, but from an indiscretion.'

The wet nurse Richmond arranged was a dour woman who fed Rosemary-Jane milk soured by a sense of abandonment directed at a husband who had 'headed inland', leaving her with his debts to pay.

The native servants – and there were many of them – were men and women whose politeness sat like a wall between her and a vague sense of companionship. She tried early on to make some conversation, to feel a sense of connection with a fellow human being.

'Do you have any children?' she asked one of the maids who brought in her breakfast.

'No, Mam.'

'Where did you learn to cook?' This to the elderly chef who, she could not deny, had excellent culinary skills.

'I do not know, Mam,' the solemn reply carrying the clear message, 'I do not want to tell you, Mam.'

She should, she knew, turn to Rosemary-Jane to find meaning and solace in this world so strange and distressing to her, but each time she picked up her child, she felt a kind of revulsion, an undeniable sense that this baby was responsible for all that was wrong in her life and this resentment was too strong for her to find it in herself to forgive.

The bed offered sanctuary. There, she did not have to try and face her new circumstances. There she could lose herself in her lukewarm existence. She would have welcomed a warm life filled with love and happiness, but likewise she would not have complained if she had become icy cold, unable to feel or care. But she sat in an in-between world, one of wanting but one that could not supply.

The sanctuary of her bed did not last long. Richmond, patient at first, understanding the need for the 'weaker sex' to recover from the ordeal of giving birth, began to grow restless and soon the restlessness turned to anger.

'Pull yourself together, woman,' he commanded gruffly. So, Agnes reluctantly dragged herself out into the social world of Mombasa, fear of her husband robbing the bed of its comfort. She met the other wives and was polite, but distant. She did not want to form friendships with them, knowing that she and Richmond were soon to head out, away from this small society into a wilderness where her exile would be complete.

After her initial protesting cry at being dragged from the womb, Rosemary-Jane settled down to accept her fate. She would lie quietly, staring at the world around her, drinking in her surroundings, alert eyes greedily trying to consume as much of life as she could.

Despite the reluctance with which the wet nurse gave up her milk, Rosemary-Jane would smile and feed sparingly, showing her gratitude through satisfied gurgles and a soft purr of contentment which slowly melted the heart of her provider. She began to be cuddled before and after feeding time and she would snuggle close to that surrogate mother, winning her over by degrees.

'You poor, poor thing,' the nurse said as she held Rosemary-Jane close to her a few weeks after starting in the job. 'Your mother does not love you; your father does not know you and soon you will be taken away and I cannot go with you.'

Rosemary-Jane smiled contently. She had wriggled her way into the heart of this woman hired to nurture her, but instinct told her that she had to win over the other woman in her life, the one who occasionally came to stare coldly at her. There was always confusion mixed with an aura of dread in that woman's eyes as if she were trying to make sense of what life had done.

Rosemary-Jane would stare back, a faint smile playing on her lips, her small arms reaching up as her hands grabbed at the air above her, trying to pull Agnes into her life.

But her mother remained resolute in her distance.

Business happened at a slower pace here in the colonies than it did back home, and this frustrated Richmond. The heat of the day sapped energy from everyone and everything as the land seemed to throb in time to a secret beat hidden in scalded skies and hazy landscapes. He tried, at first, to push things along, suggesting meetings at times when those in the know would be wanting to settle down in the shade of the veranda.

Richmond took a while to realise that they were not being difficult or deliberately stalling, this was just how things worked here. It did not help that Agnes was not settling well. He had hoped that after the pregnancy she would devote her time to the child, freeing him to go about his business. But she had become sullen and distant, both towards him and their child.

He barely noticed Rosemary-Jane. A baby was woman's work and as the child almost never cried, she was practically invisible to him. Occasionally, however, he would find himself staring at this alien creature in its cot, the strange weaving of its limbs casting an hypnotic spell on him. At moments like this, he would smile, just slightly, without knowing he was doing so.

But there was a lot to organise, and he could not be distracted by his daughter. Getting title to the farm, transportation, not only for his goods and chattels but also for his family. He needed letters of introduction to people in Voi, the strangely named town not too far from where the land was. Would there be staff to help on the farm? Where could he buy seed? Did he need seed for coffee farming? How would they get the crop to the right markets? He spent a month away, travelling to see the land and making arrangements, pulling on all his business acumen in an industry he knew nothing about.

He did not know if he could trust those around him. He barely knew them and, other than Edward Sinclair, whom he had been given a letter of introduction to via the most tenuous of connections, he had no basis, other than his own gut instincts, on which to build any confidence.

Questions were asked and answers came slowly, but the plan fell into place bit by bit and, six months after Rosemary-Jane had taken her first breath, Richmond packed his family and began the slow journey east, towards the German East Africa border and the town of Voi.

Small ugly hills and a blunt, mind-numbing heat greeted them as they lumbered into the town. Agnes felt the grime of sweat and dust cling to her as the disappointment of her surroundings dragged her mood to new depths. She had not had great expectations about this, but Voi killed off what little hope she had of a vaguely comfortable future. It took all her energy not to turn around and head straight back to Mombasa, leaving Richmond standing there where they had been unceremoniously dumped by the hired waggoner, Rosemary-Jane in her basket at his feet.

But she had no money, no family here. The journey back to Mombasa would be as long and as hard as coming had been and even if she did make if back to Mombasa, what could she do? How could she escape back to England? She could, she supposed, try to get passage on a ship, but that would require money.

She turned to look at Richmond, anger rising within her. She expected him to be his usual arrogant and confident self, standing surveying the land as if it were his kingdom to rule over. Instead, she was shocked to see a little child masquerading as a man. He looked crumpled, like something discarded by the world. He was as bewildered by all this as she was and, in that moment, she felt something shift in her emotions. This was *their* exile. They had both contributed to it, it was their punishment to be endured together.

She knew that she would never love him, not like the heroines in her books loved their heroes. But she now knew that her future happiness depended on a partnership with him. They both needed each other if they were to find even vague comfort here.

She touched his arm. 'Richmond?' she said bracing herself for an angry rebuke.

He started slightly and looked at her, the faintest expression of gratitude flittered across his face before the mask of confidence fell again as he reminded himself of his duty.

'Yes,' he said, 'I must find Mr McCallum, the farm manager. He was supposed to meet us.' He strode off, leaving Agnes feeling quite lost. But it was not long before he returned with McCallum at his side. The farm manager was a burly Scotsman who had overseen the farm for a few years. Agnes was not sure if his reddened face was a result of skin sensitive to the sun or from a love of the bottle. Despite his rugged appearance, he was well mannered, removing his hat and bowing slightly when introduced, his voice mellow and his accent soft.

'Welcome to Voi,' he said taking her hand. 'Do not be put off by its appearance,' he gestured at the settlement, for it could hardly be called a town, 'it serves us well. The scenery does get better as you head towards the German border.'

Agnes nodded her thanks for the welcome and for the words of comfort, but she kept her eye on Richmond, watching him, searching for a way in.

'And who is this pretty young lass?' McCallum asked, bending over the basket.

'Rosemary-Jane,' Agnes tried not to sound too dismissive, but if she did, McCallum didn't notice.

'Oh, she's a fine one indeed,' he said, letting the tiny hand that reached out wrap itself around the finger he offered. 'Strong grip. She'll be good on the farm, she will.'

'Do you have any children, Mr McCallum?' Agnes asked, feeling the need to respond to the attention her daughter was getting.

'Me? Ach, no. I'm a single man.' There was something not right about his response, a kind of sadness, or was it some sort of anger? Agnes was not sure. 'We had better get you inside,' he said, 'you have had a long journey, it is very warm, and the middle of the road is no place to be standing. We will go to your place in the morning when it won't be so hot. You don't want to be arriving there all worn out now, do you?'

Agnes could not help wondering what he meant by that.

Richmond paced the length of the veranda. The day was drawing to an end, the exhausting heat calming as the sun disappeared behind the low hills and the sky began to colour, light blue at first then the flaky clouds took on a pink hue. The noises of dusk emerged from their hiding places, the high whine of mosquitos, the clicking of crickets and the far-off bark of zebra contrasted with the low belly-laugh grunt of the hippopotamus in the nearby dam.

Refreshed by a bath and a shave, and with a gin in his hand, he felt ready for the task ahead. The doubts and fears that had crept up on him as they waited for McCallum in Voi had slowly evaporated as they trundled out of that rough and ready settlement. The scenery changed as they bounced along the rutted road. The drab brown and scrub of Voi giving way to rich golden-brown soil punctuated by proud baobab trees that lifted root-like branches, twisting and twirling their way to the skies as if in praise of their creator.

He had travelled the road once before when he came to view the farm, but now he had his family with him. It was not the family he had planned, nor the home he had dreamed of being lord of the manor of. But he was a practical man and knew that he needed to make the most of the situation. He had no one else to blame for his predicament and feeling sorry for himself was a luxury he could not afford. He only hoped that Agnes would emerge from her dark mood now she had seen the house.

He sipped his gin and stared into the growing darkness. A breeze carried the gentle smooth aroma of roasted coffee, a pleasant fragrance in which his future fortunes lay. He breathed in deeply, holding it in his lungs for a long while before expelling it slowly.

'The air is good here.' He had not heard Agnes come out and turned to greet her. She stood in the large doorway that opened on to the veranda, her pale skin like moonlight in the dull glow of the lanterns.

'My dear, you look lovely,' he held out his hand to her and she came and stood beside him, looking out at the hills. The clouds had taken on an orange and red tinge and wrapped themselves in the deep blue-black blanket of a sky speckled with dots of emerging evening stars. She let him put his arm around her waist, but felt the formality of the touch, feeling in that physical contact her unspoken pledge to support but not love him. She moved slightly closer as if understanding that he too was prepared to try if she was.

'Ach, now that's a lovely sight,' McCallum emerged from the house. 'You two look quite at home already.' He raised his glass. 'Here's to many happy times in your new home.'

Rosemary-Jane lay quietly in her cot. She could just about make out the low mumble of voices on the veranda, the rich tones of her father, the soft feminine ones of her mother and the slightly gruff laugh of the stranger who had peered at her after their long journey.

A mosquito whined somewhere beyond the thin netting that lay over her cot. Her eyes followed the sound, a slight sense of fear registering in her face. She had heard the sound before, but this was a different place with different surroundings.

She wanted to cry, to bring one of the adults into the room to comfort her, but experience had already told her that there would be no love in the comfort. It would be cordial at best, irritated at worst.

Her small hands reached out as if to grab at the noise, wanting to trap it inside her palm and squash it till it could no longer bother her ears. Frustration grew as her efforts proved fruitless and she gave a low whimper, stopping quickly as the whining ceased momentarily.

And in the few seconds of silence, almost unheard, came the slight susurration of something slithering across the floor and out of the room. Rosemary-Jane listened to this new sound, her face wrinkling up as she puzzled over what it could be.

Running the farm was hard work, but Richmond embraced it with vigour. Agnes had taken to the house immediately and its airy brightness and the richness of the beauty in the surrounding hills seemed to breathe life back into her.

While Richmond rode around his land, inspecting his crops, supervising the harvest, watching over the drying and roasting process and overseeing the shipments to Mombasa, she, with the help of an elderly local servant called Tobias, started to take control of the garden around the house. A beautifully manicured lawn emerged and flower bed borders appeared. Roses and azaleas splashed colour around the place while a row of trees stood sentry, marking the end of her domain and the start of Richmond's.

She would never regard herself as happy. Happy was something that she had left behind in England. But as she surveyed her handiwork a year after they arrived, she felt content. Her relationship with Richmond had become a platonic friendship. They slept in separate rooms, but felt at ease in each other's company, chatting freely over breakfast and dinner and she had even taken to giving him a sisterly peck on the cheek when he left in the morning to go about his work, but there was no deeper intimacy than this.

With just the servants around, there was no need for pretence, but whenever McCallum or other neighbours visited, they put on a show of togetherness which seemed so natural that no one suspected they were anything but a young couple in love. One or two did wonder aloud, but never in their company, why they had not yet had more children. That seemed like the right thing to do. Some guessed that Agnes might have become barren after having given birth to Rosemary-Jane, although nothing was said. But, the servants knew.

Rosemary-Jane was brought out for visitors to coo over, but was otherwise largely ignored, left in the more than capable hands of Hannah, the 'house girl' who was a year or two younger than Agnes. She cared for Rosemary-Jane as she would her own child while Agnes and Richmond took little interest in their daughter, their shame at what she represented consistently in their conscience. But things were changing slowly. The snake they had found in Rosemary-Jane's room – although not poisonous they were told – shocked Agnes and awoke in her a heightened sense of guilt about her lack of care for her child. Despite this, she still could not bring herself to love her as she should.

Letters came from home carrying news of family and friends who were fast becoming hazily remembered ghosts. The distance from home and difference of this land to England, turned those they had left behind into alien concepts. Agnes diligently wrote back, painting a picture of some comfort, but with enough sense of their exile and the pain thereof. Her aim was to make those back home feel some guilt at having banished them.

By the time Rosemary-Jane died, aged a little over two and a half, she had managed to melt some of the ice over her parents' hearts. It was enough of a softening for them to feel a sense of loss and to mourn, not just superficially for those around them to see, but with some feeling. However, the grief was never as intense as it should have been for one's offspring. Only Hannah truly grieved for the loss of this surrogate child.

It was not a snake that took Rosemary-Jane, but rather the almost inaudible mosquito that managed to creep through a tiny tear in the net above the cot in search of the child's sweet blood. Rosemary-Jane did not feel the bite but fought hard against the resultant malaria. Her tiny fists closing into hard little balls as she shook with fever, as if trying to punch this unseen enemy.

Her fight lasted just a week, during which her mother fretted. Agnes refused to let Hannah feed Rosemary-Jane the foul-smelling quinine brew that the servant suggested was needed, dismissing it as some sort of local witch-doctory and ended up barring Hannah from Rosemary-Jane's room. By the time Agnes realised that it was serious and had sent for the European doctor from Voi, Rosemary-Jane was too far gone. The doctor, a polite

German, did what he could, his European prepared quinine being accepted without question by Agnes.

McCallum showed a soft side to his gruff Scots-ness at the graveside, blowing his nose nosily on a large handkerchief while refusing to let the welling in his eyes overflow. The women from the surrounding farms gathered around Agnes, fussing and sympathising while the men stood solemnly with Richmond, smoking cigarettes and sipping their drinks. None had the heart to tell them that had Agnes let Hannah dose Rosemary-Jane with the local 'medicine' the child may well have survived. But Agnes overheard when, after everyone had left, the German doctor in his blunt but polite English chide Richmond, saying that quinine was what was needed when malaria struck. He went on to explain what symptoms they should look out for should either Richmond or Agnes fall prey to the disease.

Agnes felt the guilt of her prejudice lie heavily on her, seeing herself as some sort of ogre who had denied a child the necessary medical attention it needed. Richmond was not moved, re-assuring Agnes that she had done the right thing.

'You can't trust the local medicine men, they are barely tamed savages. What can they possibly know about diseases and cures? And that German doctor is a fool, but Germans are all like that. I will make enquiries about English doctors in the area so that at least we can get proper treatment should the need arise in the future.'

Agnes feigned agreement, nodding as he spoke, but the guilt did not ease and she found herself longing to hear the young laughter that Rosemary-Jane had coloured the house with, or even the odd cry when she stumbled and hurt herself. The silence as she walked through the large rooms seemed to accuse her and she knew that she needed to fill the void.

Richmond was reluctant but understood when Agnes broached the subject of having another child. To him it was her maternal instincts driving her. She needed someone to mother, so he agreed to her request, but not without some reservations.

The process of conceiving was awkward and fraught with self-consciousness. Where Rosemary-Jane's had been passionate – animalistic almost – and done under the cover of too much alcohol, James' creation was formal, sober and embarrassing.

But their efforts paid off and it was with a sense of relief that they returned to their separate beds, Agnes to pray that this child would be healthy and Richmond to contemplate how he may satisfy his carnal urges

– which had not diminished much since leaving England – without having to go through that again.

They were stuck with the German doctor to look after Agnes for the duration of her pregnancy. He was professional and never once mentioned the quinine issue. He was pleased with her progress and an English midwife was found in Voi which made Richmond happy. Agnes hoped that Hannah would be around when the time came, but three months into her pregnancy she noticed a thickening of her servant's features and at six months it was confirmed that Hannah would not be too far behind Agnes in delivering a child.

James' birth was easy. The storm that broke soon after Agnes' waters prevented the midwife from getting through and by the time she managed to get to the farm Agnes had, with the aid of two servants, given birth and was holding the child close to her breast.

Although not showing much emotion, Richmond was secretly pleased that it was a boy. The neighbours arrived soon after with congratulations, cigars and cognacs to welcome James, the newborn.

Three weeks later at a village half a day's walk away, Hannah gave birth to Miriam.

Mindful of the neglect that Rosemary-Jane had suffered, Agnes was determined to make up for it with James and showered him with love and attention. She fought a wordless battle with her husband for time with the child, greedily wanting to hold on to James when Richmond arrived home from his day's work and insisted on spending time with his son before going to clean up for dinner. Despite the disconnection Richmond had with Rosemary-Jane and Agnes, he found himself drawn to the concept of a son. Here was a proper heir, one who would carry on the Aitken name and one who was not technically a bastard. Without realising it, he would head straight to his son's room each evening, eager to see what progress was being made.

'Build those muscles, my boy,' he would whisper. 'Coffee farming is hard work.'

James revelled in the attention, his chubby arms reaching out to be held every time an adult peered into his cot. He did not mind the colour of the skin of those looking in at him, contentedly settling into the arms of whoever would take him.

Hannah returned to work a couple of weeks after Miriam was born and

James took to her immediately as if he could smell the sweet milk in her breasts. His own mother's milk which he was being fed was nutritious but bland and he would paw at Hannah, hoping for a treat. But Hannah knew that would not be allowed.

On Sunday evenings, when Hannah returned from her day off and time with her own child, James would clamber to be with her, his little nose picking up on the scent of another baby and, when Miriam was old enough for Hannah to bring her to work, James, on seeing the scent made flesh, crawled rapidly over to her, his limbs pumping furiously, the speed of his efforts nearly knocking a bewildered Miriam over as he clumsily tried to hug her.

Hannah secretly laughed, but the reaction of Agnes prevented her from doing so out loud.

'James, come here!' The command was sharp, and Hannah could see the disapproval in Agnes' face, a kind of fear that contact with the dirty muddy brown colour of Miriam's skin would pollute the fair white purity of James'.

The little boy turned at the command and stared at his mother, as if daring her to stop him. It was the first of many acts of defiance. In most things he was a good child, but here was something he felt strongly about and no all the disapproving words from his mother would stop him.

The confrontation lasted a short moment but felt like a lifetime to Agnes as she wrestled between the love she had for her son and her concern that mixing with the locals was not good form. But she saw the determined look in his eyes, and something told her not to try and win this battle. She softened.

'Gently, James,' she said, and he smiled a knowing smile, one that Agnes would come to love and hate as it represented a strong independent spirit, one that would serve him well in this country, but one, she could not help worrying, that could lead him to do things that would cause her pain.

She did not tell Richmond about the incident, a mixture of fear at what he would do and a sense that James would view it as a betrayal helping her keep their 'secret'. It was clear that James had identified Miriam as a friend and, Agnes argued against her doubts, it would be a temporary thing. He was still a child, barely starting to walk and only capable of sounds that were mere outlines of words. He would, as he grew, become aware of the differences and start behaving properly.

The land around Kilimanjaro was fertile, the soil rich in minerals that had been deposited millions of years back by the now extinct volcano. The coffee that the farm produced was plentiful and made a smooth tasting drink that the other settlers in the area all praised and which found an easy export market.

Richmond learned quickly, helped by McCallum who could read the weather patterns and had an uncanny sense of when the land was at its best for planting. He had a good way with the local help, was fluent in their language and engendered a sense of loyalty in them. He knew exactly how to behave around Richmond and Agnes, being a friend, but not overly familiar, when there were no other Europeans around, but fading into the background when there was company.

It became customary for Agnes and Richmond to invite him to join them for dinner each Friday evening. Initially the talk was farm business and plans for the upcoming week, but slowly more topical subjects found their way into the conversations. It began with discussions about the train line being built between Mombasa and Voi, and what that meant for business. This then broadened into the wider topic of British expansion on the continent and the possibility and practicality of a Cape to Cairo rail route.

They discussed the situation in Sudan, a few thousand miles north of where they were. The slaying of Gordon of Khartoum still reverberated around the continent and Richmond wondered why the British Government seemed to be doing nothing to avenge this brutal event. McCallum, who was well read on these events, saw something in a Major called Kitchener who had led the Egyptian cavalry at the Battle of Toski a few years back.

'Why would an Egyptian revenge Gordon's death? And what sort of an Egyptian name is Kitchener?' Richmond wanted to know.

'Kitchener is not Egyptian, he's British,' McCallum responded, 'A tough nut by all accounts. They annihilated the Mahdi troops at Toski.'

'Cut off their heads, I hope,' Richmond said, shovelling a forkful of roast beef into his mouth.

'Richmond! Please. Not at the dinner table.' Agnes was tired of war talk.

Richmond chewed his meat and gave McCallum a look as if to say, 'these women can't handle the manly things of life.' Despite the look, he did change the subject back to farm work.

McCallum took to James as quickly as he had taken to Rosemary-Jane. He had been in Mombasa when the Aitken daughter had fallen ill and carried a sense of guilt with him that he had not been at the farm to help. He was not convinced that the quinine Hannah had tried to dose Rosemary-Jane with would have helped had it been administered. Yes, quinine was the best treatment for malaria, but death had come too quickly for the poor child. Either her system was not strong enough, or the strain had been particularly virulent. He had seen it with the farm labourers' children. Some survived, others didn't. But he could say nothing of this to the Aitkens.

He liked Richmond, found him hard but fair. He liked how his new boss had taken to the task of running the farm, eager to learn and keen to master all aspects of the job, but done with an acknowledgement that he could not take on board everything in a matter of days. That had been the problem with the previous owner. Fresh from the homeland, he had been a brash and foolish man, a know-it-all, who overrode McCallum on most issues and then blamed him when things went wrong. McCallum was glad to see the back of him and more than pleased when Richmond had first said, 'You're the expert, McCallum, what should we do?' But it had not been long before Richmond was putting his newfound knowledge into practice, acting like a boss, yet still leaving space for McCallum to contradict should it be necessary.

The burly Scot relished the Friday evening dinner invites. He loved having someone he could talk to about world affairs, a place where he could express an opinion, albeit gently. It broke the monotony of the lonely evenings he would spend during the week in his cottage a mile away from the main house. He liked the soft femininity that Agnes brought to his rough bachelorhood, and he delighted in the boisterousness of James as the little one clambered over his frustrations in a mad dash to be as surefooted as the adults around him and as he struggled to colour in his noise shapes with the details of words.

McCallum would watch the youngster as he sat wide-eyed, listening as Richmond spoke about current affairs. A slight frown would play across the boy's features while he struggled to understand the significance of the conversation till eventually, he would give up and, with a slightly huffy sigh, begin to wriggle. Then McCallum would, with an open arm gesture, invite the boy to sit on his knee and bounce him gently in the hope that this would remind him not to grow up too quickly. James would snuggle back into his childhood, letting the issues of the day's lessons bed down into his sub-conscious while losing himself in the attention he was getting from McCallum.

'The poison could have killed him. He's lucky to have survived.' The German doctor seemed unaware of the young, confused eyes that watched him. Neither did he notice the sharp reproving look he got from Agnes, a look that said, 'You should not be saying this so loudly in front of the patient.'

'But he will be fine in a week or two.'

McCallum stood beside Agnes, his eyes watery as if he were about to burst into tears. Agnes had come to recognise that look but could not fathom if there was a genuine threat of tears behind it or if it was just how the man looked when he was concerned.

Richmond lay with his head on the pillow, his eyes bleary, a weak smile on his lips, James curled up next to him.

'I should have seen the blighter,' his voice was thick and laboured.

'Ach, it's not your fault, Mr Aitken,' McCallum was quick to jump in. 'Those divils are cunning. They blend in too well, like the Mahdi in the desert,' he gave a small laugh which Richmond acknowledged. 'You were lucky though, there are worse snakes out there than the one that got you.'

Agnes did not see any luck in the situation. She had seen one or two snakes in the garden which Tobias had chased away. 'Not a danger one,' he had said in his broken English and with his crooked tooth smile. Agnes often wondered if a snake were a 'danger one' whether Tobias would acknowledge it.

There had been a great commotion when they had brought Richmond into the house after the bite. McCallum barked orders as he directed those tasked with supporting the dazed victim between them while Agnes fussed over those hurriedly preparing the bed for Richmond. A man had been despatched for the doctor and various potions – Agnes suspected local cures – were produced which McCallum quickly dismissed except for one which he quietly applied to the two small puncture wounds on Richmond's hand.

No one took much notice of James, who was five at the time, and who stood wide-eyed in a corner of the room, the urgency of the adults telling him that something was not right, that his father should not be sleeping at this time of the day, but he could not understand what it was. It was only once they had settled Richmond on the bed and the potion was applied to his hand that the initial whirlwind of activity calmed and McCallum assured Agnes, 'We got the divil that did this.'

'Hannah, please take James to his room,' Agnes said, not wanting to discuss 'divils' in front of the boy. But he would not go. Instead, he climbed onto the bed and snuggled up next to his father, the same defiant look on his face as that he had given Agnes when she objected to his hugging Miriam.

The snake bite was just one of a number of little setbacks the young couple suffered. A machine broke down just at the wrong time, a fire destroyed part of the crop, a leopard made off with one of the horses ('a highly unusual occurrence,' according to McCallum). Each served as a reminder of the power of this vast land, a warning to the Aitkens never to let their guard down. Richmond was stoical about things. 'Two steps forward, one step back is still progress,' he would say and McCallum would nod sagely.

'You can only tame this land by degrees,' was the Scots' verdict.

But the setbacks chipped away at Agnes, each a reminder of the great distance between this place and home. She dropped hints about returning to England where there were no snakes, where the sky was a gentle blue, not the harsh deep blue that hurt the eyes. She longed for a place where it actually got cold in winter rather than the easing of the heat they experienced here. She wanted to live somewhere where things were neat and ordered, unlike the wild untamed land beyond the small oasis of her garden. Rosemary-Jane was gone, her little body slowly crumbling to dust in a small grave around the back of the house, a grave that she never visited. When Rosemary-Jane had died, so too had the reason for being out here.

But Richmond had fallen for the place. Despite the challenges of snake bites, buffalo getting into the fields and the constant threat of locusts that those longer in the country spoke of, he found the hard work invigorating and the connection with the land life-affirming. He satisfied his carnal lusts with the local servant women, the threat of losing their jobs enough to buy their silence. He did, however, stay clear of Hannah. Her closeness to Agnes tainting her with the same untouchable aura that his wife exuded.

Sunset was his favourite. The heat of the day lost its sting, the sky would take on different colours – pinks, reds and oranges set against a blackening background, He would sit out on the veranda, the day's sweat and ache still clinging to him while he sipped his evening drink and watched the sun disappear over the horizon. He loved the sounds of Africa, the smells. Here he would recollect the woman he had been with that day, the dusky skin, the earthy odours, the startled and somewhat frightened look in their eyes as they submitted to him.

Occasionally he would wonder out the back of the house and stare at Rosemary-Jane's gravestone. He was never quite sure how he felt about his daughter. She represented so many things, the shame with which he had been forced to leave England, the glue that meant he was stuck with Agnes for the rest of his life, a thorn in his conscience about how they had treated her. But without her he would never have come to this paradise, he would still be stuck under his father's rule being slowly shoe-horned into the family business, a business that he had never really taken to. Rosemary-Jane had been an escape route and his younger brother, Winston, would have benefitted too as he was far keener on the business then Richmond ever was.

These thoughts always led him back to James. He wanted his son to grow up and take over the farm, but did not want to be like his father, insisting on the oldest son taking over the family business. He wanted James to want it. There were days when he would smile as he watched his son's curiosity turn into a big grin when he was given a small task to do. The workers all loved him and played along, finding odd jobs for the young lad.

'Here, take this bag of coffee to the kitchen,' McCallum said, giving him a sack of a size that was just about manageable for the youngster.

'Do you want to help sort out the beans, master?' the capable foreman said one day, sitting the boy on a barrel. He gave him a selection of beans. 'These are the top-quality ones he said, pointing at a group, 'they are for export. And those ones are not as good. They are for the local market.' He let James sort out another batch and praised him when he got it right.

These moments created warm memories for Richmond, but Rosemary-Jane's grave always served as a reminder of how merciless this land could be. He would sigh, swallow the last of his drink and head inside hoping that dinner would clear his thoughts.

James loved the freedom of the farm. He loved the attention and respect the staff paid him, revelling in the tasks he was given. But as much as he wanted their approval of him, he also wanted to prove to himself that he was capable of anything. He adored his father and loved his mother. He viewed McCallum as one would a favourite uncle, always glad to see him. Even when he was still a small child the sound of 'Unca Makim,' would ring out whenever the Scot arrived at the house and he would run over to be hoisted onto the man's shoulders, or scooped and swooped like an eagle, round and round.

His young mind sensed how the differences in skin colour affected social standing in the house but he rejected this hierarchy. To him Hannah was as much a mother as Agnes was. The elderly Tobias, who let him help with the gardening, replaced the grandfather he would never know and little Miriam, who was seen more and more around the farm as she grew, was a sister substitute for the cold stone memorial out back that he had no connection with.

But he soon learned to be cautious. His mother, in particular, and to some degree his father, disapproved of him being too familiar with the servants. So, he mimicked the way his parents spoke to them but only when his mother or father were around. When he knew that they were elsewhere and unlikely to interrupt, then he would revert to an innocent familiarity, behaviour which Hannah and Tobias respected.

As he grew, he became more confident about his surroundings and began to explore the world beyond the farmhouse, wandering off, sometimes on his own but usually dragging a reluctant Miriam in his wake. Together they developed a language of their own – a mixture of English and Miriam's waTaveta with some Swahili thrown in for good measure – which helped bond them further.

They would arrange to meet at landmarks beyond the general realm of the adults, then sneak off, clambering up the small surrounding hills, feeling like the king and queen of all they could see of the relatively flat plains surrounding these lookout points. Their expeditions, always led by James, became more adventurous and Agnes began to notice his absence, never realising that he was not alone. It was only Hannah who saw that Miriam was never around whenever James went missing.

'Where were you, James? We were worried.' He was six the first time Agnes voiced her concern.

'Oh, I was not far, Mama,' he lied, 'I was playing on the other side of the fields.'

'You shouldn't play there, what about the snakes?'

'I checked, Mama, the men in the field said there were no snakes there.'

That stopped the enquiries, but not the anxiety. James was fortunate and well aware of the fact that Richmond seldom, if ever, spoke work to Agnes. Had his father mentioned that he had been hard at work on that side of the field all day and had not seen his son playing there at all, then there would have been more questions from his mother.

The cordial arrangement between his parents was not unusual to James, he knew no other way of life so the separate bedrooms, the polite but loveless conversations, the lack of touch or affection that his parents displayed to one another were normal to him and provided opportunities for him to exploit as he weaved his way through a childhood that allowed him freedoms that, had he been brought up back in the motherland, he would not have been able to conceive.

One day, he and Miriam were nearly caught playing round an old, abandoned building on a far corner of the farm. They heard a horse approach and hid behind a low wall, peeking through a small air vent hole. It was not long before they saw Richmond with his trousers round his ankles and grunting as he thrust his hips between the legs of a reluctant local woman. While fascinated, the two youngsters instinctively knew not to say anything afterwards. They were not meant to be there and any mention of seeing Richmond would have revealed their wanderings. James sensed in the look on his father's face as he finished and tidied himself up that it was something that he should not have been indulging in.

'What were they doing?' he asked Miriam after the couple left.

Miriam smiled shyly. She knew but would not say. James pressed but got no joy and eventually gave up.

That evening he found his father out the back, drink in hand, staring at the strange stone that stood upright in the earth. He went and stood next to him.

'What are you doing, father?'

Richmond, who had not heard him approach, was slightly startled, but recovered quickly. 'Oh, just remembering, son.'

'Remembering what?'

'Your sister.' Richmond indicated the grave with the hand that held his glass, the amber liquid sloshing slightly at the movement.

'My sister?'

'Yes. Rosemary-Jane. She died before you were born. Malaria.'

James nodded. The way his mother had fussed over him a few months back when he had a fever suddenly making sense. The word 'malaria' had been mentioned a lot at that time and his mother had argued with the doctor with the funny accent who kept insisting it was just a cold.

His fever had lasted just a couple of days and had, as the German doctor diagnosed, turned out to be just a cold. He was back out and playing within a matter of days and none the worse for the experience.

He stared at the headstone. 'Do people turn into a stone when they die?' he asked.

'What?' Richmond took a moment to follow his son's thoughts, then laughed dryly. 'No son. The stone marks the place where they are buried. We put them in a box, then dig a hole, put the box in the hole and cover it back up. The stone is put there to remind us where they are buried.'

'Will you bury me and put up a stone when I die?' James asked, a serious look on his face.

Richmond chuckled. 'I hope I never have to bury you, my son. You should live longer than me. You will have to put up a stone for me. But not for a long time yet, if God wills it.'

James was quiet for a while, then asked, 'So who will put up a stone for me?'

'Your children will.'

'And if I do not have children? Uncle Malcolm does not have children, who will put up a stone for him?'

'If a person does not have children, then it is the duty of someone who loves them to mark where they are buried. You do love Uncle Malcolm, don't you?'

'Yes.' The boy did not hesitate in answering.

'Then maybe it will be you.'

James nodded slowly, beginning to understand.

The next day, when he saw McCallum, he told him in all seriousness, 'I will bury you and put up a stone up when you die, Uncle Malcolm. Do not worry.'

'Ach, that's mighty kind of you,' McCallum answered, somewhat confused by the pledge.

The question of schooling caused tension between Agnes and Richmond. She did not want to send James to Mombasa to the boarding school there. She wanted to keep her son close where she could monitor his health, watch his growth and, she eventually admitted to herself, maintain some 'white' company. She liked McCallum, but he only came around occasionally. Richmond was out in the fields most of the day and wasn't really company. The distance to neighbouring farms and Voi were too great for any regular contact with other settlers, so Agnes filled the void by spending as much time with her son as she could. The thought of him being away for months on end filled her with dread at the emptiness she knew she would feel.

Richmond was pragmatic if not a little stoical. He too did not want to face a house without James, but the boy needed a proper education.

'We could get a tutor to come here. I am sure there are many good ones we could employ,' Agnes tried.

'It's not just about being taught,' Richmond replied somewhat agitated that his authority was being questioned. 'It's about getting to know people, making friends.'

'But he has...' Agnes stopped herself, realising that she could not tell Richmond about James' friendship with Miriam. It would just make him more determined to send James away. '...he has Malcolm and us for friends,' she ended lamely.

'He needs to make friends his own age, forge relationships that will stand him in good stead in the community in the future,' Richmond replied. 'He is going to Mombasa and that is final.'

Agnes started to retort but thought better of it and gave a resigned nod.

McCallum was clearly upset when they told him, but he put on a brave face.

'The laddie will do well, I am sure of it. I'll miss him around the place, but it's the right thing. He needs the education.' He did not see the look Agnes gave him, a look of one betrayed and angry. She had half hoped that the farm manager would come up with an excellent reason why they should not send her son away, but he had only repeated Richmond's frustratingly logical reasoning. As her emotions cooled, however, she knew it was a harsh judgement of McCallum and that he and Richmond were right, it was what was best for James.

James had mixed emotions. There was a certain excitement about going away. It was a sort of acknowledgement that he was a grown boy now, one who could be trusted on his own in the big wide world. But there was also a nervousness brought on by this. What would the big wide world throw at him, and would he be able to cope? It was only much later that a third emotion hit and that was when he realised that he would be separated from Miriam. There was no way he could raise this as a reason for not wanting to go, so would nod and act excited whenever someone mentioned his upcoming departure.

They held a special dinner the night before he left. McCallum came over and Hannah prepared a feast of roast chicken, James' favourite, with fresh vegetables. She had even managed to bake a cake for the occasion. Miriam helped with serving the dinner, the first time she had performed any servant duties, and it felt odd to James as he watched her carry away some plates, her face as closed to emotion as that of Hannah, Tobias and all the other workers on the farm. He felt that a door had been shut in his face and, only when he saw his mother watching him, did he close the door from his side and once more feign excitement and happiness.

Mombasa was bewildering. Before leaving home, James' experience of any sort of urban living was Voi and the occasional trip to Taveta. Both were small settlements with dusty roads, a few stores and markets and where only a few hundred people lived. Mombasa had wide, building-lined streets and people everywhere. It felt claustrophobic after the space and freedom of the farm. The school, although an oasis of calm away from the bustle of central Mombasa, was stifling with its rules, dormitories and shared ablution areas. He did not like it.

But he soon learnt that he was not alone in this. A good number of the newcomers were boys from the farms, boys used to their own vast kingdoms now stuffed into a tiny space where one jostled for attention and had little room for solitude. The first night some cried but James was determined not to. The older boys, who had been through all this, were either sympathetic and tried to comfort the new boys, or were scornful and mocked them. James would watch with fascination in his later years at the school when he realised that those of his group who mocked the new boys had been the ones who had cried the most and those more stoic amongst them on that first night were the ones who reached out to help ease the tears of the new intake.

But that was a few years away and, as James lay in his uncomfortable bed staring at the dark ceiling and blocking out the whispers and whimpers of those around him, he recalled Miriam in her servant role and with it came the realisation that his life would never be the same again. Only then did he feel the tears run down his cheeks, but he did not sob.

His mother had taught him to read and write, but books suitable for him were scarce and most of his reading had been from the family bible. School opened his horizons. Here there were books about kings and queens. There were histories of England, that mythical place his mother spoke of with much love and some sadness. As he read Shakespeare and Dickens, he tried to imagine the grandmother he had never met, living in the world described by these supposedly great writers. He found Shakespeare too sparse to place her into any of those stories and Dickens too dense and busy where she became lost in a dark and foggy London of his mind's making.

He enjoyed mathematics, the numbers seeming to fall into place, following what, to him, seemed a natural order. But he quickly realised that he was somewhat unique in this as few of the other boys grasped the concepts as well and as he did. He was soon being sought out to help with sums and equations. He didn't mind too much, especially when he struck up a friendship with Carl Muller, another 'farm boy' whose grasp of Latin outshone all the others and the two would spend hours tutoring each other in their respective specialities.

Carl came from a coastal farm down south near Tanga in German East Africa. There his German father, who had married an English woman, grew sisal. His father had a love of the romantic languages and had taught his son Latin from an early age, to the point where the boy was fluent and more skilled than their teacher. But Carl knew better than to outshine the teacher. 'It will only make him hate me,' he confided in James. James would watch his friend during the Latin classes and soon learned the facial expressions that said, 'No, that is not right,' or, 'Yes, that conjugation is correct.' But Carl would never voice any of this in class.

'If I put the correct Latin in the tests where Mr Browning has taught us differently, then he will just mark me down,' Carl explained.

'What would your father say?' James asked.

'I won't tell him. He'll just cause trouble.'

James nodded, thinking of the lies he had told his parents about where he had been when he was off with Miriam. They wouldn't understand and it would just upset things if they found out. Carl's approach made sense.

Despite their friendship, James kept Miriam from Carl. While they talked a lot, discussing life on their respective farms and the differences between growing coffee and growing sisal, James suspected that Carl would not approve of his friendship with her.

⚱

As Agnes had feared, James' absence from the farm left a great void in her life. She found herself wandering around the house, touching things of his. She hovered in the dining room, her hands on the back of his chair, she cupped the rose that he had planted as a small child, bringing it gently to her nose, inhaling the delicate scent. She sometimes found herself standing in his bedroom, not recalling how she had ended up there. She would run her hand over the bedspread, her mind recalling his little face peeking over the top of the blankets when she had come to tuck him in.

She knew it was silly. She should not be like this, but where could she turn for comfort? Richmond was out in the fields all day and Hannah was too sensible a 'lady-in-waiting' to be a confidante. The emptiness reminded her how it felt when Rosemary-Jane died and, on her darker days, it felt to her like James too had died.

She moped around the house during the day, putting on a brave face in the evenings for Richmond, fearful that he would get angry at her silliness. He had been tetchier of late and she put that down to problems with the farm, things that he didn't want to share with her. She could not conceive that he too was missing James. Even McCallum seemed a little down in the dumps.

No one noticed Miriam as she was slowly dragged into the servant ranks on the farm. She was just another of the hired help, hardly seen by either Agnes or Richmond.

Hannah was the only one who was aware of her daughter's presence in the house and she fretted about it. She knew of the relationship between her daughter and the young master but did not know what to do about it. She had tried to tell Miriam not to become too friendly with James, but the boy was a force of nature, seeming to give Miriam no space to turn him down when he wanted her to accompany him as he explored the bush around the farm. He was the master and had to be obeyed, just like those other women she had heard of who had to obey Mr Aitken's demands, fearing that they, or their husbands would lose their jobs on the estate. She could not work out why but was grateful that he had never been interested in her.

She wished that Miriam could be excused from working in the house. It was a given that she would work on the farm in some capacity, but Hannah had hoped that some work would be found outside the kitchen. However, house servants got a better deal than those working as farm labourers, so it made sense that she organise for Miriam to join her indoors. She was well aware of the possible consequences but had little choice.

She was relieved that her mistress appeared not to notice Master James' closeness to her daughter and relieved that the young master was now away at school. She hoped that while there, he would forget about Miriam, hopefully finding one of his own kind to fall in love with. So, while Agnes counted the days till James returned for his first holiday, eagerly looking forward to it, Hannah hoped that day was a long time coming.

'What are you doing for the holiday?' Carl asked a few weeks before the school was about to break up. The two friends were sitting on a small embankment that overlooked the main school building. It was late in the afternoon and the heat of the day was just climbing down from the angry state that it had been in since mid-morning.

The question surprised James. He was going home to the farm. Wasn't that what all the boys in the boarding house were doing? So many had been talking about and looking forward to seeing family again and he could not imagine that there were any other options.

'Going home. Why?'

'Of course you are,' Carl said. 'I meant what are you doing at home, on the farm?' There was something in the way he said it, a sort of sadness in the tone that made James wonder what his friend was getting at. However, feeling a bit foolish at having misunderstood the question, he went on to talk about how his mum would fuss over him, his dad would probably make him help out a bit with the farm work, but mostly he would be free to explore, maybe do a bit of hunting.

Carl nodded, recognising the similarities in their respective lives and when James asked what he would be doing, he shrugged and said, '*Ego hic moratur.*' James had to coax the English translation – 'I'm staying here' – from his friend. The banter as he struggled to work out what had been said seemed to ease the melancholy of his friend. James didn't forget about it and mulling over the answer, he began to realise that his friend was dreading the loneliness he was facing for the few weeks of holiday.

The farm south of Tanga was too far for him to go for the shorter holidays. He would only go home at the end of the year when they had six weeks off.

The answer to his friend's unhappiness was slow in coming to James, but when it did, he could have kicked himself for not realising the obvious.

'Why don't you come stay with us?' He asked the next day. Carl played it cool, pretending to mull it over and asking a number of times if it would be okay, but his eyes betrayed the reluctance he put into his words.

Letters were sent and replies came which confirmed that both sets of parents were in agreement with the arrangement. Had James been more advanced in years he may have noted a certain reluctance in his mother's reply. Agnes wanted James to herself but could not deny him this request.

With the holiday plans in place, James began to get excited about all the things they could do. He would take Carl round the farm, his farm, teach him about coffee, show him how the beans were grown, harvested, sorted, roasted, packed and shipped.

In the evenings Carl would sit and talk Latin to his father and McCallum and impress them with his knowledge. He would tell his mother about Shakespeare and Dickens and she would be so proud. The holiday was going to be perfect.

Hannah watched the young guest as he settled into his room. Master James was unpacking in his own room, but she knew she would have to re-organise everything once he was done. Neatness was not his strong point.

'This is Miriam, Master Carl. If you need anything you must ask. Miriam's English is not too good. She is learning still, so if she cannot understand, please come and find me.'

Carl nodded his understanding and thanked Hannah with barely a glance at Miriam who stood demurely just inside the doorway, her head down, studying the carpet. Hannah noted the stance and made a mental note to talk to her daughter about her posture when she got a chance. For the moment though, she was relieved that the guest took no interest in Miriam, She was yet to see how Master James would behave around Miriam now that he had been away for a while.

Having introduced Master Carl to Miriam, she felt it safe to leave her daughter to get on with her work. There were odd things that Miriam still needed to learn – her demeanour, more English and she still struggled to get the cutlery right when setting the table – but she had grasped the basics and would make a good servant in time. That was, of course if...

She knocked on Master James' door and entered on his command. 'Oh, Master James, your trousers don't go there. Here, let me sort that out for you.'

James grinned and looked at the pile of clothes on his bed which lay all jumbled up. 'Thank you, Hannah, I don't know what I would do without you. You know at school I have to do all this myself and the teachers get upset if we get it wrong. I keep getting into trouble. You will have to teach me how to sort things properly.'

Despite herself, Hannah could not help feeling a sense of pride in her work. The young master wanted her to teach him! She smiled and said she would be very happy to help, but later as the sheen of the compliment wore off, she remembered that this was all part of his charm. Master James would not be spending time learning how to sort out clothes. She would still be tidying up after him when the holiday ended.

She smiled as she realised how easily she had been taken in and, in a private moment, she found herself wishing that things in the land were different, that her daughter could freely mix with Master James and that it would not be frowned on. She dreamed of a world where her daughter could grow up and marry the man she clearly loved. But that would never be. Things were too set to be changed.

☙

'I believe your father farms sisal, Carl,' Richmond said at dinner that evening. He looked happy lauding it over the welcome home feast that had been prepared.

'Yes, sir, that is correct.' Carl was a little nervous in this strange setting despite Agnes and Richmond doing everything they could to put him at his ease.

'It's a good crop, I'm told. Lots of demand and easy to grow.'

Carl nodded politely. 'Father says that the land is so fertile one could grow just about anything here.'

Richmond smiled. 'Yes, he is right. Tell me, has he been in country long?'

'I believe it has been nearly twenty years, sir. He was to have settled in the Cape, but could not find a good farm, so came up north.'

'Just as well with the trouble they've been having down there.' Richmond sipped his wine.

'You mean the war, sir?'

'Yes, nasty business that. Those Boers are slippery characters. They need to be taught a lesson.'

Carl and James nodded although they knew little of the war other than bits they had picked up when the adults spoke of it.

Richmond went on to talk more about the war, about the tactics the Boers used and how it was unlike any previous conflict. He was almost quoting verbatim the newspaper reports he read, but the boys hung on to his words, intrigued with the romance of conflict in the way that only boys can be. James, enthralled by his father's talk, did not notice Miriam as she brought in the food dishes and cleared away.

☙

The holiday passed by in a blur as the boys played, explored, swam, lazed and helped a little with the farm work. McCallum fashioned them some wooden rifles and they would disappear into the surrounding bush, playing at being Boer and Brit, sometimes being the elusive enemy, hiding out behind rocks or bushes and ambushing poor unsuspecting guinea fowl, at other times they were proud British soldiers fighting for king and country, rooting out the pesky Boer soldiers. They held no particular allegiance to either side.

In the afternoons, when it got too hot for running around, they would swim in the small dam that served the farm and which was fenced off to keep the wild animals away. Here they would keep a watchful eye out for Boer raiders. His father had told them a story of British soldiers who were captured by the Boers while bathing in their underwear.

'There is a river in South Africa they now call Onderbroek Spruit, which the papers say is Boer for "Underpants River". It was named so after that debacle,' he had told them with a laugh, not noticing the disapproving look he got from Agnes.

'We cannot let this dam be called Onderbroek Dam,' Lieutenant James Aitken commanded one day as they took turns swimming while the other kept watch. No raiders came, but they did fend off McCallum with heavy fire from their wooden rifles and on one occasion when Miriam happened to walk near the dam, Carl went on high alert, but then dismissed the threat.

'Only a native woman,' he told his fellow combatant who nodded rather sheepishly and suggested that they finish swimming and go see if they could help with the coffee roasting.

A week before they were due to return to school, Richmond took them out hunting and taught them the basics about using a rifle. The thrill of firing a real weapon was more than compensation for the fact that they did not manage to kill any game. They came home chatting excitedly, oblivious of the bruising to their shoulders that the kick back from the weapon had caused.

Agnes did not approve. They were too young. But she knew better than to raise any objections.

'Nonsense,' she could hear Richmond saying, 'They're young men now, they need to learn.'

And maybe that was true, James was growing up fast and he would need to learn at some point, but she was not ready for him to be a young man just yet. She liked him as a boy and, with the time he spent with Carl, she felt she was missing out on the last days of his childhood.

It pained her even more when, on the boys' final night, Richmond said to Carl, 'You are most welcome to spend the short holidays here. No sense in you sitting around in Mombasa.' Agnes hoped that the boy would politely decline, but he clearly showed his excitement at the prospect, as did James.

She managed not to cry as she saw them off the following morning even though the pain of separation was made worse by James not wanting her to fuss over him. He kissed her politely but didn't hug, seemingly mindful of his new friend watching.

It was only as they drove off and she saw Miriam staring after the car that she could take some comfort from this new arrangement. At least James' friendship with Carl had made him forget his servant friend. But that did not stop the tears that she allowed herself when she was finally alone in her room. All she could hope for now was some time with her son when the longer holidays came.

Her hopes were dashed, however, as the time drew closer for the end of the year holidays. An invite came for James to spend time with Carl and his family, effectively four of the six weeks, leaving Agnes a miserly two weeks of having James to herself. And when those two weeks arrived, she found James in that no-man's land, caught between childhood and adulthood. He no longer needed or wanted to be fussed over by his mother and, with no Carl around, he was at somewhat of a loss in trying to entertain himself as he was not yet old enough to completely engage in farm work despite Richmond and McCallum encouraging him to do so.

Those two weeks were torture for him and he either moped around the house or headed out on his own to shoot at wild game with his wooden rifle. Sometimes he would catch scorpions in the small hills and then feed them to the monitor lizard he and Carl had found hanging out by the dam. He never thought to renew his friendship with Miriam who was now entrenched in the role of house girl and had little free time anyway.

In their third year, the boys were introduced to the pupils at the recently established school for European girls. Once a week they would traipse across town to be taught social etiquette and how to interact properly with members of the opposite sex. The last Saturday of each month was set aside for dances where they were taught the proper steps and the protocols for asking a young lady to be their partner.

James resented the weekly walk and having to endure the silliness of the dancing lessons. He struggled with his co-ordination and kept stepping on toes which did not endear him to others. It made him a target for good-natured banter from the other boys.

Carl, while not quite in James' league of clumsiness, was competent but mechanical. He got his timing right but lacked grace and flow. He was paired with Kate Edgeworthy, the daughter of a Mombasa based solicitor. She was a short, pretty girl with bright eyes, dark hair and a giggle that set Carl's heart racing.

At first James teased his friend when he talked about going across to the girls' school, his sense of anticipation clear in his tones. But as James began to realise that Carl was serious, he eased off teasing. Initially the change in his approach was brought on by confusion, not understanding the feelings his friend was experiencing. Where they used to talk about farming, hunting and playing at soldiers, now all Carl wanted to discuss was dances, ribbons in hair, smiles and giggles.

James' assigned dance partner was Elspeth, a slightly plump girl with bad breath, so he had no similar feelings to those Carl was having, making it difficult for him to relate. But over the weeks he would watch his friend interact with Kate and slowly he began to get some idea. His parents' formal relationship had not prepared him for this, so he struggled to process fully what was happening to Carl.

His confusion then turned to sadness as he felt he was losing his friend. Yes, they had time during the week to chat and play, but Kate became more of a presence through Carl's words and his sometimes-vacant stares. James hoped that when the holidays came, he would get his friend back, but Carl seemed worse. He dismissed playing 'Brit and Boer', saying that it was old hat and for kids. They swam a lot that holiday.

'I'm going to marry Kate,' Carl announced one day as they lay in the sun drying off. The monitor lizard, who had become used to the humans and sat nearby hoping for a tasty snack, turned its head to stare at Carl, an action mirrored by James.

'You can't marry her, you're too young. You're still at school.'

'Not now, silly. When we leave school and we are old enough.'

They were silent for a while, then Carl looked across at the lizard, his face turned from James to hide a cheeky grin and said, 'And you can marry Elspeth.'

'What?'

With some effort Carl hid his smile, turned back to James and with a straight face said, 'Elspeth. I've seen the way you dance with her. You two are a perfect match.'

James stared for a moment. 'You are joking, aren't you?'

'You don't have feelings for her?' Carl put on an incredulous face.

'No, she has bad breath,' James retorted.

'Well don't marry her breath then, just marry her feet.'

'Her feet?'

'You seem to love them so much, you are always trying to get very close to them.' Carl could not keep up his pretence at seriousness any longer and burst out laughing.

'You… you…' James launched himself at his friend and the two engaged in a good-natured rough and tumble, both of them laughing as they did so. The poor monitor lizard, startled by the sudden action, plunged into the dam and swam across to the far side to get some peace.

That night James lay awake in his bed thinking what it must be like to be in love like Carl was and wondered if he would ever fall in love like that.

While not liking it, Agnes got used to the fact that James was no longer a little boy. She took some comfort from watching him grow. Each time he returned from school he was a little taller, his scrawny pubescent body started to fill out into a well-toned muscular one as if someone were inflating him slowly when he was away from home.

His dark, alert eyes watched the world from beneath a mop of brown hair that carried its unkempt appearance with a kind of attractiveness. She could see in him the Richmond that had seduced her so many years ago now. He was a young man with a presence, one that would attract women and, if he so desired, would make them do anything he wanted.

Her heart ached for her son. She hoped and prayed fervently that he would not make the same mistake that his father had made, that he would not abuse the seductive power of his eyes or the air of confidence he seemed to exude.

But he was unaware of his growing appeal and maintained friendly, but respectable, relationships with the series of girls who ended up being assigned as his dance partner. Elspeth was eventually changed after constantly complaining about being stepped on. Winifred, a nervous skinny girl, managed to last two lessons before shaking so much that the teacher thought something untoward was happening and, blaming a confused James, switched Winifred for Meredith. Little did the teacher know that Winifred's reaction was due to her inability to control her emotions at having to be so close to a boy she found incredibly handsome. Meredith was a no-nonsense, not unattractive, girl who managed to train James not to step on her toes.

Agnes was oblivious to all this, unaware of how her son was untouched by the urges that had dramatically changed the course of his parents' lives.

She found herself studying Richmond more closely and it was not too difficult for her to recall how she had given in to his advances. His hair had started to grey slightly, the harsh African sun had darkened his skin and made it appear somewhat leathery. The physical work of the farm had kept his physique in good shape.

She watched him move around the sitting room in the evening and felt an echo of the thrill she had first experienced when she succumbed to him. She knew it was foolish to feel this way and berated herself for doing so. But she was grown up now. She was no longer that impressionable girl from so long ago and, when Richmond happened to notice her looking at him and smiled his cocky, almost lecherous smile, she had not been flustered at all.

'That button on your jacket is coming loose,' she had said suddenly noticing a way out. 'You had better let me sew it on properly before you lose it in the field.'

She had a quiet laugh to herself later as she recalled his deflated look. But there was sadness in the laugh. She had grown comfortable with their relationship, and it pained her that, despite the physical attraction she still occasionally felt, she could not bring herself to try and kindle a closer bond with her husband.

So she continued to direct her love towards her son adapting it slowly as he grew. After her initial objection to Carl, feeling that he was stealing her time with James, she had come to like the boy who had a polite charm. She soon began seeing him as a second son, part of the family and she would fuss over him nearly as much as she did James. She did, however, fret at the way the years seemed to rush by. She had barely let go of James, allowing him the freedom to grow up, when the end of their schooling loomed and Agnes wondered if they would see as much of Carl once school was over.

At seventeen, James finished his formal education and left Mombasa with enough qualifications to give him the freedom to do whatever he put his mind to as long as he could find an acquaintance amongst his father's friends who would take him on. But he had no interest in law or business, he preferred to work on the farm.

McCallum wasn't getting any younger and was starting to struggle a little with the physical side of the work while James, as his body had strengthened, found himself enjoying the more strenuous tasks and in his last few years of school would spend his two free weeks lifting, digging, planting and learning from McCallum all the time.

He discussed his options with his father and Richmond was delighted that his son chose the farm over a possible clerical role in Mombasa. Agnes too was thrilled that she would not lose her son to the city.

As a young man, James could now join in the 'men's talk' on Fridays after dinner when McCallum came over, as was the tradition. Agnes would sit in a corner reading or sewing while the three men would discuss the week's news.

'Have you heard,' Richmond said one evening with an air of superiority, 'the president of the Unites States of America is here in East Africa?'

'William Taft?' James answered trying to show that he was up to date with the news.

'No, not Taft. The previous president, Theodore Roosevelt,' McCallum said, then seemed to shrink somewhat under Richmond's glare.

'Roosevelt?' Agnes, not wanting to be left out, interjected, seemingly unaware of the look McCallum had received. 'What on earth would he want to be doing in this part of the world?'

'Hunting,' Richmond said, regaining his superior air. 'He's here on a hunting trip. They say some fellow is following him around with one of those new moving picture machines.'

'Moving pictures? What's that?' The concept intrigued James.

'From what I've read it is like a camera but instead of just taking one still picture it takes a whole lot of pictures that when viewed in quick succession it looks like the things are moving.'

'Remarkable,' Agnes said. 'And this fellow is taking all these pictures of Theodore Roosevelt? It must be costing him a fortune, if the cost of a single photograph is anything to go by.'

'Well, Mama, he was a president so I suppose he must have a fair bit of money.'

'Maybe you should start doing this moving picture thing, you could earn yourself a tidy sum.' She smiled at her son.

'What? And have to leave the farm to go running around the country with visiting dignitaries. That's not for me, Mama. I am quite happy here, helping Papa.'

It was Richmond's turn to smile.

A few months after he finished school, James went late one afternoon for a swim in the dam to cool off. It had been a day of hard labour in the field and particularly hot so instead of taking the direct route which was mostly in the open and subject to the sun's heat, he chose a more circuitous path which took him along tree lined paths that offered cool shade. The small stream that fed the dam ran alongside the path.

His mind, slightly frazzled by the day's work, drifted between thoughts like a bee lazily trying to gather pollen from different flowers. One moment he thought of the tasks he needed to accomplish the next day, then he thought of McCallum and how he had seemed sluggish in his work today. His mother passed briefly through his mind before his upcoming trip to Voi took him in a different direction. The shade and the coolness it brought caressed his mind and he marvelled at the shapes and patterns the light formed on the path as it wriggled through the leaves and branches above. This led to him thinking about the evenings where he sat and stared at the sky, mesmerised by its vastness and beauty.

Then a tune came, sung in a familiar voice. The memory of it seemed remote, almost beyond his reach and yet it had an intimacy and a nearness that made it tangible. He stopped walking, trying to place it, his lips mouthing the words as he slowly became aware that it was not just in his mind that he was hearing the song. The voice was real and while there was a familiarity to it there was also something different.

As he slowly reined in the fuzziness of his thoughts, forming focussed memories from the fluffy fragments, he remembered and could visualise Hannah singing the song as she went about her chores. But this voice was not Hannah's. It was a close approximation. There was something different. He listened carefully, trying to determine where the sound was coming from, then turned his head in the direction of the stream. He had been unaware of the gurgling of the water, a sound so natural that it blended in with the surrounding, disguising itself by hiding in plain sight. The singing too seemed to blend in with the trees and the stream, a natural sound that was at ease with nature.

Rounding a bend in the path, he knew that there was a break in the trees which opened up the stream to view. The singing, he was sure, was coming from there and he slowed his step, not wanting to startle the singer.

He peered around the corner and spotted a woman kneeling at the side of the stream bent over as she worked at washing a garment. At first he dismissed her as just one of the farm servants then, as the voice continued to sing the familiar song, he realised that it was Miriam. He suddenly recalled the games and friendship of their youth. He stood watching her work, mesmerised by the pure notes of her singing as it unwrapped his memories with the slow precision of one who dares not tear the wrapping paper and folds it neatly once done.

He had not been properly aware of the loneliness he had been experiencing now that Carl was not visiting like he used to. It had been an unidentified melancholy that coated everything he did, a sense of loss that the busyness of the farm work prevented him from exploring properly.

Seeing his childhood friend brought to the fore these feelings and he suddenly ached for that innocent companionship again, but these thoughts were quickly followed by guilt as he realised how he had dumped this friend in favour of his newfound school mate.

As he watched, Miriam straightened her back and wiped her brow with her forearm, the water like quicksilver on her warm brown skin. It was with a sense of shock that, despite her face still carrying the little girl sweetness he recalled, her body had become that of a woman's. She had developed breasts and curves, things that Carl had spoken of in relation to Kate, but which he had taken no real notice of. He now knew, in a sudden instant, what it was that Carl had been on about and it hit him like a blow in the stomach, a delicious pain suddenly knotting his gut and he struggled to breathe properly.

Yet he could do nothing but stand and stare through the foliage. Despite his instincts screaming at him that he should rush forward and take this seductive singing siren into his arms and possess her, his feet seemed leaden and unable to move.

Miriam wrung out the garment she was washing, bundled together her laundry and walked off down a path that led to the servants' village, still singing and completely oblivious to the eyes that watched her go.

*

'James, what's the matter with you?' his mother's tone mixed concern and annoyance. 'That's the second time you've spilt something tonight. First your wine, now you've got gravy all over the tablecloth.'

James glanced sheepishly around the dinner table. McCallum looked on with sympathy while his father was stern.

'Oh, I am sorry, mother. I guess I am just rather tired. It was a busy day,' he said, not daring to look at Miriam who had just entered the room to see if she was required to clean up.

Agnes softened and studied her son. 'You sure it's just that. You are not feeling unwell, are you? Feverish?'

'No, I am fine, Mother, just a little tired.'

Despite his reassurances, Agnes got up and checked his temperature, reluctantly accepting the results her hand on his forehead gave, but still worrying. The malaria that had taken Rosemary-Jane still pricked at her conscience.

He sat still, concentrating all his efforts on showing no emotion as Miriam, on instruction from Agnes, leaned over the table to clear up the spilt gravy. He could feel the warmth of her body so close to him and watched the beautiful smooth skin on her naked forearms as she worked. He wanted to reach out and touch that smoothness, to draw the warmth of her body to his. But he dared not show any of this to his parents, nor to Miriam for that matter.

That night he lay in his bed listening to the muted hum of the mosquitoes outside the netting. He stared into the darkness above him, the sound of Miriam's song bouncing around in his head while the glistening water on her skin playing with his mind's eye, the images torturing him as he tried to get comfortable with feelings that were too restless to settle.

At last he fell into a confused sleep where his dreams were skittish, coming and going, teasing him when close with their clarity and nearness but also teasing when out of his reach, their promise frustratingly just too far away.

Dawn brought no relief, no answers to his disturbed state and, while his body got on with the work of the day, his mind trudged wearily behind it, bewildered and in search of answers. The only thing keeping him going was the thought that he would again go along the shady path that evening when he went to swim and maybe she would be there.

⚍

It was nearly a week before he saw her by the stream. In the interim it had been an effort not to take too much notice of her as she went about her chores and further effort to concentrate on doing normal things without spilling, dropping or knocking something over. It did not help that his mother continued to fuss over him, convinced that something was not right with her son, fearing for his physical well-being without once thinking that the problem may well lie elsewhere.

He warded off her attentions with gentle but firm denials that anything was wrong, knowing that if he showed any of the irritation that was building in him, it would only fuel her on. Even his father was noticing something, but eventually came to his rescue with a brusque 'Enough Agnes! If he says that he's all right, then he's all right. He is grown up enough to tell us if he is not well.' This quietened Agnes, but James could feel from the look his father gave him that he was not convinced by his own words.

He considered talking to McCallum about his feelings but decided against it. Even if he could bring himself to raise the subject, it was not fair to burden Uncle Malcolm with this secret. So he suffered in silence, taking some comfort from the fact that he recognised in himself the same behaviours he had seen in Carl when he had fallen for Kate. James now fully understood why his friend had acted the way he had.

It was during that week that he recalled the time he and Miriam had spotted his father in the abandoned house with one of the servants. Back then he had not understood what they were up to, but he now knew. He also knew that it had not been an isolated incident. He had overheard conversations amongst the farm labourers and seen the way his father would sneak off then return looking flushed and, if he stared at him too long, embarrassed.

The anger that followed the thought that perhaps Miriam had been one of the women his father went with, surprised him and he began to watch closely at dinner times to see if there were any signs of unusual interest in Miriam from his father or obvious discomfort from her in his presence. But he saw only indifference from Miriam and, if anything, a slight avoidance, perhaps even a fear from his father which he could not understand. But he was more relieved by this than he was curious.

The day he saw her by the stream the second time had not been as hot. The sky had been covered by grey-tinged clouds from horizon to horizon, but the sun's strength backlit them to give a muted brightness to the land and a closeness to the air. He heard the singing and felt a stab of pain and pleasure in his heart. He moved forward slowly, not wanting to be seen, but wanting to see. The trees seemed to close in around him, as if conspiring against the forbidden love he sought.

Miriam's voice dispelled the closeness of the air, its clarity and purity dancing with the leaves that fluttered gently in a breeze which caressed the dying heat of the day. The song, another one that evoked childhood memories, played with his heart, teasing out each beat, the rhythm in sync with his soul. He felt that he could live inside this moment, cocooned in the sound of her voice.

But he was greedy. He wanted more. The allure of the song was just that, something that pulled him in, something that enslaved him and made him crave more. He wanted to give form to the sound. He wanted the visual that complimented the audio. He crept forward till at last he could see her. The cloud cover prevented the sparkle of the water on her skin and her colour was duller than his mind's image of their last meeting, but her simplicity of movement as she set about her chores enraptured him. He watched each change in her shape as she squeezed, slapped, scrubbed and shook the garment she was washing, marvelling at the fluidity and easy confidence in her limbs.

A strange ache took over his body, as if his soul wanted to tear itself away from his physical self and fly over the stream to be with her, to become one with her. But he stood rooted to the spot, anchored in the traditions and customs he had grown up with where Miriam was a servant and therefore untouchable.

Later, he would analyse his reaction, wondering why what he wanted felt so unacceptable, yet what his father got up to with the servants was somehow less offensive to the sensibilities of the European ways. But for the moment, such thoughts were kept at bay by the rapture he felt as he drank in the scene.

He did not know how long he stood there, watching, hardly daring to breathe. It felt like a lifetime yet also like the briefest of seconds, her eventual departure coming far too soon.

As he swam in the dam later, the water cooled his body, but did nothing to soothe the fire that raged in his soul.

Miriam hurried back to the village to hang up her washing, then headed quickly towards the dam, moving quietly along the path. She hoped she would not be too late. She took a circuitous route and approached the dam from the opposite side to the farm house, the thicker vegetation there allowing her to get close enough without being seen.

She found the spot where rocks and trees hid her from view yet allowed her to see the whole dam. Her eyes searched for and found the pale body that swam strongly through the muddy brown water. She could not stay long, they would miss her at the house soon, so she hoped that Master James would finish swimming before she had to go back.

While she loved watching him power his way through the water, she found herself eagerly awaiting the moment when he walked out of the dam and dried himself. She loved the paleness of his skin, so different to her own, and she loved how his hair, so straight and long, would lie slick against his head.

Her mother would not approve of her being there. It was not something that servants did, they did not spy on their masters. And her mother would have been horrified had she any insight into Miriam's feelings as she watched her childhood friend, the longing she had to be with him. Not just for the companionship and friendship they had enjoyed as children, but her feelings now extended to the physical. She wanted to touch his body, feel the strength in his muscles and caress his pale skin. She wondered how his skin would feel to the touch, the different colour must surely have a different texture.

She watched as he headed back to the far end of the dam, hoping that this would be the end of his swim and he would climb out of the water. Her patience was rewarded as he stood up, letting the water drip from his body for a moment – a moment in which Miriam held her breath – before running up the small embankment to his towel.

Miriam leaned forward to get a better view and as she did, she heard a scuttling in the undergrowth nearby which was followed immediately by the appearance of a monitor lizard who stopped and stared at her. She let out a squeal, quickly swallowing it as she remembered that she was not meant to be there. James' head swung round, and his eyes searched for the source of the sound. Miriam did not move, her heart thundering in her chest, her eyes fixed on the young master, all thoughts of his body evaporated by the heat of her fear.

The moment lasted a few seconds but felt like an age to Miriam. Eventually James gave a slight shrug and returned to drying himself. The lizard, who had stared at Miriam the whole time, a puzzled expression on its face, turned to look in the direction Miriam was staring, then looked back at her with what seemed to her to be a smile of understanding on its face.

§

The invite to Carl and Kate's wedding was not unexpected, but James found that it threw him into a state of melancholy. He was happy for his friend and he liked Kate. He had got to know her better in their later years of school when they were allowed a little more freedom and the three of them would sit and chat, under the watchful eye of a teacher, after the dancing lessons when tea was served.

She was a good match for Carl, a kind, caring young woman with an infectious laugh. She was clearly as besotted with him as he was with her, and James envied their love. He knew of his own feelings for Miriam but the invite to the wedding painfully reminded him that he could never marry the woman with whom he was in love. Apart from the huge difference in their status, he was certain that Miriam would have no feelings for him. Why would she? It had been years since they had spoken other than for him to ask her to do some domestic task and she to nod or meekly answer his questions.

'Do you know where my other sock is?'

'You left it on your chair, sir.'

'Is my father home yet?'

'He came back, but has gone out again, sir.'

Hardly the stuff of romance. She called him sir. How, he asked himself, could a woman love a man she had to call sir?

He stared at the invite for a long time, his thoughts and feelings warm and yet sad at the same time.

'What is Kate like?' his mother asked, intruding into his thoughts.

'Hmm? Oh she is lovely, Mama. Carl is a lucky man.' Being able to concentrate his mind on his friend's happiness lifted him and he began to tell his mother all about Kate, watching and wondering at the sad smile that came to his mother's features as he enthused about the young couple.

It only struck him later as he prepared for bed where his mother's sadness came from. At school they had read some of Jane Austin's novels, struggling through the stories of romance which he had found a bore, not understanding this concept of love, even after Carl had fallen for Kate. He knew that his mother devoured those books. He had often seen her engrossed in one, sometimes enduring his father's scorn and teasing about them. But he could never fathom their appeal. Later, as he recalled how he enthused about Carl and Kate's love, the formality of his parents' relationship and his father's shenanigans with the female servants now gave some hint at the reason for his mother's sadness.

He climbed into bed and stared into the darkness above. It seemed to him that his mother did not love the man she had. In contrast he could not have the woman he loved. He gave a wry smile and began to wonder if he would, like his mother, end up in a loveless marriage, feeling the need to find a partner amongst the few girls his age from the neighbouring farms. He knew some of them, not well, mostly from the occasional visits to those farms or when they went into Voi or Taveta and attended church.

He turned onto his side, the darkness above him becoming too oppressive, and stared at the frame of hazy silver light that the moon painted around the edges of the curtains.

'Who knows,' he told himself, 'I may find a girl I am happy with.' But there was little comfort in these words to himself for he knew that his heart was set on Miriam and anyone else would only be second best.

He closed his eyes and, to distance his thoughts, began to plan mentally for the trip to Tanga and the wedding.

It was Richmond who suggested that James take Miriam with to the wedding.

'You'll need someone to look after you and Carl's servants will be too busy.'

Agnes was not sure it was a good idea, but what Richmond said made sense and she did not contradict him.

James was dubious about it. He thought his father may be pushing Miriam onto him so that he could taste the forbidden fruit. His mother's look of objection supported this thought.

Despite his doubts, there was still a part of him that welcomed the suggestion. He would be close to Miriam for the three days it would take to get to Carl's and three more days for the return journey. Even though it would be torture to be so close and not be able to do anything he could not help himself craving that torment. He managed to feign indifference as he agreed to the suggestion but was agitated over the next few days, the delicious expectation of time alone with Miriam constantly clashing with the knowledge that he would be in a private hell.

The days passed slowly as he prepared for the trip. They would camp along the way so tents, cots and bedding needed to be sorted. He cleaned his rifle and checked the ammunition in case of wild animals. Clothes needed to be packed, those for travel and those for the day itself. Food for the journey and gifts for the couple also needed organising.

He still swam every evening and only once saw Miriam at the stream when he spent a few moments in voyeuristic ecstasy, taking great pleasure from seeing her in a natural state, the shackles of servanthood momentarily discarded as she, free from the masters' eyes, could move and sing in a way that was her true self and not the self that she was paid to be.

He held the scene in his mind's eye, every movement, each note of her song, the drops of water that fell from her forearms, the minutest details sticking inside his head as he clung to the image.

The cool water of the dam was a slight balm to the heat that raged inside him and the lazy stretching of his arms as he pulled himself across the water eased the tension in his body and relaxed his soul, leaving him feeling at ease with the melancholy that descended as he walked home.

The vision of his father with the servant girl, a memory that had stayed with him from his childhood, came more to the fore in his thoughts as the trip approached. He could, if he wanted, take Miriam the way his father took the other women on the farm. She would have to obey, have to submit to her master and not say anything, otherwise she and her mother would be banished.

But, while his body warmed to the idea, keen to slake the thirst it had for such an encounter, his mind was repulsed by it. Taking Miriam in such a forced way would momentarily mask the symptom but would not cure the disease. In fact, he reasoned as he lay in bed waiting for his dreams to release him from the torments of reality, such actions would sully this 'relationship'. The state of torture was far more preferable to the guilt he knew he would feel if he forced the situation. He was not, and would never be, his father.

With a sigh he turned over and lost himself in the whine of a mosquito that sought entry under the netting. He imagined that the insect was after his dreams, that it wanted to suck them from him and he smiled at its frustration. The intensity of its sound seemed to increase as if it sensed the smugness of his thoughts. With his mind thus distracted, he felt himself slowly melt into a peaceful sleep, his dreams welcoming him like an old friend.

When Agnes told her she was to accompany James to Master Carl's wedding, Miriam had bowed her servile bow, her eyes demurely denying the thudding that the news set off in her heart. There was a list of instructions that went with the news as Agnes fussed – as she always did when it involved her son – about every little detail.

'Make sure he eats. Don't let him drive in the dark. He mustn't sleep late in the mornings. Have you packed his razor and brushes? Where is the coffee I put out for him? Water, he must have clean water to drink on the journey. And matches, how can he make a fire if he doesn't have matches?'

All the time Miriam felt her mistress' eyes on her, scrutinising her as if searching for a way to peer inside her heart. 'You keep away from my son, you hear me,' the eyes seemed to say. She knew it was her own foolish guilt that created these thoughts. She knew…she hoped…that she had never revealed her feelings for Master James. Her mother suspected, but that was the job of a mother. Likewise, it followed that his mother would have her concerns for him, but Miriam knew that she was blameless in arousing suspicions. Only she and her friend the monitor lizard knew.

She set about the task as she did all her other chores, in her quiet methodical way, keeping her steps measured when she wanted to skip and her face emotionless when she wanted to smile. Not showing her feelings was made easier by the constant niggling thought that, despite the time she would have being so close to him, nothing would, or could, happen.

She pictured herself going about her servant tasks somewhere in the bush, cooking over a fire, finding a stream to wash the dishes, packing all the equipment back into the cart, the mundanity and routineness of the scene helping her control her emotions.

But when she walked home at night she would hum or sing softly to herself, the music latching onto the breeze and together they would play with the long grass that grew next to the path, causing it to dance. There she was free to let her thoughts soar above her station, there she could love and be loved in this snatched moment of release before arriving home where her dreams had to be packed away again.

McCallum came to see them off. Agnes, fussing as always, re-checked the luggage. 'Did you pack your toothbrush?'

'Yes mother.' James knew not to get impatient, it would only spur her on to further fretting, thinking he was not taking things seriously. 'And my combs.' He showed her the neatly packed toiletry bag, knowing that his father would step in soon to put an end to this inquisition.

'Oh for goodness' sake, Agnes, he's a grown boy. He spent five years going to school in Mombasa, he's been to Carl's many times before, he knows how to pack for a trip,' Richmond came in right on cue. But he had mellowed with age and, what would have been a sharp rebuke years back, was an almost playful teasing of the way she still treated her son as a little boy.

'Yes, but this trip is different,' Agnes said, recognising the teasing note in Richmond's voice and acknowledging her own silliness. She still wanted to show she cared.

'The lad will be fine,' McCallum chimed in, 'he knows these lands, he knows how to take care of himself.'

James smiled at the three of them, a relaxed and quietly confident grin playing across his lips. He knew that it would infuriate but pacify his mother. 'Yes, I'll be okay.' He hugged her and shook hands with his father and McCallum, all of them sending their best wishes to Carl. Then he climbed into the seat of the wagon, checked that Miriam was on board and cracked the reins to get the horses going.

Agnes watched the wagon bump and trundle down the long driveway till it disappeared out of sight. The two men had stood for a few moments before heading to the fields, leaving her to her motherly duty. She could not place her finger on exactly what it was, but she could not help feeling that a part of James had left the farm for good. He would return a different person, somehow changed by this adventure.

Ψ

Finally alone with Miriam, James felt an awkwardness come over him and he had to fight the temptation to give voice to the nervous babbling that bubbled inside him. He concentrated on the road ahead and steering the horses. An attempt to whistle a tune proved disastrous as the notes kept wondering off in the wrong direction. So he stopped and hummed quietly to himself, the discord within his soul not so openly on display.

The morning air was pleasant and the sun on his back warmed his muscles. He knew he should enjoy the moment as it would not be long before the heat would surpass the warmth and become something to be endured.

They would reach Taveta late in the morning where he bought further supplies, let the horses rest for a bit and made a cup of tea. They would head east from there towards the coast turning south from Tanga towards the small town of Pangani. Carl's family farm was just before one arrived at this attractive coastal town.

He had travelled the route every year with Carl, but never grew tired of it. The dusty road, the long swaying grass, the majestic baobabs and the small hills all greeting him on the way. Even the animals, the giraffe, zebra, buck and elephants seemed to nod a hello to him, and this helped ease the restlessness he felt inside.

They made good progress, stopping for lunch a little way past Holili on the German side of the border. Miriam dutifully set about preparing the food which he ate sitting at a small fold-up table set out under a shady tree. Miriam sat a little way off as she ate quickly, needing to finish before him so that she would be ready to tidy away as soon as he was done.

He glanced across at her, fighting an ache to invite her to join him. He wanted her to sit opposite him at the little table where he could see her close up and perhaps reach out and take her hands in his. But then he turned away, a sense of shame at his cowardice giving his face an appearance of disgust.

He hoped she had not noticed the glance or the emotions as he turned away. She had looked up at him at that moment, but he had not had enough time to read her face. Had she sensed his eyes on her? Had she read into his glance the thoughts that ran around in his head? Was she wary of being alone with him in the middle of nowhere, worried that he may have unsavoury designs on her? What would she have made of his looking away like he had?

The food was tasteless in his mouth and he had to force himself to finish it, eager to get back on the road again where she would be sat behind him and, being out of sight, he hoped she would be out of mind too.

He forced himself to think of Carl and Kate. He was looking forward to seeing them again, to seeing them marry. It made him feel suddenly grown up now that his friend was getting married. Being allowed to make this trip on his own, while an endorsement of his newfound adulthood, was hardly ground-breaking. He had explored the land around the farm as a young boy. This was essentially the same kind of thing with a few sleep overs and a few more miles from home. And he had travelled this route before albeit with Carl and one of the workers from his farm, sent to escort them.

Marriage was something different. Only adults got married. This was a big step in a person's life. He wondered about his parents and their marriage. They never spoke of their wedding day, never mentioned courting each other and spoke little of Rosemary-Jane, the sister he never knew. They had not had more children after him where Carl had two sisters and a brother. It suddenly struck him as odd. He had never thought about it before, and something felt wrong, but he did not like these thoughts, so sipped his coffee.

It was time to get moving again. He finished his food and watched as Miriam cleared away and repacked the wagon, then hoisted himself into the driver's seat, trying hard to supress his thoughts about what the children would look like if he and Miriam, by some miracle, could produce some.

The next two days were torture, especially the nights when he ached to invite her to join him in his tent. As evening fell on their last day before reaching the farm, he started keeping an eye out for a good place to set up camp. He recalled a spot that he and Carl had used on their trips and felt that it was close by. Then, as if his thoughts had conjured it up, the place appeared.

'We'll stop here tonight,' he turned to let Miriam know. 'There is a stream a few yards that way for water.' He turned back to the horses, the idea of another night alone with Miriam under the stars – her body so close, so touchable, yet a million miles away caused a sudden longing that was painful.

He put up the tent, welcoming the physical exercise which coaxed the stiffness from his limbs and eased the desires that had flared inside him. Miriam, following his instructions, headed off to gather some firewood and collect water from the stream.

The tent could easily sleep two, either close together, holding each other, or in separate cots with more than enough distance between them to allow respectability to stretch out. Yet he would have it all to himself while Miriam would again just have a blanket to cover herself while she slept in the back of the wagon. The driver's seat would provide shelter if it rained, but fortunately it was not the season.

The fire crackled and spat, the dull light of the flames in harmony with the quietness that the dark of night brought. Again he ate alone. Again the food, so well prepared by Miriam, was robbed of its flavour by his thoughts. Even the shot of whisky he decided to have before turning in, lacked its usual bite.

Once in his tent he undressed slowly, wanting to go and check on Miriam, to see that she was okay sleeping rough in the wagon but more than that he wanted to invite her to join him. She could curl up on a blanket in the other corner. At least she would be safe and more comfortable there. No one need know. Better still, they could lie together in his cot, her warm body touching his.

He sighed, then suddenly got up and went outside, determined to put an end to his torture.

'Master?' Miriam sat up in the wagon, the moonlight catching the whites of her eyes.

'It's fine, Miriam. I...I... just need to go into the bush.' He was grateful for the dark that hid his blushes. 'You okay in the wagon?'

'Yes, sir, I am fine.'

'Damn and blast,' he cursed his cowardice as he relieved himself. 'You have no spine.'

Miriam did not stir when he returned to the tent where, despite the chaos of his thoughts, he fell into a fitful sleep, his dreams buried too deep to disturb him or his memories the next morning.

⚜

The bustle and fuss of his welcome at the familiar Pangani farm blew away the turmoil of emotions that the trek down had stirred in his mind. The hugs, handshakes and kisses creating a whirlwind that dragged him from the wagon and into the house, leaving Miriam to unpack with the help of the other servants.

They greeted her cordially, showed her where Master James' room was and where she could store their supplies. One of the men was sent to tend to the wagon and the horses and then she joined in to help with dinner preparations.

Not being part of this farm's help, she was confined to kitchen duties, cutting, peeling, fetching, carrying and watching pots. She knew she was perfectly capable of being part of the serving team, but knew too that she was an unknown and no self-respecting 'head of staff' would allow an unproven person near the dining table. Her mother would not allow guest's servants to serve unless the guest particularly requested it. So she accepted her fate gracefully and worked hard.

Laughter and merry voices could be heard from the dining room where occasionally she could make out Master James amongst them, but mostly it was a blur of sound as she concentrated on her work.

Eventually the group moved through to the large drawing room for after dinner drinks and the last of the dishes came back to the kitchen for cleaning. Miriam went to fetch some water and helped dry. It was only once all was done and packed away that the head servant, a serious woman called Dorcus, smiled a 'thank you and well done' before asking, 'Have you eaten?'

'Not since lunch time, Mama,' Miriam addressed her politely.

'You were not expected, but there is plenty food.' She led Miriam outside where some pots sat over the dying embers of a fire. A young girl served her a spoonful of ugali, the stodgy white cornmeal porridge, and added some thin tomato gravy on the side.

Miriam felt tired. The day had been long and hot, and she had not stopped working since they arrived. The food, although only lukewarm, was good and quickly satisfied her hunger.

After she finished, Dorcus showed her to her quarters, and she was finally left alone. She undressed, completed her ablutions and climbed under the rough blanket Dorcus had provided. Despite her tiredness and the comfort of this bed after the nights in the wagon, she did not immediately fall asleep. Her mind puzzled over Master James and his behaviour on the journey. Back home he was so confident in all he did, but on the road he had been clumsy in his actions and commands. There had been a number of times she caught him looking at her and had been forced to lower her gaze, feeling the rush of blood to her cheeks. She could not understand these looks.

She wanted to believe that this was because he felt about her the same way she felt about him. She sighed as she realised that she dared not allow herself the luxury of that thought. Having resolved this, she closed her eyes and gave into the weariness of her body.

The wedding was a joyous occasion. Carl could not stop smiling and Kate looked stunning in her wedding dress, her pretty face flushed with excitement as she chattered away merrily to everyone. Mr and Mrs Muller were wonderful hosts, putting everyone at ease, Mrs Muller acting as translator wherever possible with some of the German neighbours who struggled to be understood. But James had garnered a fair smattering of German from his stays on the farm and a number of the German contingent spoke sufficient English for the conversations to flow.

A bright blue sky spread itself lazily above them, and a pleasant breeze played tug-of-war with the humidity, each taking turns to dominate but neither overstaying their welcome to become unpleasant.

The servants were dressed in gay colours, their outfits competing with their smiles for which was brighter. Hannah had ensured that Miriam took her best outfit and Miriam was grateful that her mother knew what was needed as, never having been present at a wazungu wedding, she would not have thought to dress appropriately.

She helped out with the food preparation which began soon after dawn and then, as Dorcus realised that she was good at her work, she was asked to help with laying the tables set out on the large lawn in front of the main house. When the guests arrived, Miriam was entrusted with a tray of drinks and told to circulate.

She picked up fragments of conversations as she offered the drinks around. Some talked shop – the price of sisal, would it be sensible to consider a bit of cattle farming? problems with farm hands – while others discussed the news of the rebellion happening in the south of the country – would the problem spread north? What was the governor doing? We've stocked up on ammunition, just in case.

As she walked, almost unnoticed between the guests, she would occasionally search for Master James in the crowd and spotting him, she noted how happy he looked. He was either smiling or laughing as he spoke to the other guests. But she could not help noticing how Master Carl seemed to keep introducing him to the young ladies in the group. It was good that he might find a wife here. While she had her feelings for him, she knew that nothing could come of them and the best she could hope for was that he would find someone who would make him happy.

She saw a future where the years stretched out ahead, her mother growing old and handing over the reins of senior house servant. Master Richmond and Mrs Agnes would also grow old and Master James would become the master of the house. She would serve him and his wife and would draw her happiness from making them happy. At some point, she would be married off. There were a number of young men in the village who, in the not too distant future, would make approaches.

Despite her thoughts she frowned slightly when she noted him talking to a pretty young lady who, Miriam just knew, would not be a good match. Before she could avert her gaze, or even hide her disapproving look, he glanced up and caught her eye, a puzzled expression crossing his face in the fraction of a second that they made eye contact before she quickly looked away.

The next time she looked for him, he was talking to a group of men and, as she watched him over the rest of the afternoon, he seemed determined to steer clear of the young women and she could not understand this.

As evening drew near, those guests who were not staying over, climbed into their wagons and trundled slowly off. The farm seemed to give a contented sigh as the noise and laughter of the day subsided into a blissful and relaxed state. Small groups sat around the fires that had been lit and a happy mumble rippled around the garden. Miriam and the other servants served coffee and the occasional drinks or snacks, but most had had their fill and declined the offers. The surreptitious process of tidying up began.

It was late in the evening when the guests decided to turn in. The last of the dishes were washed and tables and chairs tidied away. Dorcus thanked Miriam for her help and bid her goodnight. She made her way to her room, hoping that thoughts about Master James would leave her alone as she just wanted to sleep.

James stayed a week at the farm, enjoying the hospitality of the Mullers. The happy glow of the wedding clung to the recently married couple and all at the farm, making for a joyful time. They played croquet and lawn tennis, drank tea, went for walks and had a picnic down by the seaside.

All this served to mask the melancholy that he felt. A thin layer of happiness sat comfortably on him like a loose fitting garment and he wore it with ease, grateful for the feelings which helped him at times to forget the torment that bubbled inside.

But Carl caught him with his guard down one day towards the end of his visit. He had risen early, as he always did, and walked to the far end of the garden where the morning sun was pleasant on his back. He sat on a small bench and let the warmth massage his shoulders while he stared out across the neat rows of sisal. The deep green blades of the plant sat like giant tufts of grass in the orange-brown sand and stretched away down a slight slope. It seemed to James that they were wanting to touch the dull green hills that relaxed in the haze the distance, warmth and dust created.

He felt relieved to be able to put aside for a moment the veneer of happiness that he had been wearing and snuggled into the mysterious cosiness of his melancholy. His eyes muted the scenery to allow his feelings time with his mind.

'Thinking of changing to sisal?' He had not heard Carl come up behind him.

'What? Oh, no. Just thinking.'

'I brought coffee,' Carl said, sitting next to him and offering him a cup.

'Thanks. You used the beans I brought, I trust.'

Carl laughed, 'What else would I use?'

They were quiet a moment, sipping their coffee and staring out over the land.

'You okay?' Carl broke the silence. 'You seem happy, but I can tell you're hiding something.'

James smiled. It was good to have a friend who knew him this well.

'I am really pleased for you. You have a lovely wife who will make you happy. You are a very lucky man,' he said, looking at his friend.

'But?' Carl asked.

James looked back at the sisal field. 'But I was just wondering if I will ever be as lucky as you and marry someone I really love.'

Carl laughed. 'Don't tell me you met someone at the wedding. Let me guess. Not Susan Darby, surely? Helen Wilfred-Clark? Or was it one of the German contingent? Gretchen Schmidt, she was the pretty blonde girl who was teaching you to say, "This is a lovely wedding" in German.'

James smiled. 'She is very pretty. A nice girl, but no, it's not her, nor Susan nor Helen. In fact, it is none of the guests.'

'Then who? Anyone I know?'

James studied the neat rows of sisal, summoning up the courage. Eventually he sighed and said, 'Can you keep a secret?'

There was the usual routine of packing and loading and fussing as he prepared to leave. Carl's mother ensured he had more food for the journey home than he needed and there were gifts for his parents to be sorted. Carl's mother and father had never met his parents, and only knew from the stories their son had told. The camping equipment was packed and room had to be made for a pile of sisal mats that James had agreed to drop off in Tanga for a customer of the farm. On top of this, one of the farm labourers was going to hitch a ride as he was going north to see his family. James didn't like the way the young lad eyed Miriam but was grateful for his help in packing. Like the sisal mats, the additional passenger would be left in Tanga.

A great many hugs and kisses were exchanged and promises to visit again were made till eventually James managed to hoist himself into the driver's seat. He turned to check that Miriam and his other passenger were aboard then with a final 'farewell', cracked the reins and the wagon creaked and began to slowly bumble down the long road that ran alongside the fields.

The friendliness of the goodbye lingered and he felt a warm contentedness. But as he moved further from the farm and the young lad began chatting to Miriam, his thoughts turned back to his problem. He had expected Carl to laugh at his confession, to tell him he was being silly and that it was just lust, not love. He had expected to be told that he should, like his father with the other servants, have his way with Miriam and get it out of his system, then he could concentrate on finding the right colour wife.

But Carl had listened. He had let him explain how, as young children, he and Miriam had played together and that, despite not interacting other than on a master/servant level since then, he still longed for those carefree days of friendship. Yes, there was a strong physical pull that had now been added, but he was convinced that there was more to it than just that.

Even when he said that he thought Miriam might feel something for him, Carl had not laughed, but nodded, taking the statement on board. By his expression, James could tell that his friend was busy searching through the evidence to support or disprove the notion. Carl was like that. He would process things in a logical way and not let emotions rule his thinking. He should have become a lawyer, not a farmer, James thought.

'It is no wonder you are so sad,' Carl said when James finished his confession, 'It is a very difficult position that you are in.' He shook his head and joined James in staring at the fields. After contemplating the problem for a while he said, 'I wish you had told me earlier. I would have watched Miriam for you to see if there were any signs that she felt the same way.'

'What? And spoil your wedding day? It would not do for you to be paying too much attention to one of the women servants when you are getting married,' James responded with a laugh.

Carl smiled. 'I feel for you, James, but I am grateful that you did not ruin my wedding day with such a task. It would definitely have distracted me. I wish I could say something to help, but I fear that yours is an impossible position.'

James nodded. 'Thank you for listening. At least I have been able to talk it over with you and that has helped.'

They sat a moment longer, then James sighed and said, 'We had better get back.' They stood and walked slowly to the house, talking over what needed to be done to prepare for James' journey home.

It was late in the afternoon when the wagon trundled into Tanga. James found the shop where the mats were to be delivered and had a chat to the owner while his passenger and Miriam unloaded the goods. He felt weighed down by his problem. Carl's words, 'Yours is an impossible position', had played on his mind all the way from Pangani and the way his passenger had so freely chatted with Miriam on the journey only served to entrench the message. There was no way he could have turned round and joined in the conversation. He was an outsider.

Miriam had responded in her demure way to the friendly, bordering on flirtatious, talk. James could sense a smile in her voice. When she laughed at something that was said, the sound was simultaneously a thing of beauty that made his heart want to soar, but it was also a knife twisted in that same heart.

Suddenly, as he spoke to the shop owner about trivial things, he felt that he could not face a night on the road alone with Miriam. The pain would be too much.

'I wonder, is there somewhere I may find a room for the night?' he asked the shop owner, the question almost taking him by surprise as he had hardly thought it through. But once out there he knew that this was the right thing to do. He would treat himself to a comfortable night and face his problems again in the morning.

He was directed to a place on the outskirts of the town where he took his essentials to the room and left Miriam to fend for herself, trying not to feel guilty about doing so.

After freshening up he headed to the bar and proceeded to get drunk, finding some solace in the haze the alcohol brought, the softness of the fuzzy feeling a balm to the sharp pain his 'impossible position' brought.

A vague memory of being supported to his room by the barman accompanied him as he drifted off to sleep.

His first ever hangover was not pleasant. The dizziness, the headache and horrible dryness in his mouth that battered him as he stumbled out of his dreams became more acute under the mocking eyes of the hotel staff as he tried to eat breakfast.

It was late in the morning when he finally walked outside to the wagon and loaded his things. Miriam, who had been waiting patiently in the shade of a nearby tree gave him a concerned look.

'I drank too much last night,' he said, feeling a need to explain. He wanted to add an apology, but knew that it would not be good form for him to do so. The sun hurt his eyes as he hoisted himself into the driver's seat and, with a sigh, they set off. He felt every bump and jolt of the cart acutely and the hot sun seemed to bring the nausea inside him to the boil.

They stopped twice for him to be sick at the side of the road. The second time, just as he thought he may vomit out his very soul, he felt a hand on his back, a gentle timid hand that slowly rubbed away some of the illness and he looked up. Miriam withdrew her hand immediately, a shocked expression on her face as if she had only just become aware of what she was doing. Their eyes met for a brief second before she hurriedly moved away, mumbling an apology, But in that second he saw, through the confusion of his hangover, a look he would never forget.

Miriam stared at Master James' back as the wagon swayed slowly along the road. The memory of his strong muscles still tingled in her palm and she moved her gaze to her hand. Had she really dared to touch him? It seemed like something she should have dreamed, not something she could have done in reality.

The tenderness she felt for him as he was being sick, the ache inside her to comfort him in his discomfort, the hand that had reached out to gently rub his back as he convulsed were all things restricted to her dreams and secret thoughts. None of this was meant to overflow into the physical world.

But, as she studied the offending hand, she recalled his eyes as he had turned to her. There was something there. They had not registered repulsion nor anger, they had not said, 'don't touch me, servant'. There had, after the initial shock of realising what was happening, been the briefest hint of something that seemed to mirror her feelings for him.

'You are being foolish,' she told herself, 'why would he be interested in me?' She put her hand onto the side of the wagon and looked out beyond it to the bushes and land that drifted slowly by. It felt drab and empty in that direction devoid of hope. She knew it was foolish, but she needed hope so she shifted herself round and looked out in the opposite direction. The simplicity of the landscape, the grass, the distant hills, the baobabs, the thorn bushes on this side made sense to her and soothed her troubled mind.

She watched some birds circling lazily in the deep blue sky, wishing momentarily for the freedom that they had, the ease and apparent carefree way they hung in the sky, away from all the world's problems, away from her own problems. She lost herself in their gracefulness, only coming back to her senses when she heard Master James call 'Woah!' to the horses and saw his muscles tense as he pulled back on the reins.

'We'll camp here tonight,' he said, wearily climbing down and stretching.

'Yes sir,' she said and jumped down quickly, setting about getting the campsite ready. She helped him erect the tent, then gathered some wood for the fire. All the time she felt his eyes on her. Not a constant watching but quick, furtive glances as if he were trying to grab every second he could to look at her without having to deal with a returned glance.

She concentrated on the task at hand, feeling a slight trembling inside which she knew she needed to control. She prepared the food and served him as he sat at the little fold-up table.

'Join me, Miriam.' He gestured for her to bring her chair which she had set nearer the fire.

'Sir?' She did not understand.

'Join me. Please. There is no one around and I would like some company.' There was a look on his face as if he had been considering this for a while and was now determined to follow through on the decision.

'Yes, sir,' she was still not sure, but had a lifetime of obeying to fight against and no will nor strength to do so. She fetched her chair, dished her food and sat opposite him, her eyes averted, unsure of what was happening. She waited while he said grace.

'Please. Eat.' He was not so sure of himself now. It was less a command and more a case of imploring. She began to eat, her eyes hardly leaving her plate as she heard the clatter of cutlery on his. After a few mouthfuls she heard him take a deep breath she looked up.

'Do you remember when we were children, how we used to play together?' he asked. He was staring at her in such a strange manner that she looked away.

'Yes, sir.'

'I miss those days.'

She smiled and risked a glance at him. He smiled back.

'Me too, sir,' she said without thinking.

His smile grew bigger and this time she held his gaze.

'I don't want to do this unless you want to, do you understand?'

'Do what, sir?' She was not sure what was coming, but felt her heart beat faster in anticipation.

He reached out and gently touched her cheek. For a moment she froze, not knowing what to do or say. His hand faltered and his smile faded. He began to move it away, but she felt something within her crumble and she almost snatched at him, holding his warm hand in hers, guiding it gently back to her cheek, her smile lighting up her eyes.

During the day he had thought of nothing else but her hand on his back as the wagon trundled through familiar landscapes. He clung to the memory of that touch and his mind had engraved the look she gave him into his memory. It had been a look that went beyond concern. Somewhere in it he had seen real care of the kind that he had seen in Kate when she looked at Carl. Despite this, there were still doubts which kept sloshing around in his head like wild surf covering and revealing the rocks as it attacked and retreated.

He knew he had to make the first move if anything was going to come of this. She would never step outside her servanthood without him helping her across the gap. But he didn't know how to reach out his hand in a way that made the intention clear. Too forceful and he would come across as his father, a master demanding obedience. Too timid and the message may not get through.

He had made the decision early in the day that he would declare his love at dinner and had watched the sun make its way across the sky. At times it sped towards evening as fear and doubt took hold. At other times, it would dawdle when his courage rose, and he could not wait for the moment.

He heard one of the horses snort outside the tent and this jolted him back to the present. He felt her warm naked body lying against his in the cot and drifted back into a contented sleep, waking later to listen to the night sounds of the bush and marvelling at how he had, despite the knot of nerves in his stomach, actually reached out to her and, even more so, at how she had taken his hand when his courage and convictions had faltered. In that moment relief, gratitude and a wave of tender love had engulfed him.

In the early hours of the morning, as his passion and the warm afterglow of having made love mellowed, he began to turn his thoughts to the future. 'Yours is an impossible position.' Carl's words returned to him. How could he continue a relationship with Miriam when they returned home?

There was the expectation that he would find a nice white wife for himself, have children and take over the farm. Where in that picture was there room for a servant girl? Where was there space for a relationship other than snatched moments away from prying eyes? How could they live with the constant worry of discovery? He drifted into an uncomfortable sleep.

He finally woke just as the sun was peeping over the horizon and discovered that she was gone from his side. His heart stopped for a moment but, gathering his wits, he quickly pulled on his clothes and went out. She was there, preparing breakfast. Her smile was uncertain and he knew he needed to reassure her of his love.

'Good morning,' he said and walked over to where she stood.

'Good morning, sir.' The 'sir' was a questioning one asking what it was doing there and wondering if it was welcome in this conversation.

He took her in his arms and kissed her gently, noting the initial tension in her body that slowly dissipated as the kiss continued, her hand slowly finding its way to his cheek and then holding his head as if pulling him deeper into her love, a sense of urgency in the action.

He held her for a long time. The months of agony he had endured watching her, feeling the sharp pangs of love but not being able to touch now melted away in the warm sun. The closeness of her body was intoxicating, and he did not want the moment to end but eventually he eased himself out of the embrace, reluctantly releasing her.

'Breakfast?' he smiled.

'Yes, sir.' She gave him a last, lingering look of love, her eyes searching his for answers to the myriad of questions that he knew sat between them and which he struggled with himself.

'I don't know how we will be able to continue a relationship when we get home,' he said when they sat eating the food she had prepared. 'We cannot be seen together on the farm. You do understand that?'

She nodded. 'It will be difficult.'

'You do understand that I love you, don't you? I am not like…' he stumbled, feeling that he was somehow being disloyal to his father.

'No, you are not.' She too could not mention Mr Richmond's name. 'And I gave myself to you not because you are my master, but I gave myself out of love, sir.'

He smiled, 'Yet you still call me sir.'

Her laugh was a pure beautiful sound. 'That is my name for you, sir. If I say it with love then it is not because you are my master, but because you are my love. I cannot call you anything else when we are back home, so I must always call you sir. But I will always say it with love now.' She looked at him to see if he understood.

He nodded slowly, saddened that he could not disagree. 'I wish it were otherwise. How I wish that we were free to love whom we pleased. Free to be able to call each other by our names. It is not right that I can call you Miriam but you cannot call me James.'

'That is how it is, sir.' She said and he felt the love in his new name.

*

Agnes saw immediately that her son had changed. As she hugged him tight to welcome him home, she felt it in his embrace. His eyes were brighter, his step a dance and when he spoke it was as if he were singing. He spoke of the wedding and Carl and Kate with enthusiasm, as if trying to distract everyone from some other truth. She suspected and watched.

She dearly wished she could ask the questions that swirled in her mind. There was no doubt that he would not offer anything willingly and would angrily withdraw if she probed with the specifics of her suspicions.

He spoke a lot of Gretchen, Carl's cousin. There was warmth in his words and he seemed to take a childish pleasure in the way it riled Richmond. His father was okay with a German friend, but to marry a German was not what an Englishman did. Agnes saw Richmond's discomfort whenever James spoke of Gretchen and she saw the cheeky smile in her son's eyes as he watched his father's reaction. It frustrated and amused her at the same time.

But she was glad of her son's safe return and absorbed with pleasure the stories of Carl's happiness in his marriage, treating the news like a romance novel and a balm for those feelings that still flared up when analysing her own marriage. She liked this Gretchen about whom James spoke, as he highlighted her beauty and her soft nature. The character he created made for a good heroine and she could not help imagining her son married to this girl.

She found herself having to calm Richmond down. 'I am sure it's just a passing infatuation,' she told her husband. 'You don't need to worry, it will blow over in time and he will find a nice English girl to marry.'

'I was not worried,' Richmond retreated behind his manly façade, 'but I hope you're right.'

She had smiled to herself at his reaction, the way he seemed to feel it necessary to give the appearance of not being worried, concerned that it exposed a weakness in him.

Despite telling her husband not to worry, she could not help but feel concerned about her son. If, James had, in fact, fallen seriously in love with Gretchen, he would never be able to marry her. Richmond would see to that and James would be condemned to marry a woman he did not truly love or, even worse, never marrying at all. He would end up a Richmond or a McCallum, she thought. Both men had an aura of regret about them although neither were particularly unhappy. It was as if they had found a kind of contentment in their respective situations, an acceptance that they would never know true love.

※

The first few days back home were torture. He put on his best smiling face, chattered away about the wedding, Gretchen, the journey, how beautiful it was at Pangani beach, everything but what he most wanted to talk about.

At night he revisited the journey home, re-living every detail, each touch, each caress, every look and glance between them, how they had giggled at their secret after stopping to chat with a farmer heading in the opposite direction, the man completely oblivious to their relationship.

They had held hands, kissed and made love with an insatiable urgency, knowing they had to cram as much into the short time they had alone together.

But his thoughts also recalled the growing cloud as they approached Taveta, feeling their precious time together ebbing away and how the slow creep of uncertainty at how their relationship could flourish had taken hold. He had tried not to spoil the last few miles but could not help the knot that grew in his stomach and the feeling of despair that started to envelope him.

Miriam tried to stay buoyant, assuring him that they would find ways to be together, but he saw the sadness behind her smiles.

On their last night together, after they made love, they lay together and talked late into the night. He confessed to watching her as she washed her clothes and she had smiled and had spoken of her stolen moments watching him swim, even mentioning the monitor lizard. They laughed when she said that she was sure that the reptile had 'smiled' at her.

'At least the lizard has given us his blessing,' James chuckled. But that got him thinking. 'The dam is always deserted. We could meet on the far side and spend a few moments together, hidden amongst the rocks. We should be safe from prying eyes there.'

He had gone to the dam every evening, hoping to see her but had been disappointed as Miriam was required to catch up on some of the work she had missed while away at the wedding. It was almost a week before she could get away and even then it was for the briefest moment. The agony of letting her go was almost too much to bear and at dinner his mother had checked with him, for the first time since his return, if he was okay. 'You seem a little down,' she had said.

'Oh, I am fine,' he sighed, 'just thinking about Gretchen.' He had said it without thinking, but it had a strange effect on his mother as she gave him a look, as if to say she understood.

Miriam had been serving at the table when he said it and, fortunately, had gone unnoticed when she had looked up sharply at him for just a second before remembering the need for discretion.

'Why did you mention Gretchen at dinner the other night?' she asked when they next met at the dam.

He had smiled his warm smile and replied, 'When I said Gretchen, I thought Miriam. It is my code for you. As you call me "sir" with love so that no one will know, I will refer to you as Gretchen with love.'

She laughed and snuggled into his arms, feeling the strength of his body and the warmth of his love. When they parted that evening she grinned and said, 'I love you, sir'

'And I love you, Gretchen,' he responded.

Richmond was uneasy with all the talk about Gretchen. 'Why couldn't James fall for a proper English girl?' he asked Agnes, 'Why a foreigner?' He shook his head, then added, 'I suppose a German woman is at least better than a French one.'

Agnes, who still held the German doctor slightly responsible for Rosemary-Jane's death, was a little sympathetic but more pragmatic. 'Richmond, there are so few suitable women around here. We hardly know any English girls. Isn't it better that he marry a German than to remain a bachelor?'

Richmond 'harrumphed' and conceded that a German was better than nothing. 'Still, an English woman would be infinitely better.'

Agnes tried to encourage James, suggesting that he invite Gretchen to come and visit, but he seemed reluctant.

'The boy is a sissy,' Richmond moaned, annoyed that James appeared unwilling, almost shy, when dealing with his mother's advice. It was good in some way that he did not have the courage to follow through on his feelings with a German, but it irked Richmond that his son could be such a coward. When he wanted someone, he took them. Yes, Agnes had been a mistake, but the various farm women he had taken, and that one occasion in Voi when he had seduced the lovely wife of the hotel owner, those were signs of strength of character, he felt. It concerned him that James was turning out to be a weakling when it came to women. He blamed Agnes for this.

He tried to articulate his thoughts to McCallum, finding difficulty in expressing himself without coming across as a bigot.

'I wouldn't worry too much,' the Scot said. 'If the lad is in love, well, that's a good thing. Lassies are few and far between here. If he happens to marry a German, people understand.'

'You're a sentimental fool, just like Agnes,' Richmond said, somewhat in jest, but left feeling reassured. McCallum had been in country for a long time and knew the people here. He was, however concerned about what the family back home would make of such a relationship.

Two weeks after his conversation with McCallum, news came through that a young English doctor had arrived in Voi.

'At least we can get proper medical treatment now,' Richmond said.

James became wary around his parents. His idea to use Gretchen to deflect them from noticing his affair with Miriam was causing its own problems. His mother was becoming too encouraging while his father was clearly concerned. He had no one to turn to. A bigger concern was Hannah. Dear, wise Hannah. It always felt to him like she knew. He had never been able to deceive her when he was a child and now that he was grown, he was certain she knew the truth.

'But how could she?' he asked himself. They had been so careful to maintain the master and servant façade around the house. Despite his burning desire to take Miriam in his arms and kiss her passionately each time she walked past him, he had remained outwardly calm and treated her just as he had before. He even made a point not to be too dismissive as that could bring its own suspicions and problems.

Few people from the farm went near the dam, so it was very unlikely that anyone had spotted them there and their meeting place on the far side of the dam was secluded and kept them well hidden from any casual passer-by.

They had not made love since their return from the wedding, their time at the dam so limited, they could only steal a few kisses. They would spend most of it trying, and failing, to come up with a better way to meet.

They debated a trip to visit Gretchen. James felt that he had built up enough of a friendship with her at the wedding to warrant suggesting he make the long journey to Bagamoyo where she lived. Bagamoyo was another two days' journey south from Carl's place. But he was concerned that such a trip would send the wrong message to Gretchen and that was not fair on her.

Then things changed. While out riding on the farm, Richmond's horse was spooked by a snake, and he had been thrown. Fortunately, the damage was only a broken leg. It could have been a lot worse. One of the farm hands had been nearby and a cart was brought to carry Richmond back to the house. James was despatched to Voi to get the English doctor who turned out to be quite young, in fact he was the same age as James. But he appeared competent enough for Richmond to accept him and let him set the leg.

'You will have to rest up for a few weeks,' the doctor said, then reading the expression on the patient's face, turned to Agnes and added, 'You must make sure he rests. If the break does not set right, he may not walk properly again.'

This sent Agnes into a bit of a panic. She knew her husband. He would want to be up and about before he had healed properly.

'Richmond, you will listen to the doctor, won't you?'

Richmond gave a non-committal grunt.

'I want you to promise, and Doctor Smith you will be my witness. Promise me, Richmond.'

'All right, all right, I promise,' Richmond waved a dismissive hand and Agnes nodded her approval.

After the excitement of the injury, Agnes insisted that the doctor stay for afternoon tea before heading back into Voi. They sat out on the veranda and she introduced him to Aitkens' Coffee, 'the best in East Africa we have been told, Doctor Smith,' Agnes boasted.

'Please call me Oliver,' he said. He was a handsome man, dark hair neatly parted down the middle and gleaming with Macassar oil. He had deep brown eyes that brightened whenever he smiled. His youthful skin still clung to the memory of the pale sun of England.

'Oliver, that's a nice name,' Agnes said. 'I have an uncle called Oliver. They live in the Lake District.' She smiled sweetly.

'A lovely part of the country,' the boy doctor replied. 'I used to spend my holidays there with family.'

'Are they still in England, your family?' James asked.

'No. We moved out here together. My father is a missionary, they are busy setting up a school on the other side of Voi. My sister is helping them. She is teaching the children to read and write.'

'Your sister?' James could not help noticing the interest in his mother's voice.

'Yes, Elizabeth, Lizzy.'

'And how are your family finding things here? How are you settling in?'

'It has its difficulties, I must confess,' Oliver sipped some coffee, 'Mmm, this is very good. Meeting people has been the hardest bit. It's not too bad for me, being a doctor. I am out and about all over the district, but mother and father and Lizzy, well they spend most of their time with the natives.'

'Weekends too?' Agnes asked and James glanced at her.

'Most,' Oliver took another sip of coffee and eyed the cakes that Miriam had set on the table.

'Oh, how rude of me,' Agnes said as if noticing the cakes for the first time, 'please help yourself.' She offered the plate to Oliver.

'Thank you,' he took one then went on. 'Because they're still setting things up, there is a lot of work. They're building a proper school.'

Agnes looked disappointed, but still asked, 'Would they get a chance to come over for dinner one weekend? There's plenty of room so they can stay over. We'd love to meet them.'

Oliver smiled. 'That's very kind. I will pass on the invitation, but I really do not know if they could get away much at the moment.'

James suddenly saw a way to be with Miriam. He nearly blurted out his question as the intensity of his joy threatened to overthrow his self-control. But he managed to rein in his emotions and was able to ask in a calm voice, 'Do you want some help with the school? It's quiet on the farm just now. The harvest is in and the roasting is almost done. I am sure I can be spared to come over and help every now and then, and I've done a fair bit of construction work in my time.'

For a different reason Agnes was enthusiastic about the suggestion. 'What 'a lovely idea,' she bubbled. 'It would do James good to be with people his own age, and it would help with the school.'

'Why, that's extremely kind of you to offer. I am sure that mother and father would be delighted to accept.'

Later, as they bid farewell to the doctor and watched him gallop away, James felt a small twinge of guilt. He was using his father's accident for his own purposes, and this was not right. It struck him particularly when he went in to see how Richmond was doing. While putting on a brave face, he was clearly in some pain. But James could not help thinking that with the proposed trips to Voi he could find a plausible excuse to take Miriam along with him, and there were many spots along the road where they could be alone and that far outstripped these minor feelings of guilt.

⚱

'Can't you see, Richmond, if James goes and helps with the school, things may happen between him and Elizabeth, romantic things.' Agnes pronounced the word 'romantic' as one would a foreign phrase, a questioning tone coating its verbalisation as if asking whether it was being pronounced correctly.

Her husband looked at her from the bed where he lay, propped up by numerous pillows, his plaster encased leg lying outside the bed coverings like a log of charred wood. The pain killers the doctor had given him brought a confused look to his face as if he were trying to peer through a haze, looking for meaning in what lay beyond the fog.

Agnes repeated what she had said. 'It may mean James finally finds a wife. An English wife.'

The word 'English' seemed to jolt Richmond out of his fuzzy world.

'Yes, yes. That would be good. But we know nothing about this Smith family, do we?'

Agnes was a little surprised at this reaction. She had expected him to be happy that an opportunity had arisen for James to possibly marry an English woman, and one on the doorstep, so to speak, rather than a German one who lived a week's journey away.

'We can find out about them, ask around. I know it's too early to tell, but who knows what may happen.'

Richmond grunted and shifted himself in the bed, grimacing slightly at the pain the movement brought.

'Anyway, with you laid up like this, James will have to make the trips into Voi to deal with whatever business it is that you deal with there.'

Richmond's discomfort was barely perceptible. His current 'business' in Voi was called Geraldine, a red-haired Irish woman who had lost her husband to the jaws of a hippopotamus while he was swimming in Lake Jipe, south of Taveta.

Agnes saw the look Richmond tried to hide but chose to ignore it. She had long suspected her husband of infidelity, but reasoned that, if he found his satisfaction elsewhere, he would not come demanding it from her and she was content with that. As long as he never abandoned her.

'Well, there are things in Voi that need doing. I could send McCallum, but it is time the boy learned that side of the business.' He was warming to the idea. 'As you rightly say, at least it's not a German woman. Now I think I need to sleep. Those pills the doctor gave me have made me very tired.'

Agnes fussed over him, helping him settle back in the bed, knowing that this would annoy him and taking slight pleasure in her little game, seeing it as a small payback for his disregarding their marriage vows. I may not love him, she told herself, but I have never been untrue to him. Then she added, rather sadly, of course I have never had the opportunities to stray that he has.

James found it difficult to control his excitement at the prospect of having time with Miriam. He wanted to grab her and shout out the news, but knew he had to wait until they were alone at the dam. He also had to temper this enthusiasm with the nagging doubt that he was getting ahead of himself, and this kept threatening his joy. How would it work in reality? How could he arrange for Miriam to join him on his trips to Voi without raising suspicion? Could he eventually trust Oliver enough to enlist his help in this endeavour? Where could he and Miriam go to be alone if he was meant to be helping at the school? How long would his father be laid up?

He pushed the thought about his father to the back of his mind, but knew he needed to act quickly as this window of opportunity may not last long. But it was three days before he could tell Miriam as her work kept her from meeting him at the dam. Each day he swam quickly across to the other side, hoping she would be there, only to be disappointed. This heightened his frustration but, when she eventually came, he rushed over and grabbed her in his arms, spinning her around and causing the monitor lizard to scurry away in fright.

Miriam giggled at his joy as it bubbled through his arms into her, but was confused. Why the sudden excitement?

'What is it, sir?' she asked when she got her breath back, her voice still caressing the word 'sir', keeping her love alive in it.

'There may be a way we can be together,' his eyes sparkled and his voice sang.

'Forever?' she asked, his excitement was contagious, but her question dimmed the sparkle in his eyes.

'No, not forever,' he seemed to deflate, her one word question reducing his plan to a brief soothing of the constant ache he felt, reminding him of the enormity of their problem. This was a win in a small skirmish where the tide of the war was fully against them.

'Tell me,' she said, her voice trying to urge the happiness back into him, her eyes apologising for bursting his bubble.

He started slowly. The suddenly drained adrenaline seeping back into his system as he spoke and he watched the joy build in her. Yes it would be brief snatched moments but, if they could manage it, that would be far better than the crumbs they had to content themselves with at the moment.

'I will go to Voi tomorrow,' he said, 'and see what can be done. There must be some way that I can arrange for you to accompany me on future trips without raising suspicion.'

Their parting, which came far too soon as Miriam was needed back at the house, mixed anticipation and frustration in equal measure.

'I think I will go into Voi tomorrow,' James said as casually as he could at dinner. Richmond was still taking his meals in bed, but McCallum had joined them at the table as was their Friday custom.

'Do you need any help with that?' the Scot asked, spooning some soup into his mouth. Hannah had prepared a thick vegetable broth, the farm manager's favourite. 'The closest I've ever had to my mother's,' he had commented one evening. Since then, Hannah made a point of ensuring it was regularly on the menu.

'Thank you for the offer, Uncle Malcolm, but I should be fine. I thought I may visit Dr Smith if he's around. Does father need any more pain medicine?' He turned to his mother who was smiling a knowing smile.

'Oh that would be nice if you can see Dr Smith. I am sure he will appreciate a visit. It is so difficult settling into a new country, I'm sure he will be glad for it.'

James chuckled to himself, noting not only his mother's enthusiasm, but also the fact that she gave no answer to his question about his father's comfort. He would ask his father later. He knew where his mother's eagerness came from. She was hoping for a match with the doctor's sister. He had a fleeting moment of doubt as he wondered what complications this may throw up, but pushed the thought aside, not wanting it to interfere with the thrill the anticipation was giving him.

Hannah and Miriam cleared away the soup plates and brought in the dishes for the main meal, a hock of ham, some boiled potatoes with green peas and a tomato salad. James glanced at Miriam as she moved round the room.

'Miriam, I wonder if we have any mustard. I think it would go well with the meal.' It was a little risky asking. As a servant, Miriam would be expected to have anticipated this and already had the condiment on the table. But it gave them a brief second of being able to make eye contact and talk to each other without raising suspicion.

'Yes, sir. I have it ready in the kitchen. I will bring it through.' She glanced at him then averted her eyes as a good servant should, but the glance was all he needed for the moment and he breathed a sigh of relief that she was prepared for this and that there would be no reproaches. The 'sir' in her response tingled in his ears.

'Oh, and can you ask Josiah to have the wagon ready tomorrow after breakfast. I am going into Voi.' He felt the strain of making it sound as natural as he could, his mind's ear hearing the same instruction given so many times before and he did his best to imitate the casualness with which his father would say it.

He glanced across at his mother to see if she had noticed his disguised message to Miriam that here was some progress to the plan. He was surprised to see an unsettled look pass briefly across her face. There was a kind of concern in the look, but this seemed to struggle with a sense of happiness.

It was only later the thought struck him that, by imitating his father's tone, his mother may associate this with his father's infidelity. Did she know about that? He was unsure. However, he reasoned, even if she did, she would surely not think he was he was pursuing the same things. She must believe that his quest was far more pure. This was going to prove trickier than he thought. He would first have to establish the appearance of an interest in Dr Smith's sister before he could even think about taking Miriam along with him.

Miriam nodded at the command and left to get the mustard. James suddenly realised that he was shaking slightly. He had not fully appreciated the extent of worry he had been carrying in anticipation of announcing his trip to Voi and now that it was out there, the adrenaline withdrawal made him shiver slightly.

Fortunately, McCallum came to his rescue, talking about the various supplies that were needed, distracting his mother with mundane questions about what she required from town and checking with her whether she had asked Hannah if they needed any items for the pantry. The last thing he needed now was for his mother to start panicking that his shiver was a sign that he may be coming down with malaria. The talk was so everyday and dull that it bored the shakes from him and drew him into its ordinariness to such a degree that he did not even notice Miriam clear away the plates and the untouched dish of mustard.

After she had seen James off, Agnes went in to check on Richmond. He had finished his breakfast and sat staring out the window. He looked across at her as she entered the room and seemed to take a moment to return from his thoughts.

'Everything okay?' she asked.

'Hmm? What? Yes. All fine. Just brooding over this damned leg.' He indicated the cast. 'Darn nuisance. I should be out there, not stuck in here like an invalid.'

'Oh, don't worry yourself so much, Richmond. You have McCallum, and James is grown up now. He knows what he is doing. They have things under control. James has just left for Voi this morning. For supplies.'

'Has he now?'

'Oh, Richmond, it is time he found a wife,' Agnes picked up on the implication in his tone.

'Yes, I suppose. I'm not objecting to that. It is high time he was married. It's more that he ... Well, he's grown up too fast. It seems like just yesterday we were burying Rosemary-Jane and now we're marrying off James.'

The mention of Rosemary-Jane surprised Agnes. She could not recall Richmond ever having mentioned their daughter after she had died. She knew that he occasionally went out to the grave with his evening drink, but had put that down to him wanting some time to relax and think, away from the evening bustle of the house. She had never thought that it was any feeling for their departed daughter that took him out there. It was just a nice quiet spot.

'We live a fragile life out here. This land is tough. It took Rosemary-Jane quickly. Darn near took me with that snake bite and again with this,' he gestured at his leg. 'Could have been a lot worse. I was lucky.'

'But you will be okay. The doctor said…'

'Yes, yes, the doctor said,' he waved away her sentiment with a dismissive hand, then was silent for a while.

'It's not that I don't believe the doctor. I will be fine in a few weeks' time, a month or two maybe. It will take me a little while before I am back to full strength. And yes, we have McCallum. He is a good man, the best. James is doing nicely on the farm He has a good knack for it. But I do fear…'

He stopped and stared out the window again.

Agnes waited, her mind rushing, wondering what it was that Richmond feared so. She knew the constant worries she lived with, that malaria, or a snake, or a wild animal, or a throw from a horse, or a wagon accident, or a mishap with the farm equipment, or an uprising amongst the natives, or something she had not even thought of yet could take her son from her in an instant. She knew those fears and, while she hated them, she had learnt to live with them. However, there was something in her husband's tone that said there was a far greater and more real threat out there, one she had not contemplated. She felt a coldness creep across her heart and she shivered slightly.

🙎

'How is your father's leg doing?' Oliver asked after greeting James warmly. 'I must get over there and check on him. The cast should come off soon.'

'He's doing well. Being a real grouch, but I would expect nothing less from him,' James grinned. 'He can't stand being confined to his room.'

Oliver nodded. They sat in the little front room of the Smith's house, the smell of the coffee James had brought beginning to waft through from the kitchen.

'He's not been trying to walk, has he? It is really important that he doesn't. Those who taught me back in medicine school could not stress that enough. So many patients, they said, tried to walk too soon and never healed properly,' Oliver was serious now.

'No. Mother has been very good at keeping him on the straight path, although he has not been a bad patient. I think that you scared him enough to ensure that he behaves himself. It helps that you are English. I fear that if it had been the German doctor from Taveta telling him to rest up, he may not have been so willing to listen.'

'But Dr Holstein is an excellent doctor. Why on earth would your father not listen to him?'

'I don't know. A prejudice of sorts, I suppose. I have a feeling that he blames Dr Holstein for Rosemary-Jane's death.'

'Rosemary-Jane?'

'My sister. I never knew her. She died before I was born. Malaria.'

'Malaria? How can he blame Dr Holstein for that?'

'I don't know. My parents rarely talk about her. She was just two when she died. Sometimes McCallum, he's the farm manager, I think you met him, he sometimes talks about my sister. But it always feels strange because I never knew her.'

'Still unfair to blame Holstein,' Oliver said.

'I suppose so, although I may be being unfair on father. I am just guessing at that.'

Oliver nodded. 'Would you have liked a sister. It is just you, isn't it? No siblings?'

'Yes, just me,' James said. 'I suppose a sister or a brother would be nice, but I grew up happy enough. There was a…' He paused. Should he mention Miriam now? Even if it was to talk about her as a sisterly playmate when kids? He was just debating this when a young woman walked into the room.

'Ah, speaking of sisters, this is Elizabeth, my sister.'

James rose to greet her. She was a short, pretty woman with bright grey-blue eyes. Her auburn hair was tied in a bun, but rogue strands escaped from the knot and a wisp or two were plastered down her cheeks. Her face glowed with a thin layer of sweat and was raspberry jam red from exertion and from exposing pale skin to sunlight.

'Oh, I am sorry, I didn't realise you were with a patient,' she said, rubbing a forearm across her forehead. Her voice was light and cheery.

'This isn't a patient. This is James, James Aitken. It was his father's leg I had to go sort out two weeks ago.'

'Pleased to meet you, James. And it's Lizzy, not Elizabeth' she gave Oliver a playful look. 'You will excuse my appearance, won't you? I've been working in our vegetable garden out back.'

James liked how she was not flustered by her state, it indicated a quiet confidence in herself that appealed. It also told him that there was no immediate physical attraction to him. She would surely have been less self-assured had there been. It would complicate things if Elizabeth … Lizzy fell for him. He had to tread carefully here, but this was a good start.

'Nothing wrong with the appearance of one doing good, honest work,' he smiled.

'You are too kind, sir,' she gave a mock curtsey, 'but if you will excuse me, I must freshen up for my own comfort.'

'Join us when you're done,' Oliver called after her as she bustled out of the room. 'James brought us some freshly roasted coffee from their farm.'

When she returned about five minutes later, her hair was loose and neatly brushed. Her cheeks, while still pink, had been cleared of the deeper hue of hard work and washed clear of the shiny layer of sweat. She looked quite pretty and James marvelled at how quickly she had transformed.

'Would you like me to sort out that coffee?' she asked. 'It smells delicious.'

'Please do,' Oliver smiled and then, when she left the room, he turned to James and said, 'She'll make a great wife for someone one day.'

It did not seem to James like a hint or an invitation but he was not sure, so nodded politely and smiled.

The coffee was brought in along with some cake. Lizzy served, then settled into a chair opposite James. There was a natural ease about her that quickly had the conversation flowing. James gave a little history of his family and Oliver and Lizzy told him their story of how they came to be in Voi. Their father, a minister and a man of deep faith, had joined the Church Missionary Society and felt called to work in Africa.

Lizzy and Oliver were old enough to have remained in England, but both chose to come with. Oliver, with his medical skills and Lizzy's training as a teacher made them feel that they could contribute to the mission work.

James listened with interest. His family were not particularly religious. Yes, they went to church on the odd occasion when farm work allowed, but the family bible sat largely untouched on the shelf and would have been gathering dust were it not for Hannah's cleaning regime.

Doing something big, particularly something as drastic as moving country because God had told one to do so, was a rather alien concept to him. Yet he admired the determination and conviction of this brother and sister.

'Would you like to see the school?' Lizzy's enthusiasm for her subject bubbled over into the invite.

They walked along the dusty path to the church, pausing to listen to the choir practice that the Reverend and Mrs Smith were leading and then headed on to the school.

'We're still building it,' Lizzy explained, 'so lessons are held outside under that tree there, but we hope that by the time the rains come we will have a roof to protect us.

A group of native children came to look at the white people, giggling and pointing, their young voices skipping quickly over their words.

'I wish I could understand what they are saying,' Lizzy said, smiling and waving. 'I am trying to learn the language, but I have not found a teacher among them. I just pick up words here and there. And the adults are all too busy or have no real grasp of English to be able to help.'

James nodded. 'It's not a language that I am overly familiar with,' he said. 'I can get by with a few phrases, but I am by no means fluent.' Then an idea struck which tied a knot of excitement in his stomach. 'But I do know someone who is fluent both in their language and English. I will see if we can spare her on the weekends to come and teach you.'

'That would be marvellous,' Lizzy did a slight skip as she walked.

'I should tell you that she is one of our servants, a native woman. But Miriam is very good in both languages,' James struggled to keep the excitement out of his voice. Here was the opening he had been looking for.

There was a spot not too far off the road between Voi and the farm where they made love for the first time since their journey home from Carl's wedding. There was sufficient bush and long grass for them to pull the wagon off the road and out of sight. The ground was level and the grass gave way to a rocky area. The trees that were dotted around provided shade for the couple and made a good viewing point for the curious monkeys.

They could not linger too long as they needed to get back to the farm before sundown, but they were grateful for this short time together, the grass and the trees and rocks forming a natural barrier between them and the social norms that prowled the land beyond this private Eden.

They explored each other's bodies, hungry for the smooth warmness of skin, marvelling at the soft ripple of muscled limbs, caressing the gentle contours, tasting the slippery wetness of each other's mouths, then shuddering at that delicious moment when they became one, joining together to climb to the point of pleasure, then holding on tight as they slowly slid back down from the peak.

Every Saturday morning they set off early from the farm. If Oliver was free, he and James would help with building the school while Miriam would teach Miss Elizabeth the Dawida language of the locals. They would lunch together with Miriam helping the Smith's servants in preparing and serving, both her and Lizzy reverting to their respective roles with ease.

While he enjoyed these mornings, the easy friendship with Oliver, the relaxed labour in building the school, James would always feel the nagging irritation of anticipation. He could not wait for the day's charade to be over so he could escape with Miriam to their little paradise. Keeping the restlessness in check as he sawed wood for the school, or helped with the laying of bricks, was a torture he resented and yet savoured. The anticipation of the moment he could take Miriam in his arms, was as thrilling and as frustrating as the act of love making itself. Wanting to get there in a hurry but not wanting to miss the journey as it would all be over too soon and he would then have the long wait for the next weekend to come around.

He also came to resent how quickly the school building was going up and how his father's leg was healing. The progress of both hastening the time when he would no longer have an excuse to make these trips. He was certain that once fully healed, his father, who was now hobbling around the house with the aid of a crutch and the blessing of the doctor, would want to resume his duties. And this included going into Voi for supplies. He was less concerned about the school building being finished as his friendship with Oliver and Lizzy had developed enough for him to continue making the journey. And Lizzy's progress with the Dawida language was slow, not because she wasn't a quick learner, but because the language was so different to her mother tongue. It was also taking longer because she wished to be fluent and not just proficient, spending long periods perfecting her pronunciation of each word.

The Reverend and Mrs Smith had taken to James and welcomed him into their home, making him feel like one of the family, although he could not say for sure if the familial feel was for a son or a potential son-in-law. They seemed to encourage, but never push, interaction with Lizzy. The Reverend had a stern face but a gentle nature. He was a man who carried God with him wherever he went. Mrs Smith was a short woman made out of smiles who showed little loss of the looks she had passed on to her daughter. Her nature, which was somewhat reserved, was amplified in Lizzy.

Despite their welcoming nature, James could not help feeling ill at ease around them, always aware of the deceit in his visits.

While their time together on a Saturday travelling back from the Smith's was more susceptible to discovery than the quick moments shared at the dam, it was at the latter spot that McCallum stumbled upon them. It had been a particularly hot day. A fierce sun had scalded the blue from the sky leaving it white hot and glaring down on the land. The air cowered in the face of this onslaught, too frightened to move and wrapped a cloying blanket of humidity around everything.

James and McCallum worked slowly in the fields, their energy levels sapped by carrying the additional weight of the sweat that drenched their clothes. As soon as the day's work was done, James headed off to the dam, eager for the coolness and cleanness the water would bring. He had not been expecting Miriam but was glad to see her waiting for him on the far side.

Despite his eagerness to grab at the few moments with her, he swam slowly, letting the water cool his heated body.

McCallum hardly ever went to the dam, but the heat of the day made him decide to go for a swim to cool off. He arrived just in time to see James emerging from the water on the far side and was about to call out when James quickly disappeared into the bushes. He undressed to his bathing suit and eased himself into the water, watching for the reappearance of the young lad. When he did not return, McCallum began to get a bit worried and swam slowly across.

He found them kissing passionately, James pawing at her breasts while Miriam held his face in her hands, her fingers interlaced with his hair. It took him a moment to realise this was not the same kind of liaison that Richmond had with the other farm women. Miriam was not simply obeying a master's command.

'Ach!' The cry was out of his mouth before he could stop it. Had he not cried out, he would have withdrawn quietly and left the two in peace. He was the farm manager. It was none of his business what Richmond, or James for that matter, got up to with the workers. But his involuntary outburst denied him the luxury of an unnoticed retreat.

There was a quick fumbling and shock as the couple untangled themselves. McCallum took a few steps backwards, his brain not yet fully realising that he was as much caught out as they were.

'I'm so sorry, laddie. I didn't realise that you were...' He managed to find his voice while simultaneously James was trying to utter a defence.

'It's not... it's...'

Miriam took advantage of the confusion to flee the scene, leaving the two men to stutter their wild machine gun excuses till they both quickly ran out of ammunition and just stared at each other, both waiting for the other to formalise the ceasefire.

'Ach, laddie. I'm so sorry,' McCallum broke the moment of silence. 'I saw you come in here and, well, I had no idea what you were up to and I started to worry when you didn't reappear.'

'It's not what you think, Uncle Malcolm. I am in love with her... and she is with me.' James suddenly seemed to find his voice and he stood with his hands on his hips, legs slightly apart as if preparing to launch a physical attack on McCallum if necessary. 'I'm not like my father.' There was a mixture of defiance, disdain and petulance in the comment.

'Ach, no. No you're not, my laddie. You're not.' McCallum shook his head and held out his hands in a gesture of surrender. 'No, you're not. I could see it the moment I spotted you together,' he added with some level of sadness.

'You could?' James' voice showed his surprise and his stance became less aggressive.

'That was young Miriam, wasn't it?' McCallum asked gently.

James nodded slowly.

'She's a lovely lass. Pretty too. Like her mother. Both of them very bright. But you know you can't...' he shook his head again. 'You know...'

James stared at him for a moment, then a horrid thought struck and stumbled back a step. 'She's not ... no, she can't be, she's not one of my father's?' There was a note of terror in his voice and a welling up in his eyes.

'No, no, no,' McCallum was quick to calm him. 'No, she's not your father's daughter,' despite himself, he gave a chuckle. 'For some reason your father has always kept away from Hannah.'

James took a moment to process this and a moment more to calm himself, then his defiance suddenly reappeared.

'She's not yours, is she?'

McCallum gave a little chuckle. 'No, laddie, not mine. As far as I know Miriam is the daughter of Hannah's deceased husband, but come, let's go and swim. I can't think in this heat, and we need cool minds now. We can talk in the water.'

James nodded slowly and they waded back into the dam swimming slowly back to the other side where they found a couple of submerged rocks to sit on, their bodies submerged, but heads and shoulders above the water.

'There are undoubtedly some of your father's offspring walking this earth somewhere, but it is unlikely you will ever meet your half-sisters or brothers.' McCallum said once they had settled.

'Why not?' James asked, the term 'half-sister' sitting strangely with him.

'They send them away. To family or friends on other farms. Somewhere where they can't cause trouble.'

'Trouble? For my father, or for them?'

'A bit of both, I think.' McCallum replied. 'Sending them away helps reduce the possibility of your father firing them, particularly if the child's skin ends up being fair.'

James stared out across the dam as he processed this, his heart trying to convince his mind that his father would never have done such a thing, but he knew that even his heart was not convinced of its own argument.

'And how does it prevent trouble for them?'

McCallum shifted in the water. 'Well, I'm guessing, but surely such a child would be a source of tension between the woman and her husband. The husband would not take responsibility and the woman does not have the means to support the child.'

James nodded slowly. 'That is terrible, but surely...'

'Surely nothing, laddie,' McCallum's tone was suddenly sharp. 'Life is not always fair and Africa is tough. Tougher if you're a native rather than a settler. What chance does a mixed blood child have? Sometimes they are lucky and come out dark. They can mix in and be accepted as native, if not amongst their own family, at least in the towns and other farms. But the fairer ones will always be too dark to be a settler and too light to be a native. They live in the in-between, suspended in a kind of no-man's land. You must have seen some of them in Voi. Usually they are beggars. No one will employ them.' His voice became slightly fraught.

James stared at him, the penny slowly starting to drop. 'Is your offspring one of those in Voi?' he asked.

Richmond sat on the veranda looking out at the garden. He had never really appreciated the work that Agnes put in to tame, and keep tame, the lawn and flower beds. The neat borders, mix of colours and well-trimmed grass created a garden that could almost be at home in a country estate back in England. He remembered some of the gardens he had visited as a youngster. But there was something softer about those. Was it just his memory that had taken the edge off his vision of those gardens, or was Agnes' garden just that little bit tougher?

There was a hardness to the blue sky that England did not have, but it was more than just the light. The grass here was coarser, a kind of gnarled green root. And the flowers seemed brighter and spikier. There were none of the gentle roses that flourished back home. Here were fiery red balls of spikes and the near violent lavender of the bougainvillea.

He liked this difference, the toughness of local plants. He saw himself reflected in these hardy flora, a survivor ... no, a flourisher in a land where the odds were stacked against one. He was proud of what he had achieved since coming here. If truth be told, he had been far more successful than he would have been had he stayed in England and taken over his father's business.

He watched as James walked round the garden with the doctor and the doctor's sister who had linked arms with the two men. She was very pretty and Richmond had to fight the stirring inside him, his mind telling him that she could end up being his daughter-in-law, but other parts of his body could not see what the issue was. As if responding to his conscience, a twinge of pain shot up his leg and he gave a sharp intake of breath.

'Are you okay?' Agnes looked up from her sewing.

He gave an unconvincing grunt accompanied by a non-committal nod, then rubbed his leg. 'Just a twinge,' he said and settled back with a sigh. Even if this Elizabeth was not forbidden fruit, he did not think he would be able to perform properly with this confounded leg and that caused him more pain than the physical twinges he occasionally felt.

He longed to be fully healed so that he could resume his trips into Voi to meet with Geraldine. Even being able to get around the farm and have his way with the servants would relieve his frustration.

'What do you think of Elizabeth?' Agnes asked, indicating the youngsters in the garden.

For a brief moment Richmond wished to tell his wife what he really thought, what he would like to do with the pretty girl on his son's arm. 'She seems very nice. A bit too talkative and confident for my liking, but otherwise nice.'

Agnes clicked her tongue quietly but did not say anything. He knew that she liked Elizabeth, or at least fancied the girl as a match for her son. He also knew that the click was a disapproval of what she would regard as his bigotry, but he was not going to be intimidated. That is what he thought of Elizabeth. The girl had too much confidence for her age, and even more so for her sex. He blamed that Emily Hobblehorse, or whatever her name was, the one who had caused all that trouble in South Africa.

He sighed. 'I suppose that's just the modern woman for you. Can't say that I like it much.' He knew it was pointless getting into a debate with Agnes.

'Well, James seems to like her and that's what is important,' Agnes insisted.

Richmond looked over at the trio as they neared the end of their circuit of the garden and were making their way back towards the house. He could see that James had great affection for Elizabeth but, to him, it was the love of siblings that he saw there. He could not see the love one should observe between a man and his intended. 'But then,' he thought to himself, 'what do I know about that kind of love.'

He looked across at Agnes and felt again his care and affection for her that had grown out of years of living together. But if he sought passion, or love of the kind a good marriage was supposed to be made of, his first thought would be of someone more akin to Geraldine than to his wife.

'You do have a lovely garden, Mrs Aitken,' Elizabeth said as the three youngsters climbed the stairs to the veranda.

'Why thank you, Elizabeth. Ah here's the tea,' Agnes responded as Miriam brought out the tray.

For a fleeting moment, Richmond thought he saw in James the look that he expected to see from one in love, but thinking it was directed at Elizabeth, he said to himself, 'Maybe there is hope after all.'

⚇

McCallum sat at the small table that served both as a work desk and a dining table where he had his meals. The front and back doors of his small house were open, allowing the breeze to pass lazily through. Despite the movement of air, the room felt close, a stagnant heat oppressing the lone occupant.

On the table in front of him was a small shot glass of as yet untouched neat whisky, encircled loosely by his freckled pinky-brown fingers. The physical contact with it his only thread of interaction with the present as his mind was elsewhere. He stared out the window, a window which faced in the direction of Voi. But his thoughts went beyond Voi, travelling further on to the coast, to a town called Malindi.

He had visited there once and recalled the blue blue sea and golden sands of the beach. He remembered standing, staring out across the great Indian Ocean, the bustle of the busy town coming to him as breeze-blown noises, the stench of the fish market colouring the sound.

Somewhere amongst that noise, probably hidden down one of those grubby side streets, was his daughter. She would be about five, possibly fair-skinned, possibly not. However, one thing was certain, she would be completely unaware that the man who stood alone on the beach staring out to sea, was her father. Would she ever know that her father was a mzungu, a white man? Jana, the girl's mother, would be there too. Sweet Jana, so unfairly treated. Of course that was in the time before the Aitkens took over the farm. The previous owner had banished mother and child the moment he realised that McCallum was the father. McCallum had been down in Taveta for a week on business and returned to get the news that Jana and her child had been sent away.

It had taken a long time to establish that they were in Malindi and a further time to get a chance to visit. But as he stood on the beach, wondering about them, he realised that to try and make something of this relationship, which seemed so natural to him, but was anathema to both his and her worlds, was never going to work. They would be outcasts wherever they went. It was best, despite the ache it caused his heart, if he simply let them be.

He had turned slowly from the ocean and trudged back into the town to his lodgings where he packed then made his way back to the farm, trying to work out why the emptiness he dragged with him felt so heavy.

'Well, here's to you laddie,' he said, his voice slightly cracked. 'I hope it works out better for you than it did for me.' He raised the whisky glass in a toast and downed the drink, feeling its fiery tentacles spread through his veins.

ꚛ

James sat quietly on the veranda. Stars freckled the night sky and the merest slither of moon hooked itself onto an invisible nail. The house was dark and quiet except for the odd creak as it cooled after the warmth of the day. The night sounds of crickets and frogs seemed to crinkle the darkness that lay beyond.

He very rarely sat out at night like this, but his mind was too crowded by thoughts to allow sleep. Questions raced and spun around with a dizzying effect.

It had taken more than a day for McCallum's story to really sink in. After the confession at the dam, James had had little time to process it as Oliver and Lizzy arrived for dinner and to stay over. Oliver was there at Agnes' behest to check on Richmond's leg and Elizabeth was invited 'because we've heard so much about her'. A thinly disguised attempt at aiding match-making, James thought.

While he loved Oliver and Lizzy, he could have done without their company just then. He needed time to think. But circumstances forced him to put the newly acquired information to one side as he entertained the guests. Dinner had slowly drawn out the sting of distraction as the Smiths were such good company. They sat till late in the evening, chatting and laughing. Even after McCallum made his excuses and left and his mother and father retired, the three continued talking. This, he imagined, would be what it was like to have a brother and a sister, and he liked it.

When they finally turned in, he was exhausted from the heat of the day and the weight of his new knowledge. The warmth of the friendship also helped to send him to sleep quickly before his mind could re-settle on McCallum's confession. The whole of Saturday had been taken with Oliver and Elizabeth. He showed them around the farm explaining the roasting and grinding process and even paused at Rosemary-Jane's grave. It was late in the afternoon when the visitors took their leave, giving just enough time for them to get back to Voi before dark.

Then there was dinner to get through and waiting for his parents to retire before he could creep quietly onto the veranda. He knew that his mother would not be happy with him sitting outside like this, the spectre of malaria always making her cautious.

He eased himself quietly back in the chair and let the cool dark air calm his mind and body. Before he could properly process all that McCallum had told him, he needed a clear head.

He had never stopped to think what would happen if Miriam got pregnant. They had been lucky so far, but they needed to be careful. He could not bear to think what he would do if she was sent away from the farm because of a child. Quite how he felt about this not yet conceived child was uncertain. It was a bit like his sister where he felt he should have some emotional attachment but could find nothing to convert her from a concept into a feeling. Likewise, his theoretical love child could not make the leap from 'what if' to attachment.

Yet, he had seen in McCallum's face the pain of loss and knew that it extended beyond the woman he had loved to the child he had never known.

And what of his half-brothers and sisters? How many of his father's illegitimate offspring were out there, children who would never know their true father, never know of their mixed heritage?

But they were not his problem, his problem was with Miriam and how he could love her and make love to her without the worry of what a pregnancy would mean. McCallum could offer no advice other than 'be careful, laddie, be very careful.' And, he concluded, that was all he could do. There were no easy answers.

'Your mother is keen to see us married,' Lizzy said one Saturday when he sat alone with her in the front room of the Smith's house. Oliver had been called away suddenly for a medical emergency and the Reverend and Mrs Smith were leading the choir practice in preparation for Sunday's service.

'What? What makes you say that?' He was somewhat taken aback.

'Oh, don't come on all innocent with me James Aitken. Your mother wants us to marry. It's as plain as the nose on your face.' There was a smile in her eyes as she said this.

'Yes. Yes, you are right.' He tried, unsuccessfully, to keep the sadness out of his voice.

'So what are we to do?' she asked.

'Do?'

'Yes. Your mother clearly wishes us to be married and, I must admit, my parents are keen on the match too.'

'They are?' James was feeling well out of his depth. Love and marriage were not something he had much experience of. Love, yes, but the two together?

Lizzy gave a slight laugh. 'Yes, they are. They are very fond of you, James. They like you a lot. Your generosity in helping with the school and our work has endeared you to them. They can tell that you are a good man. They would be delighted to have you as a son-in-law. They already see you as part of the family.'

'They do?' Guilt was beginning to flood his emotions. Helping out with building the school had been purely from selfish motives, allowing him time alone with Miriam. But here was Lizzy practically proposing to him. He had no idea how he could let her down without hurting her.

'But you don't love me, do you?'

James was shocked but slightly confused as he searched for the hurt she must surely be feeling. But her voice was calm, teasing almost.

'No. Not like one should a woman he wants to take for a wife. I do love you, but it is more...' he searched for the right words, '...it's more like one would feel for sister. I think. As you know I never knew my real sister, but my feelings for you are how I imagine I would have felt for Rosemary-Jane, had she lived.' He looked up, not wanting to, but feeling he owed it to her.

'And...?' She left the sentence hanging. James searched her face. Where he had expected to find hurt, he saw a vague suppressed smile. She seemed to be toying with him, but he could not fathom why.

'And?' he pleaded for help.

'And you love Miriam,' she concluded for him.

'I...I...'

'Oh James, it is so obvious. I've seen the way you look at her and how she looks at you.' She started to giggle. 'And I am perfectly fine with that. I love you James Aitken, but my love for you is like my love for Oliver. You are like another brother to me.'

'I am?' He was not sure whether he was allowed to feel relieved or not.

'Yes, you are.' The lightness left her voice and the glow of humour dimmed slightly in her face. 'And that is why I will say yes when you ask me to marry you.'

James stared at her. None of what she was saying made sense. He was still reeling from the fact that Lizzy knew about Miriam. They had been so careful about concealing their love, yet she had spotted it. Not only spotted it but had said that it was obvious.

'Don't you see, James, you have no choice. You will never be able to marry Miriam.'

He did not need reminding of that and winced slightly at the familiar stab of pain in his heart each time this reality struck at his thoughts.

Lizzy leaned forward in her chair and took his hands in hers, her eyes no longer bright with the humour she usually carried in them. In its place was a gentleness and, James felt, a look of deep care.

'James,' she said, 'I am offering you a solution. It's not perfect, but I think it will make things easier. Marry me. This will take away any suspicion people may have that there is anything between you and Miriam, or at the very least, temper such thoughts. We can then build our own house, somewhere on the farm, perhaps rebuild on that spot where those ruins were that you showed us when we visited. It's far enough away from your parents' house and we will need a servant to look after us…' she left the rest for James to work out.

Mention of the ruins brought back memories of his father and the servant whom he and Miriam had seen when they were children. He had not mentioned that episode to Lizzy.

'You mean…? But what about you? I mean, shouldn't you be looking for a husband who you love and who will love you?'

'James,' she tugged slightly at his hands, emphasising her word, 'I am already married to my work. This is what I have always dreamed of doing. A proper husband will get in the way of that. He would probably insist that I stop working and be a good housewife. I do not want that and this is what I would ask in return for helping you and Miriam. I want to be allowed to continue working at the school unhindered.'

'But the farm is not close to the school.'

'I can ride. It will only take twenty minutes on a fast horse and, if I finish too late on the odd occasion, I can sleep over here. We can make this work. For both of us. I know we can. What do you say, James Aitken, will you marry me on these terms?'

He took a week to think about it. Not only was it an audacious proposition which had left him nearly speechless, he had also been struck by how determined and strong-willed Lizzy was beneath her pretty exterior. Her gentle, smiling eyes and small frame belied her headstrong personality.

He had not said anything to Miriam on their way home that evening. She had sensed something was up, but he had kept everything to himself. He used tiredness as an excuse for being distracted. By the Wednesday, after clearly having aroused suspicions in his mother, and to a much lesser degree, his father, he decided to seek council from McCallum and invited him for a swim that evening. He was relieved, when they arrived at the dam, to see that Miriam was not there.

McCallum's eyes grew wider and wider as James explained Lizzy's proposal and, by the time he had laid out the whole deal, McCallum was shaking his head in disbelief.

'Remarkable, quite remarkable,' was all he could manage as an initial response.

James waited, realising that McCallum needed time to process things. He had already had a few days to absorb it himself and was still not certain if he had managed to fully grasp the extent of the offer. But his impatience got the better of him as McCallum kept staring off into the distance and shaking his head.

'Well, Uncle Malcolm, what do you think?'

'Ach laddie. It is a quite remarkable offer, I must say.'

'Yes, but what should I do?' James tried to keep the frustration out of his voice.

'I don't know, laddie. Are you sure this is a genuine offer by the lass?'

James nodded. 'She sounded very serious about it.'

'And Miriam? What does she say?'

'I've not told her yet. I don't know how she will react.'

McCallum gave a stifled laugh. 'Well that's where you must start. I don't think you will have an issue there. In her culture, they are used to the man taking more than one wife. But as the lassie said, it's not a perfect solution, however I think it's the best offer you're ever going to get. It's got its potential problems, for instance what if this Elizabeth lassie meets someone else after you are married and then resents the decision she made? Or if Miriam agrees but later gets jealous of you being married to Elizabeth, even if it is just for show?'

James nodded. These things had crossed his mind too.

'There is also the risk that Elizabeth falls in love with you and then demands that you get rid of Miriam,' McCallum added.

'I guess that is possible,' James said.

'And then, what if you and Miriam have children?' he gave a knowing look.

'That too is possible,' James nodded becoming more miserable.

'I suppose what I am saying is that there are risks attached to accepting this proposal. Things you need to think through. You need to be able to deal with whatever may arise. But I guess it boils down to whether you, and here I mean all three of you, are prepared to take the risk or not.'

'Would you take the risk if you were in my shoes, Uncle Malcolm?'

'Oh, absolutely, my lad.' He did not even hesitate. 'This may well be your only chance at happiness in this situation. You know my story, you know my regrets. You don't want to live with regrets.'

The following Saturday, as they rode from the farm to Voi, James explained to Miriam the offer Lizzy had made. He deliberately kept the horses at a slow pace to allow as much time as possible to discuss things.

Her reaction was much like McCallum's – wide-eyed incredulity at first, then thoughtful silence followed by a gradual warming to the idea as the significance of it sunk in. Then, despite her reservations, she began to get excited at the prospect.

'This could be a way,' she smiled. 'It could work.'

'There will be risks,' he said pulling up on the reins so that the cart came to a standstill. They needed the silence to discuss this bit. The squeak of the turning wheels, the clip-clop of the horses' hoofs on the dusty road and the creak of the seats as the cart lolled from side to side, cluttered things too much.

One of the horses shook its head and sighed loudly before the two settled, patiently waiting for the command to move. A slight breeze sent a low whisper through the grass as if unseen creatures were excitedly discussing the couple.

'What will they decide?'

'Can this work?'

'Who is Elizabeth?'

The grass swayed in time to the debate. The morning air was warm and seemed to hold the couple in its embrace.

James went through the possibilities that McCallum had raised, without mentioning that he had discussed things with the farm manager. After being caught together at the lake, James had conveyed to her the Scotsman's undertaking that he would not say anything to anyone.

Miriam nodded at each scenario, agreeing that these were very real possibilities, her brow furrowing deeper and deeper as James laid them out.

She was quiet for a long time after James finished. Eventually she turned to him and, before she opened her mouth, he could see the answer in her eyes.

On the journey home, they stopped at their usually hiding place and held each other.

'Maybe next week I will have time alone with Lizzy to let her know,' he said.

Agnes stood on the veranda watching James ride off into the fields.

'There's something up with that boy,' Richmond's voice caused her to turn. He stood in the doorway also staring out at their departing son. He was walking with a cane now which was almost only used as a means of attracting sympathy, although occasionally a twinge of pain would make him lean more heavily on it.

'You feel that too?' Agnes replied, moving quickly to her husband's side.

Richmond grunted. He had never felt comfortable being in agreement with his wife. She should be in agreement with him.

'What do we know about the Smiths?' he asked.

'The Smiths?'

'Yes. If they are going to be our son's in-laws, we should at least know a little bit about them.'

'In-laws?'

'There's no need to repeat everything I say,' Richmond said gruffly. 'It's quite obvious that the boy is smitten with this Elizabeth Smith girl, just look at the way he wanders around all starry-eyed. I thought women were supposed to be the ones who notice these things. Clearly James is in love with this Smith girl and quite likely is going to propose to her. So we should find out a bit more about the family, should we not?'

'They are a good family. Well respected in Voi. You know Oliver. He did a good job with your leg and has already built up a reputation as an excellent doctor.' Agnes deflected her husband's irritation. She was not sure that he was right about James' mood. There was something funny about it. A mother knew these things. There was a strange nervousness about her son that went beyond being in love and thinking about proposing. But she could not say that to Richmond.

'And how do you know all this?' Richmond, unaware of her thoughts, questioned her knowledge about the Smiths. The implication in his question being that Agnes never went into Voi and never socialised with people in the area, so how could she have any knowledge.

'Hannah. She hears things. From the staff who go into Voi.'

'So, we are to entrust our son's future happiness to the rumours of the natives,' Richmond snorted.

Agnes remained silent. She trusted Hannah and had come to realise just how much the settlers did and said in front of their servants, regarding them as less than human and incapable of comprehending what is being said. But surely a person's true nature comes through when they speak freely, thinking that their words are only heard by close family and 'dumb as a doorpost' servants. She had often steered Richmond away from saying anything harmful about others when Hannah or one of the other servants were around. What servants heard and saw were people at their truest and if the servants were hearing only good reports about the Smiths, then they were most likely to be accurate assessments.

'I suppose we could ask Mr McCallum if he has heard anything,' she suggested as Richmond seemed to be incapable of thinking outside his prejudices.

Richmond nodded slowly. 'I suppose we could.' He stared out along the road. James was almost out of sight.

The week seemed to drag for James. Everything he did felt like he was trying to pull a cart through black cotton soil after the rains. The sticky mud of life seemed to pull him back as he tried desperately to move forward. To make matters worse, it was a particularly hot week and it constantly felt like he was walking through a wall of hot water and breathing was something one had to concentrate on.

Every evening he went to the dam, hoping to see Miriam. He longed to be held in her arms. Even if they didn't talk, he would at least be touching someone who shared his worries and concerns. The urge to try and communicate some of his frustrations to her while in the house was strong, but he knew that now, more than ever, they needed to be discrete.

He was vaguely aware of some unease in his parents but did not have the energy to analyse it. There was often tension between them, but this was slightly different in that they seemed united in their unease instead of adversaries.

While he could not wait for Saturday to come, he also dreaded it. He was not sure he could handle the disappointment if he was unable to talk to Lizzy alone and let her know of their decision to accept her offer. In his more desperate moments, he would panic, imagining that she had changed her mind, or that her proposal had all been a cruel joke just to make him confess that there was something between him and Miriam. Oliver was also dragged into his thoughts as he imagined his friend putting his sister up to this prank.

His mind felt fried by the heat of the day and the heat of the debate that raged within. Then on the Wednesday, news came through that Carl was going to visit. He had some business to do in Mombasa and planned to stop over on his way through. The message was only a few days ahead of him and he expected to arrive on Friday evening.

James was torn. It would be good to see Carl again. Apart from McCallum, Lizzy and Oliver, Carl was the only other one who knew about Miriam. But this meant that he could not go into Voi at the weekend. As he swam that evening, thoughts waged war with emotions. What if Carl told him that this plan with Lizzy was ludicrous, that he should not go through with it. Could he stand to be told that. He felt his whole world was as brittle as eggshells and could be shattered at any moment. Each stroke, as he swam, seemed like he was stretching out to try and grasp something to hold on to and steady himself. But the water never offered him this stability. Even when he reached the shallows of the dam and stood up, he felt that the stony ground would crumble under his feet.

'With Carl coming, I won't be able to go into Voi this weekend,' he announced at dinner. Of course his parents knew this, but James waited until Miriam was in the room before stating the obvious. A slight rattling of the plates she was carrying told him that his love was as disappointed about this as he was, but he dared not look at her.

'Well of course not, Son,' Agnes said. 'We would not expect you to. I don't need anything that could not wait. Richmond you don't want anything either, do you?'

Richmond looked about to contradict her, then grunted that he could wait till the following weekend for his tobacco and newspaper.

But he did not have to wait a week for the news as Carl arrived with a paper from Taveta and a smile the size of a coffee field.

Richmond sat on the veranda, his leg up on a small stool. The pain had mostly disappeared, but he had grown accustomed to sitting like this. Somewhere past the dam, four vultures circled slowly in the sky and a fifth was hurrying across from the south. He felt ill at ease. The news from Europe was not good, like something unnatural was about to happen.

He shook his head to dispel his discomfort and looked at the circling birds, taking some comfort that the laws of nature were still working. The land out there was inhabited by wild animals. Lions and leopard killed impala or zebra or even giraffe on a daily basis. This was the natural order of things in this land and just as natural were the scavengers of the skies. They would circle, waiting their turn to complete the job started by the big cats. Whatever happened in Europe would never stop that.

He looked across the lawn to where James and his friend were walking, deep in conversation, and realised that his sense of foreboding was for things much closer to home. Would James move away from the farm if he married this Smith girl? He liked to think not, but he could not be sure. Since starting to go to Voi regularly, there had been a change in James which he was convinced was more than just the result of his love for Elizabeth. James was being urbanised.

Why should that worry me? he asked himself. It is only natural for a lad of his age to marry, and that Smith girl is, by all accounts, a good enough match. Yes, James would have a better choice if they had been in England. Then again, an impertinent part of his mind reminded him, if we were still in England, James would not exist. Not this James. Had it not been for the misfortune of Agnes falling pregnant, who knows? Instead of coming here to Africa, he could have married Matilda Evans or Emily Deerhart.

He began to feel a little aroused thinking of those girls who would forever be eighteen in his mind. What children would he have had with either of them? Would he have had a son who he would now be worrying about marrying off?

He looked across at James and Carl and realised that he was proud of his boy and loved him. He was just being silly worrying about James and that Smith girl.

He sat back for a bit, trying to convince himself that everything would be all right, but his mind could not convince and the itch that the memory of Matilda and Emily had created began to take over. He found himself wondering what had happened to the petite servant he particularly fancied. She had just disappeared from the farm one day. McCallum had said that the natives were like that, they would up sticks and leave for the slightest reason.

He stood. James and Carl would be catching up for a good while and Agnes was tending to the garden. He hadn't been with a farm woman for a while and he really felt like one now.

James could not discuss Lizzy's proposal with Carl immediately. He first had to catch up on his friend's news. Carl and Katy had recently had a daughter and that needed to be dealt with in their manly way, Carl pretending it was no big deal but was puffed with pride, his bright eyes at odds with the stoicism in his voice.

There was news of his parents and some of the extended family. Gretchen, his cousin, had married a hunter from the south of German East Africa. As Carl related this piece of news, James recalled feigning interest in her to try and throw his parents off the scent of the real love of his life.

'Don't tell my mother,' James said with a grin, 'I think she still holds out hope that we might become family through marriage.'

Carl laughed. He had grown plumper since James had last seen him. Married life was obviously treating him well. He looked content and James found himself envying his friend's state. All seemed so simple, so natural. Carl was married to a woman he loved, had produced an heir, his farm was flourishing. Everything about his life appeared good.

Lunch interrupted them and Carl spent most of the meal answering Richmond's questions about the sisal trade.

James watched his father as Carl spoke about the current market conditions and wondered if he might be considering branching out, trying something other than coffee. Carl certainly made it sound an attractive business.

Then his mother monopolised Carl as they sat drinking coffee on the veranda after lunch, talking about everything and nothing. James sat politely, keeping his patience in check, hoping his mother would release them soon so he could talk to his friend alone.

'Has James told you about the young lady in his life?' Hearing his name, he quickly returned from his thoughts.

For a moment he panicked, thinking that his mother was referring to Miriam, then quickly composed himself as he realised it was Lizzy who was being alluded to. Then he panicked again as he saw Carl's somewhat shocked features. He is thinking that I've told them about Miriam, he said to himself so quickly jumped in.

'Oh, Elizabeth,' he used her full name to try and give the impression of a formality. 'Yes, she's very nice. The sister of the local doctor, Oliver … my friend, Oliver I should say. They moved here from England about a year ago. We got to know them when father broke his leg and Oliver came over to fix it. Their parents are missionaries, building a school in Voi. I've been helping them out. With the school. Helping them build the school. They are very nice people.' He was babbling and he realised it, but he did not know how to stop.

Fortunately, Carl came to his rescue, perhaps sensing something was not right in all of this, or perhaps just curious and wanting to know more. Whatever the reason, James was grateful for the interruption.

'They sound very nice to me,' there was an enquiring tone in his friend's voice. 'What about Miriam?' was the unasked question behind the statement. 'Perhaps you can introduce us if we get a chance. I have to go through Voi tomorrow. I would love to meet them but tell me more about Elizabeth.'

The interruption not only gave James time to regroup his thoughts but also acted as a cue for Agnes to withdraw.

'I will leave you two alone to talk,' she said, excusing herself. James noticed the self-satisfaction in her voice as if she were proud of herself for getting him to admit that he may have feelings for Lizzy.

He smiled to himself. If only she knew what was really going on between us, she might not be so smug.

He and Carl stood as Agnes went back into the house, dragging a slightly annoyed Richmond with her. When they had left, the two friends sat down again,

'Elizabeth?' Carl asked. 'What about…?'

'Not here,' James half whispered, the urgency in his voice trying to convey to Carl that they could easily be heard while chatting and, in all likelihood, his mother was just inside the door, trying to pick up titbits of information. So he told Carl about Lizzy, describing her, dropping hints about potential nuptials without actually saying that he may propose soon, picking his words carefully and hoping that his expressions were letting Carl know that there was a lot more to the story. He began to enjoy this deception, convinced that his mother was eavesdropping, but he knew it was unfair on Carl to keep him in the dark for too long, so after what he hoped was sufficient to satisfy his mother's curiosity, he said, 'Well that's about all to tell at the moment,' and suggested that they stretch their legs in the garden. At least there, away from prying ears, he could talk freely about Miriam and Lizzy and the offer that he was contemplating.

Miriam watched Agnes standing just inside the door that led on to the veranda, her mistress' head cocked slightly as she tried to hear what was being said by the young men who sat outside. Miriam could barely hear the voices coming in through the open door. From where she stood it was just a low mumble, a breeze blowing through the coffee plants. Occasionally a word or phrase would flutter through, like a leaf blown free from the plants and landing at one's feet. She heard Elizabeth's name mentioned and the word 'proposal' floated in. But mostly it was meaningless fragments, '...teacher...', '...although I...', '...that was when...'

She moved off quietly when she saw Agnes preparing to withdraw. Had James told Master Carl everything, or had he realised that his mother was listening in. The two words, 'proposal' and 'Lizzy' kept flying around in her mind. But, she reminded herself, hoping her recollection of English was correct, 'proposal' could mean asking someone to marry. But it could also mean suggesting a plan. Had James been talking about Miss Elizabeth's proposal or had he skipped that and was rather talking of the proposal of marriage he was going to make to Miss Elizabeth?'

Miriam had been unable to see Mrs Agnes' face, so had no idea how she had reacted to what she had heard and hated the not knowing. She hated the sneaking around quietly, the need for their moments together to be clandestine. She felt guilty every time her mother looked at her strangely, panicking that she, as mothers so often do, knew what was going on.

She would love to tell her mother of her love for James. She would love to shout out to all in the servants' quarters that she was in love with Master James and that he loves her. She wished she could tell those who looked at her like she was another victim of the white man's lust, that they were wrong in this case. Master James was not the same as Master Richmond. The old man used, the young man cared.

Her days were spent doing mindless chores which helped numb the constant ache she had to be with James, to feel the touch of his strong hands on her body. Making up the beds, sweeping the rooms, dusting every corner that Mrs Agnes was likely to check, cooking, cleaning, fetching firewood, washing dishes, all helped wrap her desperate longing in a fuzzy blanket, keeping the precious treasure of her love safe, but out of sight, only unwrapping it during those few precious moments when she could be with him.

She still struggled to comprehend the offer Miss Elizabeth had made. It was something she could never see one of her kind doing. But, judging by James' reaction, it was also not something the white people usually did. Part of her was suspicious about it, wondering what Miss Elizabeth would be getting out of the arrangement, but part of her wanted to believe that Miss Elizabeth was being honourable in all this. She liked Miss Elizabeth, she was kind to her and helped her with her English.

Once Mrs Agnes was out the way, Miriam went quietly out to the veranda to clear away the tea things. James and Master Carl had moved off somewhere and the place was quiet, except for the almost audible buzz of the heat as it pulsed around the green grass of the lawn. On the far side she saw Tobias as he tended to the flower beds, moving with the slow dignity of his age. She put the last of the plates onto her tray and carried them through to the kitchen, her mind turning to another of her worries. Her time to bleed had come and gone and she knew what that could mean.

⚱

A week after Carl headed on to Mombasa, James at last managed to grab a few moments with Lizzy and accept her proposal. The Reverend and Mrs Smith were delighted when he asked for their daughter's hand. Oliver was as pleased and Agnes cried when they announced their engagement at dinner the next day. Richmond was more reserved.

Two weeks later they were married in a simple ceremony in the Smith's church in Voi. They had a short honeymoon in Malindi where they first realised the awkwardness of their decision as they were forced to share a room and a bed. Surprisingly, neither of them had considered how they would cope with this. They had been too caught up with the romance of the idea. James devised a small curtain to divide the room but had to dismantle it every day so that the chamber maid did not suspect anything. All the time they fretted about how they would deal with this when they returned to the farm. There they would be expected to share James' room while their own house was being built and that could take a few months.

'It'll be fine once the house is ready,' Lizzy assured James as they walked arm in arm along the beach.

James nodded, but his mind was elsewhere. He was missing Miriam and there was another thing they hadn't contemplated which was beginning to occupy his thoughts.

'They'll be expecting us to have children,' he said stopping and staring out to sea.

Lizzy's grip on his arm tightened just slightly and only for a moment, then she said, 'We will have to pretend I'm barren.'

'But…' he thought of mentioning the stigma that being barren would bring should they spread that story then decided against it. '…Are you sure you won't mind.'

The hesitation was there and he noticed it, but her voice betrayed no doubt. 'Yes. I will be fine with that story. Besides, silly, how can I devote my life to the school and the children if I am too busy being a mother. No, this is the best thing to do.'

She seemed to gain confidence from her words and they walked on in silence for a bit.

'The school and those kids mean a lot to you, don't they?' James said after a while.

'Yes. They are God's children and they deserve a chance in life.'

He nodded but McCallum's story of how the children of mixed heritage were treated, pricked his mind. Surely they deserved a chance too.

'Mother won't be happy,' he said after a while, his mind returning to the issue of producing offspring. 'She will want grandchildren.'

'So will my parents, but I'm sure Oliver will do the honours in that department.'

They were quiet for a moment as the realisation sunk in that there was no brother or sister to oblige and continue the family name on James' side.

'I'm sorry, James, I had not thought that through from your side.'

He nodded and to be fair, confessed that he too had not contemplated that.

They walked on in silence till they reached a river mouth and turned back.

'James, I am prepared to have a child if you want to.' There was a determined undertone to the softly spoken words, but he could tell that she had not completely convinced herself that she was prepared to go through with this offer.

James looked at her, searching her face for clues as to her commitment to this proposal.

'Lizzy, this is a huge step. We need to think carefully about this. Both of us, all three of us. We must see what Miriam thinks too.'

'You are right, James. We don't need to sort this out today. We need to think it through properly but my offer stands.' There was more assuredness in her voice this time.

'The house should be ready in about a month,' Richmond informed the newly weds at dinner on the evening of their return.

'I still don't see why they need to move out,' Agnes said. 'There's plenty of room here.'

'Oh do stop being silly,' Richmond retorted, 'they are only going to be a few minute's ride away. It's not as though they are moving to another continent.'

That hit a nerve as their rushed departure from England to a strange and foreign shore came back to them both. Richmond gave a quick glance at his wife, but not wanting to lose face, added, 'They will want their privacy.'

'I suppose,' Agnes agreed, then with a forced smile turned to Elizabeth and said, 'I guess I haven't got used to the idea of James not being in his room. I hope you will be happy in your new home.'

Elizabeth smiled back. 'I am sure we will be. And we will visit everyday, won't we darling?'

'Of course we will, Mama,' James assured his mother.

Agnes nodded, 'Of course you will. It is only good and proper that you look after your ageing mother.' She pattered her hair to draw attention to the few grey strands that were starting to show amongst her dark locks.

'Mother! You're not that old,' James laughed.

'Oh, she is not getting any younger, Son,' Richmond mocked in a good-natured way.

'You bite your tongue, Richmond Aitken,' Agnes replied with a laugh. It won't be too long before I am a grandmother, won't it my dear?' She looked at James, then back at Richmond, 'And you will be a grandfather.'

The brief exchange between his parents allowed James time for a quick glance over at Elizabeth who gave a small nod of her head as if reaffirming her agreement to have a child.

'Aye, and if you'll let me, I'll be a grand uncle to the laddie,' McCallum, who had been quiet to that point, added.

'It could be a lassie,' Elizabeth said quickly and with some emotion.

'Or lassie,' McCallum bowed his head slightly as he conceded the point.

'Well, you will have to have at least one "laddie" so you can leave the farm to them,' Richmond said, not realising the additional complication he had just added to the young couple's lives.

They slept side by side in the same bed with no curtain dividing them that night. It felt strange and almost sinful, even more so when James' leg accidentally touched hers. But, tired from their journey home, they soon fell asleep and when they woke, it was Elizabeth who broke the ice, giggling at their embarrassment.

'We will get through this, James, we will. Yes, it is awkward at the moment, and will get more awkward, but we will get through this. Your mother and father, from what you have told me, get along just fine despite not being intimate, so we can do it too.'

'But what about the "laddie" or "lassie" they are expecting?'

'I suggest we get working on that as soon as possible. Once we have satisfied their requirement, we can relax and live the life together that we have planned.'

'And the "laddie" or "lassie?"'

'James,' she took his hands in hers and looked him straight in the eye, 'if we bring a child into this world, even if it isn't for the same reason others have children, then we are duty bound to love and care for that child as if it was conceived … I don't know how one puts this … but you understand what I am saying. I will love any child we have and you too, James Aitken. You are a good man. I have no doubt you will.'

They were interrupted by Miriam knocking at the door to bring in their morning cup of tea.

'Good morning, Miriam,' Elizabeth greeted her cheerfully. 'Please put the tea on the table, then help me with the mosquito net, I am going to get dressed.'

Miriam put the tray down then held the net back so Elizabeth could climb out of the bed. But instead of immediately heading off behind the screen to change, Elizabeth turned and held the net up, gesturing for Miriam to get into the bed with James.

'Two minutes,' she whispered with a smile, 'just while I get dressed.'

Miriam looked at her, then across at James who was also staring. She nodded at James who, after a second to process what was happening, nodded back.

Once Elizabeth was behind the screen, he took Miriam in his arms and they kissed passionately, enjoying this snatched moment and revelling in the strange naughtiness of the situation. The couple of minutes Elizabeth took to change seemed a matter of seconds to them and before they knew it, she was calling out to Miriam to pour the tea as a warning that she was about to reappear.

They disentangled themselves and, as she climbed out of the bed, Miriam whispered, 'Tonight at the dam.' By the time Elizabeth emerged from behind the dressing screen, Miriam was at the table pouring the tea as if nothing had happened.

The day was a busy one for James as he caught up on what had been happening in his absence. First his father at breakfast, then McCallum as they headed out to the fields, told him how the crops were progressing, explained the issues they had been having with the grinding machine and how one of the young farm hands had fixed the problem.

'He is quite bright for a native,' Richmond said, 'one we should try and keep. He could be an asset.'

James nodded. He knew the young lad and he was a good worker, but had noticed that he seemed a little too interested in Miriam, so had not taken to him. He found himself wondering about the challenges Miriam faced with her family and the other servants. What was expected of her? Was she, like him, expected to marry and have children? He knew it was not her role to fall in love with the master's son. She never spoke much about what sort of issues she faced, but he was sure there must be pressures on her too.

He was tired by the time evening came and was not really in the mood for a swim, but the thought of seeing Miriam helped him set out for the dam. The water cooled him and, as she was not there when he first arrived, he did a few more lengths and felt refreshed by the time she appeared.

Her body felt slightly firmer to him as they embraced and kissed, but when he moved to go further, she gently resisted.

'We must talk,' she said.

'Talk?' He was a little annoyed. Apart from the brief kiss in bed that morning they had not been together for a week and all he wanted was to make love to her. But something in her look told him this was serious, so he sat back, his arms reluctantly falling to his side.

'Come, sit.' She gestured to the flat rock where they would often lie together.

Once seated, she gazed in the direction of the dam and it felt to him that she was gathering her thoughts, so he gave her time while his mind started to conjure up all sorts of possibilities of what she was about to say, none of them good. Her demeanour warned him to expect bad news.

'I am pregnant,' she said at last. Her words seemed devoid of emotion and this somehow spoke volumes of how the news had exhausted her of feeling. It had clearly been playing heavily on her mind for some days now.

'Pregnant?' The word sounded as heavy as the condition itself. 'Are you sure?'

'Yes, I am sure. I have not bled when I should have.'

He looked at her, shocked and confused. She laughed a gentle laugh. Despite knowing that the laughter was mocking his lack of understanding, it somehow eased the shock of the news.

'It is what happens with women. We bleed. Once a month. When we don't bleed, it means we are pregnant. I have not bled.'

'Bled? Where?' The biology was momentarily distracting him from dealing with the enormity of what Miriam was really saying.

She gave another laugh. 'It is private,' she said and looked away for a moment. When she looked back, her face told him that the lesson was over, he would get no further explanation and they now had to deal with the real issue.

'Pregnant?' was all he could think to say.

She nodded and they were silent for a while.

Eventually he said, 'So what happens now?'

'I will be sent away,' she said.

'Away? Where?'

'I do not know. Msambweni perhaps. My mother talks of a brother there.'

'Msambweni. That is not too far away. About a day and a half's ride.'

'Yes, it is not too far, but what reason would you have to go there? And if you do come, my mother's brother will not let you see me, especially if the child has your skin.'

He was struggling to believe her news even though he had thought a lot about what would happen if Miriam did fall pregnant. Despite his thoughts, he had never really believed that it would actually occur. This felt surreal to him. This was only meant to happen in his thoughts, not in real life.

'Surely you don't have to go. We can work something out. No one needs to know who the child's father is. You can pretend that it is my father's child if it has my skin.'

'That would be worse,' Miriam responded, 'You father is a...' she stopped suddenly as if realising that she was going to say something she shouldn't.

'My father is what?' he pressed, his growing anger not with Miriam, but with the realisation of the hopelessness of their situation which he was trying hard to ignore.

'Your father is a tough man, he would not let others stay, so why will he let me stay?'

James knew she was right, but fought hard against this truth, knowing that it was not a battle he would win.

Miriam took his hands in hers. 'Look at me, my love.' She repeated the command when he continued to stare out across the dam. 'Look at me, Sir. We can be together again, but I must go now. If I leave before I show I am pregnant, then I have a chance of coming back. But I must go soon. I will be away, maybe a year, maybe a bit longer. I will come back. But if I wait, if everyone knows I am pregnant, then there will be no coming back.'

He nodded slowly. Her words made sense despite the pain they caused.

'I shall miss you,' he said at last.

⚱

'There were complications. I did everything I could, but...' Oliver hung his head. He was exhausted not only from his work, but also his emotions. Agnes led him gently to a chair while James stood staring at the door to their bedroom which stood open. He vaguely felt his father's hand on his shoulder, but his surroundings were just memories of reality, as if reality were deliberately blurring his senses.

'Son.' His father's voice was unusually gentle. He wanted to shrug off the consoling hand and march into the room, demanding Elizabeth not to be dead. It was not fair. She had sacrificed so much for him. Why did she have to pay the ultimate price? And for a child neither of them really wanted. This was not right.

He turned and looked around the room as if searching for someone who he could talk to about what had really happened, someone who knew. But the only one who was aware of things was McCallum. He was the only one who knew that their marriage was one of convenience, he knew the reason behind Miriam's sudden disappearance and that Elizabeth's pregnancy had been a necessary complication in an even more complex situation. But McCallum was in Taveta.

His eyes settled on Oliver who sat with his head in his hands. Guilt flooded though him and a desire to confess all nearly overwhelmed him. But even in his guilt-wracked state, he knew he had to keep everything a secret. He did not know if Elizabeth had ever confided in Oliver but, unless his friend said anything, he had to assume the answer was no.

'Can I see her?' His voice seemed to come from somewhere far off, floating like a circling vulture in the blue skies. Oliver looked up and nodded slowly.

He moved, somewhat trance-like, into the bedroom. Hannah had just finished arranging Elizabeth's body in the bed. He was struck by how pale her face was, yet her hair was plastered against her brow from the sweat of exertion. He recalled the first time he had seen her when she had just come in from gardening, her hair, as it was now, stuck to her forehead.

Hannah picked up an enamel dish full of a red liquid which he only later realised had been blood and water. She left the room quietly, closing the door behind her, but leaving with a quizzical glance at him. He knew that he would have to analyse that look at some point, but now was not the time. He moved over to the bed and took one of Elizabeth's hands in his. It felt cool and at odds with the heat of the day and the closeness of the room.

'I am so sorry, Lizzy, so very sorry.' Somewhere in the fog of his mind he knew he should sob or at the very least be choked with emotion, but his apology seemed to accuse him with its blandness and apparent lack of remorse. She would understand, he told himself. She would know that his tone of voice had little relation to the emotions behind it. His lack of tears was the result of a shocked numbness rather than from an absence of feeling.

There had been no warning signs. Her pregnancy had progressed as it should. Oliver had been pleased with things and Elizabeth had seemed healthy and, as she swelled up, James had noticed a change in her. There was a bond forming between her and the unborn child and there was a sense that she was as surprised about this as he was. It now felt brutal to him that she had not lived to enjoy the full extent of those maternal feelings that had grown as her body had.

His thoughts were interrupted by his mother who had come quietly into the room.

'Her parents are arriving,' she said, her voice an almost reverential whisper. 'We will have to break the news to them.'

'I'll be there in a moment,' he said, feeling that he owed Elizabeth a little more time.

Agnes nodded and withdrew.

'Thank you for everything,' he said to Elizabeth once he heard the door close. 'You gave me hope. I don't know what has happened with Miriam. I have no news. I only hope that your sacrifice was not in vain. I will always remember you and will always be indebted to you for what you did.' He kissed her gently on the forehead and turned to leave the room. At the door he paused and looked around. There was no sign of the still born child and, he realised that he did not know if he had missed out on having a son or a daughter.

                        ☿

Miriam's absence and the lack of news about her played more heavily on his mind in the days following Elizabeth's death. In his more morbid moments, he imagined her also having died in childbirth, of having lost a wife and a lover. And not only that but also having lost two children in quick succession, neither of whom he had got to see.

The time between Miriam having left the farm and Elizabeth's death had not been quite as bad as he had expected. They had moved into the small house they had built on the site of the old ruins. Supervising the building works in his spare time and then helping Elizabeth as she made it her home had alleviated some of his frustrations while the task of arranging an acceptable heir, which was fraught with tension and embarrassment on both sides, had been difficult but it had at least concentrated his mind elsewhere.

Their happiness when they announced Elizabeth's pregnancy came from a sense of relief rather than expectation. Had either of them known back then what the consequences of their news would be, they would not have been so joyful.

Despite his mother's protests, he had remained in the small house after Elizabeth's death.

'It's not good for you to be all alone in that house,' Agnes pleaded, 'you should move back in here.' She said 'that house' as if the ghosts of Richmond's infidelities haunted it. But James knew it was just her grief talking. In the short time Elizabeth had been a daughter-in-law, she had established a good relationship with his mother. He saw his mother's animosity towards 'that house' stemming from the fact that it just reminded his mother of all that could have been.

'I'm not ready to move out. Not yet. Maybe at some point.'

She nodded, saying that she understood but did not like the answer.

'You will always have a room here if you want.'

He smiled, but in his mind the house had been built for him and Miriam and he clung to the hope that one day he would be able to be with her there. But there was more to it. The house also held memories of Elizabeth and they had had fun together setting it up. There was a sense of camaraderie in building their home together. They had planned the two bedrooms for the time when their duty was done and they could settle into their connected, but separate lives.

His grief at the loss of Elizabeth was real. He had been very fond of her and would visit her grave, which sat next to Rosemary-Jane's, as often as he could, invariably thinking that one gravestone represented the sister he never knew and the other, with the exception of a few necessary moments of incest, represented the sister he had known.

It was about a fortnight after Elizabeth's death that Hannah came round. He had just finished his morning toilet and found her in the kitchen preparing breakfast for him.

'Mrs Agnes said I must come. She said you are not eating properly, Mr James.'

James grunted. Yes, breakfast had been overlooked on more than one occasion since Lizzy's death, but he had dined at the main house every night, so he was hardly starved.

'Thank you, Hannah,' despite his annoyance at his mother, he did not forget his manners.

'Please sit, it is almost ready.' She had cooked a large breakfast with bacon, sausages, fried eggs, tomato and a thick chunk of fresh bread. The smell quickly built up an appetite in him and he waited at the table while Hannah finished preparing the food.

'This is very good, Hannah,' he smiled at her and she nodded, her wise eyes showing no emotion. She turned to go back to the kitchen table to tidy up, then paused and turned back to him, a look of uncertainty on her face.

He looked up, wondering what was bothering her.

'You have a son,' she said, her voice betraying no emotion.

He nodded, thinking that Hannah had just mixed up her tenses. 'Lizzy would have liked that,' he thought.

'He has her skin. She has named him Musa in our tongue but calls him Samwelli in your language.'

Before James could process this news, Hannah had disappeared into the kitchen. He was about to call after her, then realised the effort it had taken to pass on the news and he nodded to himself, a smile spreading across his face.

As he left to go to the fields, he popped his head around the kitchen door.

'Thanks, Hannah. I like the name.'

She did not turn from the sink where she was washing the dishes, but merely nodded her head.

With Richmond's leg back to good working order and James having no excuse to go to Voi, they began to take turns making the supply run each Saturday. Richmond renewed his relationship with Geraldine while once a month James would take Agnes who, in the wake of Elizabeth's death, felt a need to spend some time with Lizzy's mother and the two women built up a friendship, Agnes' first since arriving in Africa. The Smiths' grief over the loss of their daughter was pragmatic, their faith seeming to bear the worst of the load.

'She is with her child in heaven. Our Lord is looking after her,' and similar comments were voiced whenever Elizabeth's name came up. Agnes found herself struggling with this. Her years of only occasionally attending church had blurred her beliefs.

'Yes, she is probably looking after all the orphans there,' Agnes found herself saying, her conviction only loosely attached to the words. 'Any news of a new teacher?' Her sense of hypocrisy prompting her to change the subject.

'We have had a number of applications. Mostly from Mombasa, some from England, and even one from Nairobi.'

'Nairobi?'

'Yes, it has grown so quickly as a town, I can hardly believe they have made it the capital.'

'The capital? When?'

'Oh, a few years back. Did you not know?' Mrs Smith offered more cake.

'I must admit that I do not follow the news much,' Agnes gave an embarrassed smile.

'I am sure you will hear a lot more of it in time to come. They say it is becoming an important centre for the coffee and sisal trade. Your Richmond will have dealings with them soon, you can count on it. From what I heard, it is going to create competition for the farms closer to the coast, like yours. These railways have really changed things dramatically since we have been here.'

Agnes nodded, feeling acutely how remote and distant from the world her life had become. Richmond never discussed his work with her and her knowledge of the farm business was built on scraps of 'work talk' at the dinner table when her husband or her son or even McCallum deigned to mention something. Presumably they reserved the serious talk for when she was not around.

'Nairobi?' Richmond asked and then laughed when Agnes repeated what Mrs Smith had said about the threat that the new capital posed.

'What competition can come from up country. Even if they do send the coffee on the railways, they will have to pay more to send it such a distance.'

She felt foolish. Of course it made sense that it would cost more and she was annoyed with herself for not realising this. Why had Mrs Smith ... Judith ... not thought of that? Agnes felt slightly betrayed. Judith was supposed to be intelligent. As the wife of a minister, she should surely have been better informed. But after her initial irritation she forgave Judith, realising that this whole business with the railways and coffee was just that, business. And business was for the menfolk. As women, they had responsibility for the family and at the moment, her family, well her son anyway, needed healing. Ever since Elizabeth's death he had been distracted and she worried about him.

It was only natural that he mourn the loss of his wife, but she could not help thinking that there was more to his mood, an underlying something. Despite wracking her brain, she could not work out what it could possibly be. She tried to tell herself she was looking for things that weren't there.

It was while going home one Saturday that she noticed James pull back slightly on the reins, slowing the horses just a bit and gazing off into the bushes. 'Why are you slowing down?' she asked and was taken aback at how this seemed to fluster him.

'I ... um ... well ... er ... somebody told me that there was...' he seemed to be desperately searching in the bush for the answer. '...there was ... that they had seen a leopard around this spot.'

'A leopard?'

'Yes, a leopard.' He suddenly grew confident in his story.

'Who told you that?'

'Oh, um, I think it was Mr Jeffries, you know the station master at Voi.'

'Mr Jeffries?'

He nodded but she knew he was lying. She looked around the area and it struck her that the monkeys that sat in the nearby trees were far too relaxed for there to be a leopard nearby. She started to say something, but suddenly realised that this spot had a special meaning to her son, probably connected to Elizabeth, judging by his face.

So, instead of interrogating him further, she asked, 'Are we safe then?'

'Safe? Oh yes, we'll be fine. Leopards don't tend to attack humans.' Despite this, he urged the horses on.

The following month when they passed the same spot, Agnes watched him stare determinedly in front of him, as if deliberately ignoring the place.

The news of Miriam left James both elated and frustrated. The worry that something had happened to her, that she had died in childbirth, was lifted from him. Those simple words, 'he has her skin', which Hannah had spoken had been a relief too. Miriam and the child would not be shunned by her community. But it had also hit home the distance between them, not only in terms of miles, but also time. Miriam would not be able to return to the farm for a good while yet, if at all.

Hannah came to his house more regularly now, almost every morning, to prepare his breakfast. It was his mother's doing and, where normally this would have irritated, he welcomed it as a tiny thread keeping him connected to Miriam. Hannah almost never said anything directly about her daughter but occasionally would, in a short sentence casually dropped, renew his link to Miriam, reminding him that she was still alive and with this, keep his hope alive. They started out very unspecific.

'It has been very hot in Msambweni.'

'My brother in Msambweni is doing very well.'

'The missionaries, like Mrs Elizabeth, are going to build a school in Msambweni. It will be good for the children there.'

These comments, James felt, were designed to let him know that things were okay and Miriam and child were doing well. They were always positive comments.

On occasion, a plea for financial support came along.

'My brother needs to build a new room to his house. He nearly has enough money.'

The offered funds were accepted with an almost imperceptible nod of the head and a slight lowering of the eyes. No words of thanks, but James knew that it was his obligation to support Miriam and Samwelli and he should not have to be thanked for doing his duty.

It was a strange time, and he found the system of coded messages odd as there was no need to be discrete as it was only the two of them in the house. No one could overhear if she were to say something outright and clear like, 'Miriam and your son are doing well.' But he needed to respect Hannah's way of dealing with the issue. He had no idea how this whole thing had played out in her community. All he had to go on was McCallum's experiences and, if he was honest, McCallum was probably less informed than he was. McCallum had never spoken of a go-between when it came to the mother of his child.

Despite the irregularity of the news and, at the time, very cryptic nature of the messages, he found himself beginning to slowly climb out of the despair he had fallen into since Elizabeth's death. He began to look forward to seeing Hannah each morning, hoping that there would be another crumb of news for him to store away, another seemingly throw-away sentence for him to cling to and renew this tenuous connection to Miriam.

The breakfasts themselves were welcomed too. Immediately after Elizabeth's death, his mother had sent Wamuhu to prepare his morning meal. She was a young servant, still learning and not a very good cook. James had found it somewhat amusing that her name meant one born of ashes as it showed in the blackened food that was placed in front of him with an almost apologetic smile.

He had not complained, but his mother must have picked up on something as Wamuhu didn't last long in the kitchen and was soon confined to cleaning duties. There were times when he wondered if his mother had deliberately sent Hannah, knowing that she would reconnect him with Miriam. But he knew this was just a strange fantasy as, if she knew about Miriam, his mother would surely have said something by now.

But he did not spend too much time dwelling on the question. He was just thankful for this arrangement, which not only allowed him to get his scraps of news about Miriam, it also meant that he was probably having the best breakfasts on the farm.

'You spoil that boy,' Richmond had said one evening at dinner when James had alluded to the good breakfasts he was getting. While there was a tone of lightness in his father's voice, James also detected a note of annoyance and he wondered who was making breakfast at the main house these days and was it really that bad?

'Richmond, he deserves to be spoilt a bit,' Agnes retorted, not seeming to pick up on the teasing meant by her husband's remark. 'He has just lost his wife.'

'It was six months ago, Mama,' James said, trying to avoid an escalation.

It was the wrong thing to say as his mother saw it as a sign that he did not care and as soon as he said it, he realised how insensitive it must have sounded.

'It's not that I don't care. Mama. I loved Lizzy.' It was not a lie, it was just a different meaning of the word 'love' he was using to the one his mother was hearing. 'And I really do appreciate you sending Hannah. I was just trying to say that you don't need to spoil me if it means you and father suffer.' He grinned at Richmond who scowled back at him, but as soon as Agnes was not looking Richmond gave him a wink. He had prevented an argument and his father appreciated that. He had also probably secured Hannah's services for a good while longer as his mother would sacrifice her own comfort if it added to Richmond's discomfort.

'No, Son, it is a parent's duty to care for their offspring more than themselves,' she gave Richmond a sharp look. 'You can still have Hannah. Maybe when Miriam gets back we can swap and Hannah can return to the main house and Miriam can take care of you.'

'Is Miriam coming back?' It took all the strength he could muster to try and sound casual.

'Oh yes. I asked Hannah this morning and she said maybe in about six months.'

'Where did Miriam go? I must admit I hadn't really noticed that she was gone.' He hoped that he was not overdoing things.

'She went to look after a sick uncle in Msambweni.'

'Msambweni? I've heard it is very nice there, beautiful beaches.'

'I wouldn't know,' his mother said.

'Maybe I should go there ... for a holiday. I think it was Uncle Malcolm who told me how attractive the place is. But there are not many settlers there, mostly natives. If I did go, I guess that I would have to camp on the beach.'

'You're not going off on your own, camping on a beach surrounded by natives. It's too dangerous,' Agnes snapped.

'Maybe Uncle Malcolm would come with me. I was thinking that I needed a bit of a holiday after everything that has happened.' James was beginning to see a way to be with Miriam and possibly a chance to see his son for the first time, even if just briefly. 'It would do me good to get away from the farm for a bit, gather my thoughts without being haunted by memories.'

'Take Hannah as well,' Richmond suddenly piped in.

'Richmond! Don't encourage him.' Agnes turned on her husband.

'Oh come now, dear. You heard the boy. He needs some time to mourn properly and Hannah has family there. If she goes with, she will ensure that no harm comes to James from the natives.'

Agnes was not convinced, but James could see that his mother could be brought round to the idea. He held his breath for a second, hoping she would agree.

Two weeks passed with no further talk of Msambweni. During ths time some sad new came through from Carl. His daughter, like Rosemary-Jane, had succumbed to malaria. James could feel the grief in his friend's words and wrote a reply full of sympathy, the acuteness of feeling in the letter heightened by his own grief at not being able to find a way of seeing Miriam again. He had felt his mood sink when Agnes had not relented that night at dinner and, as the subject was not mentioned the following few evenings, he had become more morose. He made a point though of not coming across as sulking.

He had almost forgotten the idea of getting to Msambweni when his mother suggested at dinner one evening that he should go.

'I've been thinking about it and I think you were right. A change, time away from here, would do you good.'

He was so taken aback that he nearly choked on the pork cutlet he was eating.

'And I have checked with Hannah, the natives there are fine, you should have no problems with them. But I still want you to take McCallum and Hannah with. I forbid you to go on your own.' She gave James a smile of the kind she gave him as a little boy when he was about to open a birthday or Christmas present.

'Thank you, Mama. I am sure the break will do me good.' He marvelled at how calm his voice sounded despite the lava-like excitement that suddenly bubbled inside him, threatening to erupt at any minute.

'I'll be glad to accompany you, laddie,' McCullum said. 'Your mother has already discussed this with me. And don't you worry, I'll sort out all camping goods and food. Hannah will come too. She will cook for us. I believe that one can get some good fresh fish there, so we won't have to take along too much, the ocean will provide.'

The little details distracted him from his joy long enough to get his emotions in check and, he realised, it had been a deliberate ploy on McCallum's part. However, he still needed to get rid of some of the excess gas that the sudden build up of excitement had created in his stomach and the resultant belch was louder than he had expected.

'I do beg your pardon,' he said, looking round the table.

'James, really!' His mother shook her head. 'I hope you won't behave like that when you are away.'

He suppressed a second burp, swallowing hard and hoping that he looked contrite enough. While unlikely, he did not want a small lapse of manners to derail this gift from his mother.

Fortunately, the rest of the dinner went well. They talked a little bit about the plans for his holiday and then moved on to other things.

The week of preparations seemed to drag. Each day it felt to him that the sun took an age to stroll from one horizon to the other, while the nights would fumble around blindly in the darkness of their own making, trying to find the door by which to leave.

He had wanted to know from Hannah if Miriam was expecting him, or would it be a surprise? But he found no route into a conversation that would answer this and Hannah had become decidedly uncommunicative at breakfast.

At last the day came. He was up early and ready to leave when his parents appeared soon after Hannah. Agnes had ensured that a particularly large breakfast was prepared.

'It's a long journey, so you'll need your strength,' his mother said when he tried to protest.

So he ate the bacon, eggs, ham hock, bread and fried banana that Hannah prepared and drank coffee till he could manage no more. Then he had to wait until Hannah had washed the dishes and tidied up. All the time his frustration grew. McCallum eventually arrived with the loaded cart and, after the usual fuss from his mother, they finally trundled down the road towards Voi.

'Well, my lad,' McCallum said when they were safely out of earshot of Richmond and Agnes, 'looks like you have had a lucky break.' He smiled kindly and James grinned back.

They stayed the night in Mombasa before heading along the coast to Msambweni. As they neared the small settlement, James felt his excitement grow and found he could barely talk. But McCallum, as he had done almost the entire journey, did most of the talking. It seemed to James that the farm manager was unaware he was talking so much yet at the same time, he got a sense that McCallum knew exactly what he was doing, that he was deliberately talking to take James' mind off the frustration at how long the journey was taking.

It was late afternoon when they arrived in Msambweni. James was a little disappointed that Miriam was not standing by the roadside waiting to greet them and even more so when they went to the village to pay respects to the local chief and ask permission to camp on the beach, as there was still no sign of her.

The long politeness of custom meant that a lot of talking needed to be done before they could even start to discuss business and they also needed to meet Hannah's brother who was an important man in the village hierarchy. But when he began to get restless, McCallum spoke in a low voice,

'Patience, laddie. You need to be on your best behaviour. You are being assessed.'

'Assessed?' He asked, then suddenly realised. The village all knew. They knew of his relationship with Miriam, they knew he was the father of Miriam's child, but most importantly, they also knew that he loved her and that she loved him. This was not a case of a settler taking advantage of a native woman. They knew his love was true.

He was now acutely aware that most eyes were on him. They were sitting in the shade of a large tree, a pleasant breeze coming from the direction of the ocean, which eased the discomfort of the humidity. But now that he knew he was being observed, the heat seemed to jump to the forefront of his thoughts and the sweat rolling down his back beneath his thin cotton shirt, demanded promotion from his subconscious to his mainstream thoughts.

He sat up straight and smiled nervously at the gathered group. The woman and children, and some of the younger men smiled back, some seeming to have genuine smiles of approval while others looked as though they had just caught a prized prey in a trap. The elders, however, remained stony faced as they watched and analysed him. He stopped smiling and tried to concentrate on the conversation. McCallum was doing most of the talking with the elders, occasionally asking questions.

As he started to pay attention to what was being said, he realised that what he thought were negotiations about being allowed to camp on the beach were actually dowry discussions and McCallum was his arbiter. His heart stopped momentarily, questioning if this was actually happening.

'Uncle Malcolm,' he hissed.

'Not now, laddie,' McCallum spoke out of the side of his mouth.

'But…'

'It's what you want, isn't it, laddie?'

He nodded.

'Then leave it to me. Now is not the time to argue.'

James started to speak, but a look from the farm manager silenced him and he sat back, his mind spinning with excitement and fear. Was this really happening? He looked from McCallum to the elders, then back at McCallum. Then he sought out Hannah in the crowd of villagers who sat watching him. At first he could not see her. Eventually he spotted her on the edge of the group. Their eyes met and her soft smile told him that everything was going to be okay. He could have jumped up and hugged her at that minute, but knew he could not.

McCallum had stopped talking and the elders huddled together to come to their verdict, but even James could see that this was only for the sake of appearances. The serious faces of the old men belied a sense of excitement and happiness that seemed to buzz around the group.

McCallum turned to him and whispered, 'I think we have been successful, laddie.'

Three nights later, James lay in his tent going over the events of the last few days. Miriam slept next to him, her breathing, a soft susurration, seeming at one with the gentle rhythm of the waves that lazily lapped against the beach a short distance from the tent. In a small, crudely constructed cot, Samwelli, his son Samwelli, slept. It all seemed surreal. He had never dreamed that he would ever find such happiness.

McCallum eventually confessed that he had approached Hannah as soon as he heard James talk of coming here. After a lot of discussion, she had agreed to seek the elders' approval for them to open negotiations. Hannah knew of their relationship as Miriam, no longer able to conceal her condition, had confessed everything. McCallum used his experience with Jana, the woman he had loved, to convince Hannah to help.

'She was reluctant at first,' he told James. 'But I saw something in her eyes that told me this was not a closed door. She sent messages to her brother and the village elders while I worked on your mother to get her to agree to you coming here for a holiday.

'We didn't say anything to you in case things fell apart and we failed to convince the elders to be open to the idea of marriage. We did not want to build up false hopes. But the elders obliged and, it should be said, did not even ask for an outlandish dowry.'

Miriam stirred next to him and he kissed her gently on the forehead. She settled again, her breathing falling back into a contented rhythm at one with the ocean.

His thoughts turned to Hannah's brother, Jacob. With Miriam's father having died while she was still young, it fell to him to have the final say on whether or not his niece could marry this mzungu, this white man.

Jacob, a tall man with a gentle face, had been warm to him from the start, smiling and welcoming him with a hearty handshake. He had looked elegant at the wedding ceremony in his spotless white robe and fez, watching the proceedings with a hint of a smile on his face.

Despite the warmth of welcome he had received in this small community and their joyful acceptance of him, all did not sit well with James. It had nothing to do with these people who had taken them into their hearts, but it revolved around those of his family who he would have to face on his return to the farm. And these thoughts began to bleed through the happiness he had felt in the last few days.

He eased himself out of bed and quietly went outside. The moonlight was bright and seemed to create a shiny path across the water as it reflected off its surface. The sand was cool on his bare feet as he walked slowly towards the surf, the warm air carried the slight heaviness of humidity and was scented with the smell of seaweed.

He found a spot not too far from the water and sat down, staring out across the inky black ocean, his eye following the line of the moon path. The beauty of his surroundings and the tranquillity of the setting served to cool his mind which had been ruffled by thoughts of his parents.

'Couldn't sleep, laddie?' McCallum's voice, although soft, made him jump. He had not noticed the Scot sitting a few yards away.

'Oh, Uncle Malcolm. I didn't see you there.'

'Sorry, I didn't startle you, did I?'

'A bit,' James admitted.

McCallum came up and sat next to him. 'Too hot?' he asked.

'No, not really.'

'No, it is not,' McCallum conceded, 'the breeze is pleasant.' His tone hinted that he knew the real reason for James' restlessness.

'Yes, it is pleasant.'

They stared out at the sea, letting their surroundings soak into their thoughts providing a kind of protective layer as a defence against the difficulties of the conversation that was to come.

James hoped that McCallum would say something, prompt him to open up about what was on his mind. But the Scot was silent and James knew that he had to start.

'I am worried, Uncle Malcolm.'

'About what, laddie?'

'About going home with Miriam as my wife. My parents will never accept her. Mother would be devastated if she knew, not just because Miriam is a servant, but also she would be upset that I got married again without her being there. And you know my father's views on the indigenous people.'

'Aye, laddie. It is a real quandary you have there.'

'And it won't be too long before mother will be trying to find a new wife for me, one they regards as suitable.'

'That she will,' McCallum agreed.

'And father wants an heir, one who can take over the farm in due course. He won't want Samwelli to have it.'

'No.'

'I just don't think I can tell them I am married to Miriam.'

'No you can't, laddie.'

'I suppose I could take on a second wife. Miriam's people won't object as it is perfectly acceptable, and in fact expected, in their culture.'

'Yes, that is true,' McCallum nodded.

'So, I could do as Lizzy and I had planned. Take Miriam as if she were my house servant, well at least that is how we can make it appear to mother and father, but we could live like husband and wife when no one else was around. And Hannah knows so that is a least one less person to worry about'.

'You're right there, laddie.' McCallum put a reassuring hand on James' shoulder.

'Thank you Uncle Malcolm, you have helped me a lot.'

'My pleasure, laddie.'

James looked over at the farm manager and saw that he was smiling, the moonglow reflecting from the ocean lighting up his face.

'Uncle Malcolm,' he laughed, 'you knew that I knew the answers to my problems, but you didn't say anything!'

'No, laddie,' McCallum chuckled, 'if I had told you the answers, you would still be unsure, but as you have come up with the ideas yourself, you will be more sure of them and maybe you will be able to sleep.'

'You are a canny man, Uncle Malcolm,' James smiled. 'And yes, I think I will be able to sleep now. After all it is almost exactly what we had planned, the only difference is that Elizabeth will not be there, God rest her soul.'

They stared out at the sea again, respecting the memory of Elizabeth for a moment. Then James stood and dusted the sand from his shorts. 'I'm off to bed,' he said. 'Goodnight, Uncle Malcolm.'

'Goodnight, laddie.'

He walked towards his tent, then paused to look back at McCallum who still sat staring out to sea. He wondered what thoughts were going through the Scots' mind. Was he thinking about what could have been in his life? A momentary wave of sadness for the man passed over James. He turned and headed back to his wife and son.

It was three months after his return from Msambweni that Miriam came back to the farm. She brought Samwelli with. Agnes and Richmond did not notice the child, assuming it was just another offspring of one of the servants.

To James' relief, no one raised an eyebrow when he suggested that Miriam take over duties at his place so that Hannah could return to the main house. In fact, Richmond openly welcomed the idea while Agnes made a slight show of reluctance to deprive her son of the services of the best servant on the farm. 'Why settle for second best?' her minor protestation seemed to say.

'If only you knew,' James smiled back a silent riposte.

They built a small servant's room just outside James' house which they furnished to give the appearance that this was where Miriam was living. In reality though, they lived as man and wife whenever Richmond and Agnes were not around. And it was quite easy as his parents seldom ventured to his place.

He still went to the main house most evenings for dinner, but every now and then he would send a message saying he was tired and would eat at home. Those nights were special when he and Miriam would eat dinner together. Often they would sit outside the back of the house afterwards, drinking coffee, listening to the night sounds and marvelling at the sky. Sometimes they would make love out there, enjoying the cool night air on their naked skin.

It was a very happy time for James, but he found he had to temper his happiness when around his mother.

'You must miss Elizabeth terribly,' she would say occasionally.

'Yes I do, Mama,' he would truthfully answer. He did miss her company. She had been fun to be with and, as a co-conspirator regarding his love of Miriam, she had been someone he could share his secret with. He was still pricked by feelings of guilt whenever her name was mentioned. He could not help blaming himself in part for her early death. But he hid those thoughts whenever his mother mentioned her and he knew that once a suitable period of mourning had passed, she would start hinting that he should re-marry. He dreaded that day. He had been lucky with Elizabeth. She understood and her own dreams and hopes had meant that she could aid him in achieving his. But he knew he had little chance of finding another like her.

Five years passed and his life became settled. His marriage to Miriam remained a secret and he managed to fend off the pressure from his mother about finding a wife. For the first few years after Elizabeth's death Agnes had only occasionally hinted at it, her comments coated in caution, not wanting to stir up memories of his recently departed wife. But as time went on, the caution faded and the comments became more frequent and more forceful. Then, just as she began to really apply pressure, news came through from Europe that Archduke Ferdinand of Austria had been assassinated. While shocking, the distance between those in the colonies and Europe muted the harsh reality of the act and no one, not even Richmond at his most pessimistic could foresee where this would lead.

While he had always maintained an interest in England and the politics of the country, Richmond struggled to instil a similar interest in his son. However, James found it difficult to connect with this foreign land that he had never visited. All he knew was Africa. He knew the heat, the brilliant blue sky, the bush, the whine of the mosquito, the roar of a lion, the sad, yet beautiful call of the fish eagle and the golden brown of sun burnt grass.

His parents spoke of milky blue skies and misty rain, of snow and it getting dark mid-afternoon. They spoke of a cold that bit into your bones, of lush green meadows and the sounds of carriages on cobbled stones. All this was alien to him. While it existed in his parents' memories, for him, it was an artist's impression created by his imagination. The fading sepia photographs his mother had shown him of the family home could not convey temperature, aroma, sound or colour.

News of the growing tensions in Europe, while concerning to his father, laboured under this fuzzy imagined view James had and his lack of clarity coupled easily with his lack of engagement and real concern.

Even a letter from Carl could not push home the seriousness of what was happening.

My Dear Friend, I am writing to you with both good news and a concern. First the good news. Kate has given birth to a boy. He is a beautiful child and we have named him Heinrich George. Both mother and son are doing well.

That is the good news in these troubled times. I am also writing to you now as I fear that soon I may not be able to. Never before have I imagined that our differing heritages could cause any difficulties between us and, I speak for myself here, I hope, no it is more than hope, I believe that it will never have any impact on our friendship. However, the forces of the world conspire to drive a wedge into that friendship. It does not seem long now before Britain will be at war with Germany and, while I sincerely hope that this was will not come to the colonies, there is a real chance that relationships between British East and German East Africa will become strained. Crossing the border to visit and trade may become problematic.

I worry too about Kate and my mother for, as you know, they are both English and everybody here is aware of this. I fear for what people may do.

Father has suggested that I ask if your family would offer them refuge until all this passes. Please do consider this request, although we pray that it will not be necessary. Write soon and let me know your views. I sincerely hope that our fears are unfounded, but realistically, I don't think they are.

Please pass on my love to your parents.

Your friend,

Carl

'That seems a bit excessive, do you not think?' James said after reading the letter at dinner. 'Sending his mother and Kate away like that over some silly spat in Europe.'

'I imagine it is just a precaution,' Richmond said, chewing on a lamb chop, some grease dribbling out the corner of his mouth.

'Oh, do eat properly, Richmond,' Agnes said, pointing at his chin. 'And maybe it is more than caution. You said yourself that war looks imminent in Europe, so why would it not affect us here. And you know what the Germans can be like.'

James glanced at his mother. She hardly knew any Germans so why would she say such a thing? Then he remembered her telling him how the German doctor was responsible for Rosemary-Jane's death, so remained silent.

'Why would it affect us here?' Richmond asked. 'We are thousand of miles away. They will be too busy sorting out Europe, they won't have time to worry about the colonies. And besides, we need to stick together as Europeans, one never knows if the native will get ideas.' He wiped his chin with a napkin then proceeded to dribble more grease with his next bite.

'So you are happy to have Carl's mother and Kate come and stay?' James asked.

'Why, of course. We are always happy to have guests, aren't we, Richmond?'

Richmond grunted. 'By the time they get here they will be able to head home as it will all have been sorted. But,' he dismissed Agnes' protest before she could make it, 'I am happy for them to come if it makes everyone feel better.'

'That's settled then,' Agnes smiled at James then, seeming to have an idea, she added, 'They can stay in your house and you can move back into your old room. They will be more comfortable there as they can each have a room. Here they would have to share.'

James' pleasure at seeing Carl's mother and Kate again suddenly faded. He knew he could not argue with his mother's logic about the accommodation arrangements, but it would mean that he and Miriam would not be able to be together easily.

'Yes, it makes sense,' he said, trying to sound positive about it.

'Remind me, what is Mrs Muller's Christian name?'

'Hortensia if memory serves me correctly. I really only know her as Mrs Muller.'

Agnes smiled. 'What a lovely name.'

'Sounds rather la-di-da to me,' Richmond said. He was attacking his third chop now.

'Richmond!' Agnes chided.

But James laughed. 'We don't say "la-di-da" anymore, father, the word is "posh".'

'Posh? That sounds like a la-di-da word to me.'

'Stop it! Both of you!' Agnes snapped. 'If there is going to be tension between the Germans and us, then we must do all we can to help our friends and not be making fun of their names.'

'Friends?' Richmond looked bemused, 'You have never even met Hortensia.'

'No, but we have had Carl here so often and he is James' closest friend. By helping his mother and wife, we are helping our friend Carl. Surely?'

Richmond gave the non-committal grunt that James had come to recognise as his way of conceding defeat without losing face.

Letters were sent off the next day saying that they hoped it never came to it, but should Mrs Muller and Kate need refuge, the Aitkens would be delighted to have them come and stay until things settled again.

The day after the letter was sent, Oliver Smith arrived with the news that the Royal Navy had shelled the German wireless station at Dar es Salaam.

'There is trouble amongst the wazungu,' Hannah said to Miriam while the two tidied the kitchen after dinner.

'Trouble?' They spoke in soft tones, using their mother tongue.

'Yes, Master Oliver came over today to say that the English people had attacked the German people in Dar es Salaam.'

'Attacked. That is terrible. But why?'

'I do not know,' Hannah said, handing her daughter another plate to dry, 'but I think it is because of something in Europe. I have heard there is a war starting there and the English are going to be fighting.'

Miriam dried and stacked the plate, digesting this news. 'But why are they fighting in Dar es Salaam? If there is a war in Europe, then why do they not just fight there?'

Hannah clicked her tongue. 'I do not know, my daughter. The wazungu do many strange things.'

Miriam was quiet and Hannah, realising the implications of what she had said, added, 'Some of their strange ways are good … very good. Fighting each other is not a good thing.'

Miriam smiled at the way her mother had smoothed things over. They continued with their chores in silence for a few moments, then Miriam asked, 'Do you think the wazungu will start a war here?'

'I do not know, my daughter. The fighting is in Dar es Salaam only. If it is big fighting, then maybe. War is a restless beast. It moves from place to place, looking for food to keep its belly full. Maybe it will go south and we will be safe.'

'And if it comes north?'

Hannah dried her hands on a tea towel, then turned to her daughter. 'I think it will come north. It is Germany and England at war in Europe. I have heard that it is the Portuguese to the south of the Germans and I have not heard that they are at war with England or Germany.'

Miriam stopped drying the dish she was busy with and stared at her mother.

'Do not worry, my child. This is a war between the white men. It will not affect us.'

'It will affect my husband. And Master Richmond and Mistress Agnes, will it not?'

Hannah turned back to the sink. She had finished her work but could not face her daughter as she told her the truth. 'Yes, I fear it will affect them all.'

That night, as she waited for James to come from the main house, Miriam held Samwelli close to her and kissed the top of his head gently. 'Pray that this war goes south, my child,' she whispered.

⚐

'Please do call me Tensi,' Hortensia Muller said as they sat on the veranda watching the setting sun wrap the small hills in a hazy orange gauze.

'And do call me Aggie,' Agnes replied. Richmond and James exchanged glances. No one had ever called her Aggie. Why a sudden need for this less formal version of her name? James, finding it funny gave a smile, but Richmond scowled slightly.

Then James looked across at Kate. She was giving her mother-in-law a queer look and he realised that the two women were just trying to put each other at ease.

'How was your journey, Mrs Muller?' he knew he was not included in the invite to be informal.

The simple question helped dispel the slight awkwardness of this first meeting between his and Carl's mother as Mrs Muller went on to talk at length about the discomforts associated with travelling such distances.

'I had forgotten what that is like,' Agnes said when she got a chance. 'The only journey of any distance I have undertaken in Africa was when we travelled here from Mombasa. Of course I was much younger then, but I did have Rosemary-Jane to think about. She was only a few months old then.'

'Rosemary-Jane?' Hortensia enquired.

'My first child. She sadly succumbed to malaria when very young, poor thing.'

'Dreadful business this malaria,' Hortensia shook her head and looked across at Kate. 'It took Kate and Carl's first child too.' She patted Kate's arm.

'Quinine, that's the thing,' Agnes said.

'Yes, we would mix it with a little fruit juice to try and hide the bitterness.'

'Would you like to see the garden, Kate?' James, sensing that the conversation was going to turn very dull, offered his friend's wife a get out.

'That would be lovely,' Kate said, her dark eyes sparkling. 'Let me just check on Heinrich first.'

They took their leave of the two older women and headed inside to see that Kate's son was settling down. Richmond took the opportunity to make his excuses and, pleading farm work, headed off after downing his second whisky of the afternoon.

Heinrich George was sleeping peacefully in his cot and Wamuhu rose as they came into the room. She was already proving to be a far better nurse than cook.

'Thanks, Wamuhu,' James whispered. 'We are just going for a walk, but wanted to check on Heinrich first. Please sit, we won't be long.'

They spent a few moments looking at the child, then left quietly.

'He has Carl's eyes,' Kate said, looping her arm in his as they walked across the lawn. 'Carl adores his son.'

James smiled. 'I can well believe that. He spoke with such love for Heinrich in his letters. He is a very proud father.'

Kate turned to face him. Motherhood had filled her out a bit, but she still had a girlish tinge to her pretty features. Her eyes sparkled momentarily at this comment, then a sadness dulled her looks.

'I am worried James. This news of war is a terrible business.'

'Don't worry,' he assured her, 'it is all happening in Europe, it won't affect us here.'

'Do you really think so?' She searched his face.

'Why would we fight here? We have been good neighbours for so long. There is no need.'

'Carl does not share your views,' she responded. 'And that recent attack at Dar es Salaam has made things very tense down south.'

'An over-zealous navy captain,' James dismissed the incident. 'And they've agreed that Dar will remain an open city. There is nothing to worry about. It will all be over and forgotten very quickly. They are saying that the problems in Europe will be sorted out before the end of the year.'

'I wish I had your optimism,' Kate said. 'Carl and his father are very concerned. They have sent us here and Carl set off the same day we did to go and join the German army.'

'Carl is joining the army? But why?' James pulled up. They were standing in the middle of the lawn.

'He had no choice. They are conscripting and would have called him up eventually.'

James stared at her and Kate tugged his arm. 'Let's go look at some flowers. His mother does not know this, she thinks Carl was heading off on business. If we stand here in the middle of the lawn, she may think something is wrong. She is good at sensing things. I don't want her to be worrying.' They moved over to an area of particularly colourful flowers and pretended to admire them.

'Carl was really angry about the attack at Dar. He says there was a gentleman's agreement not to attack but the British broke that. That is why he has gone to do his duty.'

James stared at Kate. He could hardly believe what he was hearing. Carl, or at least the Carl he knew, was never that caught up in the politics of the day.

'I really don't know what to say, Kate. I never would have thought that Carl … anyway I am sure it will all work out okay. From what I have heard, the attack on Dar was a mistake. I am sure they will resolve all this and we can return to normal soon.'

'I do hope so. But I am scared James. What if things don't blow over. What if Carl has to go and fight. Heinrich is too young to lose his father. Oh, I must stop calling him Heinrich. Carl said I was to use his middle name while we are here. George, that's Carl's maternal grandfather's name. Carl says that I must call him George so that we don't have any trouble here.'

'Trouble. What sort of trouble?' James was beginning to feel out of his depth, as though he had missed something significant.

'Oh, I don't know,' Kate shook her head, her dark curls bouncing as she did so. 'He just said that the British may take offence at a child with a German name. He said it was best if I just called our son George while we are here.'

While James wanted to dismiss all this as nonsense, he could not help seeing the concern in Kate's eyes and he had always held Carl's opinion in high esteem. If his friend was concerned, then there was probably good reason for him to be so. And if Carl was worried then, James realised, that he too should take note of what was happening.

'Oh, I've upset you now,' there was a tremble in Kate's voice and a threat of tears in her eyes. 'I'm so sorry James, but I just didn't know who I could turn to. I cannot tell my mother-in-law anything and I feel so alone and afraid.'

'You haven't upset me,' James said, turning his head back to the house so that his face did not betray his lie. 'And do not feel alone,' he turned back as the lie passed, 'You are with friends here and Miriam will take care of you.'

'Miriam?'

'The servant girl who looks after the house where you are staying.' He felt guilty calling his wife 'the servant girl' but he did not know if Carl had said anything to Kate about his relationship. Kate nodded as he quickly went on to say that Miriam was one of their best servants and if they needed anything they just had to ask and she would sort it.

Kate smiled a sad smile. 'We are grateful to you and your family for all that you are doing for us.'

'Oh nonsense. Carl would have done exactly the same if we had been the ones in need.'

Kate nodded and stared out at the hills for a moment, then looked back at the house where her mother-in-law sat merrily chatting away to Agnes.

'And what about you?' she said changing the subject. 'How are you doing since Elizabeth died?'

'Oh, I am doing okay. I miss her, and always will. She was an amazing person and a good friend. You would have liked her.'

'I am sorry we never got to meet. Carl spoke highly of her.' She squeezed his arm gently. 'Is it too soon for you to be looking to remarry?'

James gave a little chuckle, 'I am not ready just yet,' he said. 'I don't know if I will ever get married again.' He now laughed at his own private joke, then realising that this may look a little odd, he added, 'But one should never say never.'

Kate nodded and said nothing further on the topic. They walked slowly back to join the two ladies on the veranda, James wondering how much pressure about remarrying he would have to endure over the next while.

McCallum brought the news of the German attack at Taveta, the small border town that James knew so well from his trips to see Carl. There was a stunned silence around the dinner table as the Scot told them how a small band of Germans had attacked and taken the town.

'Fortunately not too many casualties. One dead on our side, a local policeman, Mwiti. I think you may have dealt with him once or twice, Mr Aitken.'

Richmond nodded slowly. 'Mwiti, a good man, very helpful.'

'They think they got one of the Germans as they retreated. There was hardly anyone there to defend the town, just a handful of policemen really,' McCallum continued. 'I am told the Germans were led by a guy called von Prince. The man is supposed to be half Scottish, he should be on our side.'

'Tom von Prince?' There was a quiver in Kate's voice.

'Yes, Tom von Prince. Scottish father, German mother. Do you know him?'

'Yes. Well, no. I've never met him, but I am sure Carl was heading over to see him as we were leaving to come here.' She gave James a knowing look.

'You don't think he was going to enlist?' It was Hortensia's turn to quiver. 'Kate? Did he? You don't think...'

'Ach, no Mrs Muller. I am sure he wasn't there. They say it was mostly natives on the German side, Askari they call them.'

'Mostly natives? But you can't be sure that Carl wasn't there, can you?' Kate's voice was icily calm.

McCallum could not hold her gaze. 'No, I cannae be sure. But the chances...'

'Chances! Don't talk to me about chances,' her composure seemed to melt.

'Now Kate, we can't assume...' Hortensia tried to calm her daughter-in-law, but she too looked pale and shocked. 'Mr McCallum was only reporting what he had heard.'

'Ach, Mrs Muller, Kate. I wish I knew more and I will try and find out. But the news was scanty at best.' James could see that McCallum was clearly distressed by the upset he had caused. How was he to know that this von Prince character was the one Carl had gone to join.

McCallum's discomfort had a calming effect on Kate who, while still upset, took a deep breath and placed her delicate hands on the table either side of her plate. 'I am sorry Mr McCallum, I did not mean to be short with you. I am grateful for the news you have brought. I wish you knew more about the soldier on the German side who was killed. I would rest easier if I knew for sure that it was not Carl.' His name was almost swallowed as she choked and a tear ran down her cheek. 'Would you excuse me please. I would like to be alone for a moment.' She stood up and the men present, taken by surprise, fumbled to their feet as Kate swished out of the dining room. Hortensia stared after her, a grim expression on her face. And then nodded, as if noting her suspicions had been confirmed.

'I'll go after her,' Agnes said, causing the men to half stumble as they looked to sit down and had to suddenly stand again. They watched Agnes go, then looked at Hortensia to see if she was going to leave as well.

'I had better go too,' she said and the men remained standing as she took her leave.

Once the women had left, the three men sat down and a sombre mood descended. Suddenly this war that was meant to happen so far away, was on their doorstep and there was a real chance that one of the first casualties was a good friend.

Richmond stared at his wine glass, twirling it slowly in his fingers. McCallum pushed the food around his plate while James looked from one to the other, hoping that the two older men would give him some advice on how to deal with the emotions that rushed through him.

'It's outrageous, attacking Taveta like that,' Richmond eventually broke the silence although he did not look up.

'That it is,' McCallum forked a carrot, lifted it to his mouth, then returned it to his plate.

James wanted to remind them that it was the British who had attacked first. Had they forgotten what happened in Dar es Salaam? But he thought better of it and held his tongue.

'This means war,' Richmond said, again not looking up.

They sat in silence for a while. Eventually Richmond raised his head. 'We will have to evacuate the farm. Move up to Mombasa. McCallum, can you start making the arrangements tomorrow.'

'Move to Mombasa?' James was dumbfounded. 'Why?' His concern was for Miriam and Samwelli, what would happen to them?

'Because I'm not bloody sitting here waiting for the Germans to come and take us prisoner … or worse.' Richmond's voice was terse.

'What about the farm hands? The servants?' McCallum stepped in to help James out.

'They can look after themselves. The war is not with the locals. They will be safe. And it will only be temporary. The British will not just sit back and let the Germans advance. There are soldiers, British soldiers, between us and Taveta. They are stationed at Maktau. I am sure they are already being mobilised. And there are bound to be reinforcements being sent as we speak.'

'If there are soldiers at Maktau, then why must we evacuate? Surely they will stop a small group of Germans from getting here.' James said, bewildered by these sudden developments.

'It's just precautionary,' Richmond said, his tone less harsh than before.

⚱

'Miss Kate?'

'Is that you Miriam?'

'Yes, Mam. I have brought you your shawl. The mosquitos can be a problem here at night.' She helped wrap the garment over Kate's shoulders. The sky was charcoal grey and flecked with indigo blue clouds making their silent, solemn trek across the wide expanse covered the dark land. A slither of moon sliced a small gash in the grey, allowing a muted brightness to leak out and gave enough light for the two women to make out the other's outline, but failed to colour in any details.

Kate thanked Miriam and pulled the shawl closer around her, seeking warmth from it, despite the balmy night air.

'It is an ominous looking sky, do you not think?'

Miriam, who had started to move off, turned back.

'Mam?'

'The sky. It looks ominous.'

'I am sorry, Miss Kate, I do not know that word.'

Kate slowly looked away from the sky and tried to focus on Miriam.

'Ominous. It is like it is saying that something bad is going to happen.'

Miriam looked up at the sky, then back at Kate.

'Yes, Miss Kate, it is that,' she agreed and looked to move off.

'Stay with me a moment, will you Miriam? Please.'

'Mam?'

'Stay with me for a bit please. Mrs Muller is asleep and I don't want to be alone.'

'Yes Mam.'

Kate sat down on the bench where James and Miriam often sat in the evenings. It was on the opposite side of the building to the main farm house and looked over some of the fields and the hills beyond, but the dark night had censored the view.

'Come and sit,' Kate invited Miriam over and repeated the request adding a 'please' when Miriam hesitated.

Miriam eased herself onto the bench, leaving a respectable distance between her and the white mistress.

'Master Carl told me all about you, Miriam. He said that you looked after him very well when he stayed here.'

'Master Carl is a good, kind man,' Miriam said, unsure where this was leading. She knew that James had told Carl about their relationship, but was unsure if this news had passed on to Master Carl's wife.

'Yes, he is.' Kate said and Miriam heard the concerned tone in her voice. 'He has joined the army. On the German side. You know about the war, don't you?'

'Yes, Mam. It is a terrible thing, this fighting.'

'You heard that there was an attack on Taveta?'

'Yes, Mam.'

Kate stared out into the darkness for a bit then, without turning back to Miriam, said, 'I am so afraid that Master Carl was there. They say one German was killed and I do not know if it was my husband. I have no way of finding out and the worry is too much to bear.' A soundless sob sent a spasm through her slight frame.

Miriam hesitated, then gently put her hand on Kate's shoulder. 'Do not worry, Miss Kate. Master Carl was not the German man killed.'

'Thank you Miriam, but you cannot know that for sure.' Kate continued to stare out at the blackness.

'But I do know, Mam. It was not Master Carl.'

Kate turned and grabbed Miriam's hands desperate for any news. 'But how could you know?' Her voice fought to bring reason back to a heart that dared hope.

'One of the workers here on the farm was in Taveta when the attack came. He saw it all happen. Jeremiah knows Master Carl from his visits here. He would have said it was Master Carl who was shot if it had been so. He did not even say that Master Carl was there. He would have said so if he had seen him.'

'Are you absolutely sure?' Kate's grip on Miriam's hands tightened.

'I can ask Jeremiah again, but I am sure that if he had seen Master Carl, he would have told us, and he said that the Germans called the man who was shot by the name Brooka, or something like that.'

'Oh, Miriam. Thank you so much,' Kate suddenly grabbed and hugged her, taking her by surprise. Then just as suddenly Kate let go and sat up straight. 'Thank you,' she said again, but this time the tone was formal and Miriam edged slightly, almost imperceivably further from her on the bench. Her relationship with James had trained her to be extra formal around the white settlers. In order to hide an intimacy, she had to maintain a distance.

'I am sorry, Miriam. I did not mean to embarrass you,' Kate's voice was soothing and eased her bewilderment. 'I was just so excited at hearing that Carl was okay. Please forgive me.'

'That is fine. Miss Kate. I understand.' Despite the dark, Miriam could feel Kate's eyes on her, sizing her up. 'Does she know about me and James?' she wondered.

Then Kate suddenly laughed.

'Mam?' Miriam was confused,

'Oh, sorry Miriam, I should not laugh like that. It is just that Master Carl has said such good things about you that I had begun to think that he might be ... well, you know ... that he might have had a relationship with you. You are a beautiful woman and, you know men. I thought that maybe he had been intimate with you when he stayed here.'

'Oh, no Mam. Master Carl has always been good to me. He has never...'

Kate nodded. 'No, I don't think my Carl would ever. But some men do, you know. I have heard stories how they take advantage of their servants.'

Miriam said nothing, then began to wonder if her silence would be seen as an admission that something had happened to her. 'Yes, I have heard such stories too, but this has never happened to me.'

'No, I suppose it wouldn't. Mr Aitken and James are good people.'

Miriam was glad that it was dark as she was unsure if her face would betray her thoughts. She hoped that Mrs Kate would not pursue this conversation and was relieved when the young white woman was silent for a bit.

The burbling trill of a nightjar filled the void and gave a pebble-dashed texture to the dark.

'What will happen to you, Miriam, when everyone goes to Mombasa?'

'Mombasa, Mam?'

'Have you not heard? We are to move to Mombasa. Mr Aitken is concerned about the Germans advancing.'

'I had not been told,' Miriam replied.

'They will probably tell you tomorrow. Mr Aitken only made the decision this evening.'

Miriam nodded, her mind racing. What would become of her and Samwelli. They would be separated from James.

'I am sure that you will come with us. We will need help in Mombasa,' Kate's voice was suddenly cheerful, but her words worried Miriam. Yes, she and James may still be together in Mombasa, and with a bit of luck they may be able to snatch some moments together, but it will be far more risky. And what of Samwelli?

Kate interrupted her thoughts by standing up. 'I had better turn in. We have some busy days ahead of us. Thank you for listening to me Miriam. And a special thank you for the news about Carl. I will be able to sleep now.'

Miriam stood while Kate took her leave, but then sat down again once the white mistress was inside. She stared into the dark, feeling the nightjar's call tickling her ears.

James stared into the darkness above his bed. It was strange being back in the main house and hearing the snoring coming from his father's room. The rumbling sound seemed to be duelling with the gentle trill of the nightjar, a rough masculine bass note to the almost soprano bird song.

He was worried about this talk of moving to Mombasa. In fact, this whole war business was disturbing. Kate's concern for Carl, the upheaval at Taveta which was too close for comfort, and his father's suggested move all served to heighten his discomfort. But worst of all was the thought that this may mean a separation from Miriam and Samwelli.

He would have to try and talk to Miriam tomorrow. He could, he thought, persuade his parents that Miriam should come with to look after them in Mombasa. In fact, he thought they would probably suggest it themselves. 'We will need to take Hannah and Miriam,' he could hear his mother saying and his father would reluctantly agree, reluctant because he had not thought of it first and now had to act like he was making a concession. But would they allow Samwelli? Unlikely.

He had only been back to Mombasa twice since leaving school, both business trips with his father. Most of the time they had been in offices or restaurants or clubs, concluding deals with other men for the purchase of the farm's produce. He had visited the school once when his father had disappeared for an afternoon saying that he needed to conclude a particular piece of business on his own. This had been in that desperate time between falling in love with Miriam and the trip to Pangani for the wedding when their relationship had begun.

James had walked around the school for a while, reminiscing about his time there, then had followed the route over to the girls' school, thinking about Carl and Kate. The short walk between schools had been filled with thoughts of Miriam and whether he would ever find happiness.

Now, as he lay awake thinking back to that time, he reflected on how things had changed since that Mombasa trip. He was married to the woman who had so consumed his thoughts back then. He had a son with that same woman. But his parents knew nothing of the relationship, nothing of a daughter-in-law or a grandson. As he considered these things, he marvelled at the fact that they had managed to keep the relationship from his mother and father for so long.

He wondered if he and Miriam would be able to maintain any sort of contact in Mombasa other than a formal master and servant footing. The risks would be far greater as it was unlikely they would have any opportunity for privacy. There would be no trips to Voi where they could stop off at the side of the road. No dam where he and Miriam could meet, no house of his own where they could enjoy the comforts of a soft bed.

McCallum had instructions to start evacuating the farm first thing in the morning. He knew that there would be little or no opportunity to speak to Miriam before the mad scramble of packing began. Mother would be fretting, wanting to take every last plate and teaspoon while father would be oh-for-goodness-saking, fretting about the second harvest which was due in a month or so.

He turned onto his side and listened to the night sounds. The nightjar had fallen silent, but the crickets and frogs continued their serenade. Occasionally a whoop or cry would come from somewhere far off. He recalled his first few nights at school in Mombasa where those sounds were suddenly absent and how that had left a strange emptiness in him. Those sounds were a comfort and he only realised their value when they were not there. Going to Mombasa now would rob him once again of this simple pleasure.

He sighed and then let himself drift off to sleep. His dreams came quickly, like a crowd gathering after some event, hungry for news of what was happening. They filled his head, chatting away, the lines between sounds and colours blurred and uncertain.

※

'I want you to escort the women to Mombasa, Son.' Richmond took James aside before breakfast. 'They can stay at The Mombasa Club.'

'You are not coming with?'

'No, of course not. I have to look after the farm. And it won't be for long. It is just a precaution, but we need to keep the women safe.'

'Am I to stay with them in Mombasa?' James was beginning to realise something.

'No, of course not. I want you back here, I will need your help with the harvest. Get them settled, then return as quickly as possible.'

James nodded. So it was just the women being evacuated. His father had given the impression that they were all to go to Mombasa when they had spoken last night. This was not like him and James wondered if his father was getting soft as he grew older. Just sending the women away made more sense. But the more he thought about it he could not help feeling that his father had meant a full evacuation when he spoke last night. Having had time to think about it, he was now back-tracking and saying only the women.

He knew that if he challenged his father, he would be rebuked and told he was being silly, so he played along, pretending that he had understood from the start.

His views were confirmed a short while later as McCallum looked a little puzzled when told that James was going to accompany the women and then come straight back. He exchanged a glance with the farm manager as if to say, 'No, you did not misunderstand last night, father has changed his mind overnight.' There was a slight nod of acknowledgement from McCallum.

As predicted, his mother fretted, but there was less fuss than he had anticipated.

'I wish you had made yourself clear last night, Richmond. I could hardly sleep worrying about how we would pack up the whole house and now you are telling me it is just the women who are going,' she moaned at breakfast.

'I thought I was quite clear,' Richmond responded in a tone that said, 'do not make a fuss in front of our guests.' He then helped out his wife by adding, 'I am sorry if you did not understand.'

'All this upheaval. I don't know how many long journeys I can endure,' Hortensia said. 'This beastly war business is certainly making life uncomfortable.' Whether she said this to help ease the tension at the table, or if she was unaware of it and was just having a moan, James could not tell.

'It is only a precaution and won't be for too long,' James repeated his father's earlier words and hoped that, by backing up his father, it would be accepted by the women. He was, however, motivated by getting the Mombassa trip out the way quickly so he could return to be with Miriam. His ploy worked. His mother smiled, reached over and put her hand on his.

'You are quite right. Do you not think my son is very sensible, Tensi?'

Hortensia nodded and said, 'He has always shown himself to have a good head on his shoulders. I have thought that ever since he first came to visit us.'

Agnes smiled proudly at him while his father gave him a grateful nod. Kate was the only one who did not respond in the same way, but when James caught her eye, she inclined her head just slightly as if saying that she understood.

Later, when just the two of them were on the veranda together, she said, 'You don't believe what you said at breakfast, do you? When you said that it would only be for a short while?'

'I don't know, if I am honest. I hope it will only be temporary but, I must admit, I have never paid much attention to these sort of things, so I could not even begin to guess. But I know Carl follows these news events closely and has a far better understanding than I do. If he thinks this is serious, then I am sure it is. And serious things don't tend to go away overnight.'

They looked out over the garden. The brilliant blue of the morning sky competed with the deep green of the grass while the rusty red paths through the fields tried to tempt the eye away from the sky and the grass and lead one's gaze to the grey rocks of the hills beyond.

'McCallum says that there are British soldiers at Maktau. They should keep the Germans from invading too far into British territory. Hopefully they will see that it is foolish to try and advance further and coming close to us here. Then we can forget this all happened and go back to our normal lives. Let them have their war in Europe if they want. Surely we don't have to get involved. If we in the colonies have any sense, we will call a truce quickly. Besides, what would the natives think if they saw us squabbling like this?'

Kate nodded without much conviction then, after a moment, said, 'Carl was not the German soldier shot at Taveta.'

James looked at her. Something about the way she said it told him that this was not just wishful thinking. 'How do you know?' he asked.

'Miriam told me. She said one of your workers, Jeremiah, was there and he saw what happened. He knows Carl from his visits here and he would have said if it had been Carl, wouldn't he?'

'Jeremiah? Yes of course. I had forgotten that we sent him to Taveta to pick up some goods. I should have thought to ask him about it.' He paused, then said, 'You spoke to Miriam, you said?'

'Yes. Why? Was I not supposed to?'

'Oh no. No ... I ... er ... I told you she would look after you ... and she has.' He stopped, suddenly aware of the strange look he was getting from Kate. He took a breath and said, 'You had better go and pack. We will want to leave by midday so we can stop overnight in Voi. We can then go on from there. It's going to be a long journey.'

⚱

Miriam was grateful that James managed to arrange a few private moments with her before heading off with the women. Mrs Agnes was fretting as usual, checking and double checking that they had packed this, or that. Mrs Hortensia was slightly calmer, not having as much of her worldly goods with her, while Kate seemed almost oblivious to the hubbub, moving as if in a trance, her mind clearly on her husband.

Once the guests had finished packing, they were sent up to the main house. James, who was meant to escort them, said that he needed to check on something in the field first and would be up at the main house shortly. He saw them off, then headed back the moment they were out of sight. He and Miriam embraced quickly in his room, kissing each other tenderly. He hugged Samwelli who, sensing that something big was happening, flung his arms around his father's neck and had to be pried off when James said he had to leave.

'Go carefully,' Miriam said and then in response to his questioning look, she added, 'There may be more war.'

He laughed but without conviction. 'I'll be fine. I am not a soldier, and I will be travelling with the womenfolk. No one will bother us. And besides, we are travelling way from the fighting.'

Miriam nodded and she held Samwelli tighter as a kind of comfort against the upcoming separation. He was getting to be a little too heavy to carry these days but, under the circumstances, she knew she had to hold on to him, as much for his comfort as for hers.

James kissed first the top of his son's head, then her on the cheek before turning and heading off. She watched him go till he was out of sight, then put Samwelli down but held on to his hand. Eventually she said, 'Come, my son, we must go and tidy up now that the people are gone.'

The boy looked at his mother, then back to where his father had just disappeared.

'He'll be back soon, don't you worry,' she said. 'Come on. When we have finished cleaning, we can have some bread and jam. Would you like that?'

The boy nodded and smiled.

Miriam set about taking the bedclothes off the bed and putting fresh linen on. 'Who knows when the bed will next be needed?' she thought. Samwelli helped as best he could.

'Ma, what is war?' he asked after helping to pack the dirty bedclothes into Miriam's washing basket.

'War? That is when people fight with each other.'

'Why are they fighting in Taveta?'

'I do not know my son. They say it is because of something happening in Europe. Europe is a land far far away. It is where the wazungu come from.'

'Is Mr James a wazungu?'

It saddened Miriam every time Samwelli called his father 'Mr James' but knew that it had to be in order to protect them all. At his age, Samwelli would not understand why he should not call him 'father' or 'papa', so they agreed to train him to use the formal master/servant version to avoid the child giving away their secret. When he was old enough, they would tell him the truth.

'Mah-zungu, mah…mah. It is mzungu. He is only one so mzungu. If there are more than one, then it is wazungu.' She gently corrected his Kiswahili.

'Mzungu,' the boy's brow furrowed as he committed this new bit of learning to memory. 'Is Mr James a mzungu?'

Miriam laughed. 'What is a mzungu?'

Samwelli handed her the pillowcase he had been folding. 'A mzungu is a white person.'

Miriam took the pillowcase and refolded it while distracting her son with another question, 'Is Mr James a white person?'

'Yes.'

'So is Mr James a mzungu?'

Samwelli thought for a minute, then smiled. 'Yes, he is.' Then, after some further thought, he asked, 'Is he from Europe?'

'No,' Miriam laughed again. 'Mr James was born right here on the farm. He was born three weeks before me. His mother and father, Mrs Agnes and Mr Richmond, they came from Europe. They are wazungu and that makes Mr James a mzungu.'

The little boy's eyes closed slightly as the effort of processing this information meant he had to shut out visual stimuli to allow the brain to focus on understanding it.

Miriam put the last of the bed linen into the washing basket and hoisted the load onto her head, taking just a second to balance it.

'Come on,' she said, holding out her hand to her son. 'We need to go and do some washing.'

The boy took her hand and walked silently next to her. They were about halfway to the stream when he asked, 'Is my father from Europe?'

The washing basket teetered for just a second before rebalancing itself.

'No, my son, he is from around here.'

Further processing was required before the next question came, 'Where is my father?'

Miriam put a hand up to steady the basket. 'Your father? He is ... he is dancing with the monkeys.'

They stopped in Voi to spend the night at the Smiths'. Mrs Smith insisted that Kate and Hortensia sleep in their spare bedroom and Agnes could sleep in Oliver's.

'And where will Oliver sleep?' Agnes asked.

'I can share the tent with James. It is only for one night,' Oliver said with a smile.

'You really don't need to go to such bother,' Agnes said, although it was clear that the objection was merely for politeness' sake and that the offer was very gratefully accepted.

'Nonsense,' Oliver dismissed the protest with a wave of his hand. 'Besides, it will be quite fun to sleep under canvas for a change. I have not done so in a good while. And James and I can have a good catch up. It's been ages ... too long ... since we last saw each other.'

They dined well that evening. The talk around the table was light-hearted and there was no mention of the war. Hortensia and Mrs Smith got on well and Kate chattered away with James and Oliver. Between soup and the main course, James looked around the room and it struck him that Elizabeth was missing. His mother sat in the chair where his first wife used to sit whenever they had visited.

Agnes caught his eye as he stared at the spot. At first a questioning look passed over her face, then one of realisation. She opened her mouth to say something but he quickly gave a slight shake of his head and a smile. The atmosphere was warm and jovial, he did not want to put a damper on it with talk of the departed. And, he was sure, Elizabeth would not have wanted it. Perhaps later, when he and Oliver had a chance to chat, he would find out how the Smiths were really doing.

Reluctantly they ended the dinner around eight o'clock. The travelling party wanted an early start in the morning. It was only then that the question was raised about whether the Smiths were going to stay where they were or relocate to Mombasa.

'We are staying here,' Reverend Smith said, his voice was calm. 'We are running a mission school for the locals. I do not believe we will be affected by the war, if indeed it does progress this far into British territory. I am sure we will be fine.' There was just a hint in his tone, James thought, which questioned why Richmond had felt it necessary to relocate the women. He was glad the Reverend did not give voice to the question as he did not really know the answer himself.

The women retired to their bedrooms and James and Oliver made their way to the tent that the servants had erected around the back of the house.

'What do you make of all these war shenanigans?' Oliver asked as they settled themselves for the night.

'I don't know,' James replied. 'Some say it will be over quickly, but Carl, Kate's husband, is fighting on the German side. Kate says he thinks it is a serious thing and will certainly affect us here.'

Oliver climbed into his camping cot. 'I think he might be right. I hope not, but I cannot see this coming to a swift conclusion.'

They put out the lamp and let the darkness settle in the tent. The night sounds in Voi were different to those on the farm or in Mombasa. Here they did not have the full range of wildlife one heard on the farm. Neither did it have that big city bustle of Mombasa. Here, the occasional passing mumble as locals walked by in the street and a cricket chorus were about the sum total of sound.

James felt tired. The journey itself was not too arduous, but the strain of the last few days, worrying about Carl and fretting about not being able to be with Miriam and Samwelli had exhausted him.

'Do you think you will enlist?' Oliver's question disturbed the rhythm of his thoughts.

'Will you?' He did not want to answer this.

'Yes, definitely. It would be my duty as an Englishman.' There was no doubt in Oliver's voice and, James knew this made his answer even more difficult. Oliver would expect him, as an Englishman, to fight for his country. Even his own father would, most probably, expect it too. But he did not feel English. Not in the same way Oliver and his father would. Both had been born and grew up back in the motherland. It was different if you were born here in Africa. This land was all he had ever known.

Yes, there were times when he felt like an interloper in this place. He had watched the natives and had some sense of the way they were connected to the land. There was a natural harmony between them, and it showed in the ease with which the people walked across the paths and climbed over the rocks. He felt it in the way they seemed to glide through the heat of the day. Even the animals responded differently to them, as if they had some sort of understanding.

'I suppose I should. Father would expect it.'

'You don't sound convinced,' Oliver responded.

'Well, it's difficult for me. I have never been to England, so I don't have the connection to it that you do. It seems strange to me to fight for a country I've never even visited. But I do feel a sense of duty because my parents are from there. Does that make sense?'

Oliver's reply took a moment to come, and James could imagine him nodding in the dark.

'Yes, I think it does. I hadn't really thought about that.'

'But I don't have to do anything just yet. I need to get Mama and Mrs Muller and Kate settled in Mombasa first. With a bit of luck, it will all be over by then and I can bring everyone back home.'

'Let's hope so.' Oliver's tone was not very positive.

The farm felt strange without Mrs Aitken. As far back as she could remember, Miriam could not recall a day when she was absent. There had been the occasional day trip into Voi, but she had always returned home by nightfall.

Her mother had gone with the women to Mombasa and Miriam was left behind to look after Mr Richmond. She had never felt at ease around him.

The image of him with his trousers down around his ankles while he did his business with that poor servant girl had stayed with her. She had not said anything at the time, but the woman being forced to please her master was the young mother of a friend of hers. She would never tell James this and sometimes she wondered if he even remembered the event.

How different James was from his father. His father showed no respect for others. Even the way he treated Mrs Agnes was not with love. Miriam often wondered about the relationship between Mrs Agnes and Mr Richmond. It seemed to her to be a miracle that James was even conceived. His parents lived separate lives, had separate bedrooms, never touched each other. She could not imagine herself being happy in a marriage like that. And yet, in their strange way, Mr Richmond and Mrs Agnes while not happy, were not unhappy.

She cleared away the plates from the dinner table. Mr Richmond had had a few drinks more than usual. She heard him belch softly then sigh.

'Miriam.' His voice sounded a little strange, but then having dinner on his own was strange.

'Yes, sir.' She turned. The pile of dishes she was carrying was heavy and she hoped that he would not detain her long.

He looked her up and down in a way that made her feel uncomfortable, as if he were assessing her for something. She felt her stomach knot and had to concentrate hard in order not to let the dishes rattle.

The moment seemed to last forever while his eyes clawed at her like grabbing hands. She felt almost forgotten in that moment as if he had physically ripped her body from her inner being, as if she were watching him from the other side of the room while he violated the body of another woman who looked like her.

Her voice was buried deep inside her, hidden from her mouth. She wanted to speak, even if just to ask a questioning, 'Sir?' to try and break this strange moment, try and tell him that she was a human being, not just an object subject to his lustful desires. She clambered around, searching desperately for a word or even something to make her move, shift her weight to her other leg. But nothing came.

Then he shook his head, just a tiny, almost imperceivable shake, and said, 'I'll have my coffee on the veranda.'

The room breathed again and colour returned as it came back into focus. Details, the smeared gravy on the plate, the blink of the lamplight on the silverware, the dull green of the untouched beans, all rushed to embrace her senses, their mundaneness a balm to the intense fear she had felt a moment ago.

'Yes, sir,' she nodded and turned to go.

'Oh, and Miriam.'

The plates, which a second ago had suddenly felt weightless, now tugged at her arms, sending a short spasm of pain up them which ricocheted into her heart and knocked the air from her lungs. 'Yes, sir.' The words came from years of obedience rather than from a conscious action on her behalf.

'Ask Wamuhu to come and see me please.'

Mombasa felt muted. There was an air of nervous tension that manifested itself in a kind of gloom which clung to the humidity. This was not helped by the clouds which obscured the usually sunny skies.

The women did not notice it. They were far more concerned about coping with the heat, finding their rooms and unpacking. But then, James told himself, they had not spent much, if any, time in this city. His mother had a brief spell there when they first arrived, a time she rarely spoke of. From what he gathered, mostly from others who knew the family, she had kept to herself. But that was not too surprising, they said, as she had just given birth. Rosemary-Jane, the sister he never knew, had been born in this very club where they were now settling. He wondered if it brought back any memories for her. She didn't show anything if it did.

Hortensia had never been here before. It was only Kate who knew the city.

'It's a bit subdued,' she commented when they had a few moments unhindered by the fuss of the mothers.

'Yes, I felt that too. Must be this war business,' James said.

'It is partly the war itself, but people are more concerned about the impact it will have on business,' was the opinion of Edwards Sinclair, the man whom, so his father had told him, was the one who had suggested coffee farming when the Aitkens first arrived in country. James met with Edward out of politeness. He did not really like the man, but they had had dealings a few times before and James felt a sense of duty to his father to keep that relationship on a good footing. They had some drinks before dinner and then, thankfully, he went off to another engagement.

There were a number of men who greeted him when they went into dinner, men whom his father did business with, but whom he only vaguely knew. Some had names that attached themselves quickly to the face, while for others, the name floated around their aura, but never came into focus.

They all smiled politely when he introduced his mother, Hortensia and Kate. One or two vaguely remembered Agnes and had brief conversations. He nearly corrected the man, Albert White if his memory served him correctly, who said, 'Your son has grown quite a bit since coming into the world in this very club.'

'Yes, he has. We are very proud of him.' His mother's answer puzzled him, especially as he could see that there was no sign on her face to show that she was just going along with Albert's mistake. Perhaps the journey had confused her, he thought, but said nothing.

As if tuned into the mood of the city, dinner was a muted affair, but the four of them were travel weary and Hortensia and Kate said their good-nights straight after finishing.

'I'll just have a last cup of tea before going to bed,' Agnes said. 'You don't have to sit up with me, James.'

'I'm fine, Mama. I'll sit up a bit longer.' He could have gone to bed, but the sense of duty to his mother kept him. He could not leave her alone in a room full of strangers.

The tea arrived and his mother fussed over the pouring as she always did, checking again that he did not want some.

'No, Mama. I am happy with my brandy.'

They sat back and James sipped his drink while his mother looked around the room.

'You know, I don't remember any of this,' she gestured at the room.

'Well, it was a long time ago,' he replied.

She nodded slowly but continued to scan her surroundings as if searching for something to latch on to, something to anchor her memories.

'Why did you not correct that man earlier about me being born here. I was born on the farm, wasn't I?' His curiosity got the better of him.

'Hmm?' She continued to look around, but he could tell she was avoiding the question and he decided not to pursue the issue.

But then she looked back at him and said, 'I don't know. I guess this place just brings back memories, ones I don't really want to recall.'

He nodded and was silent, wondering what it was that made her not want to remember, but knowing he may never get an answer.

'It was your sister who brought us here, do you know that?' She spoke as if to herself so he didn't answer, letting her have the space she needed.

'She was conceived before we were married. Your father seduced me at a party so we had to leave England and come here to cover the shame of it.

It was a silly moment of weakness and yet it changed our lives so much. I hated your sister because of what she had done to me. She had dragged me halfway across the globe to a land I had only vaguely heard of and never wanted to come to. I hated this place. This club, the people, the wretched heat. Everything.'

He stared at his mother, struggling to find words with which to respond to this confession, then realised that she was not yet done.

'I wasted a year of Rosemary-Jane's short life hating her. And that was so unfair. It was not her fault. It was also not your father's fault. I gave into his charms. I could have said no. I could have pushed him away and none of this would have happened. But I was young.'

She stared at her teacup and he knew that if she looked at him, she would not be able to complete her confession, so remained silent, not moving.

'I only began to love Rosemary-Jane just before she died and not a day goes by when I don't regret the time I wasted not loving her as a mother should. I wish I could get those days back and I would smother her with a lifetime of love to cram it all into those few years that she lived. She deserved so much more.'

She picked up her teacup. It rattled so in the saucer that she replaced it on the table. She looked up now, but could not hold his gaze for more than a second, shame burning in her eyes.

'I am a terrible mother,' she said staring down at her hands which now lay on her lap.

'No, you are not, Mama,' he said it with some force, causing her to look at him.

'No, you are not.' He was more gentle this time. 'You made a mistake Mama. That does not make you a bad person. You have been a wonderful mother to me.'

She smiled a sad smile. 'You are a good son, James. I really didn't deserve you, but I am glad I had you.' She looked around the room again. 'I was dreading coming back here, dreading the memories. And it has certainly done that.' She gave a small laugh and picked up her tea. This time there was no rattle.

'I'll be all right,' she responded to his look of concern. 'Don't worry about me. It may take a day or so, but I cannot let the past haunt me. Things happened, things I regret but I will never regret having you. You brought sanity to my world.'

A waiter came to clear the tea things while they sat in silence. After he left, she stood and announced she was now ready for bed.

'Don't worry about me,' she repeated, 'I will be fine. I hope I haven't shocked you too much with my confession.'

He shook his head but knew that the action lacked conviction.

She turned to leave, then stopped and turned back. 'Oh, and please don't mention any of this to your father.'

He nodded and watched her go.

'Do you require anything else tonight, Sir?' The waiter had returned without him noticing.

'No. Thanks. Actually, yes. Another brandy if I may.' He seldom had more than one after dinner drink but he needed to think.

After a week in the city, James began to grow restless. He was keen to get back to the farm, to Miriam and Samwelli. But he felt he could not leave his mother just yet. Not after her confession. She arrived at breakfast the next morning and behaved as if nothing had happened and it didn't seem to James it was just because Hortensia and Kate were there. He sensed a restlessness in her and occasionally caught her looking around the room as she had done the night before, as if searching for an answer to a question she didn't really understand.

She appeared cheerful. Too cheerful in James' opinion. He could see that she was overcompensating, acting as if nothing was wrong. He felt torn. He knew his father would be impatiently awaiting his return and that the harvest would not wait for him, but he could not just leave his mother until he was certain she was fine.

In the end he confided in Kate who had sensed something.

'Is your mother all right? She's been acting a bit strange ever since we got here,' Kate observed when they took a stroll through the club grounds one day.

'She has memories of this place,' he replied and went on to tell Kate about Rosemary-Jane, leaving out the bit about her illegitimate conception. Rather he spoke about a difficult birth which his mother had only recently confessed to. Then he went on to speculate that the club had obviously brought back memories of the daughter lost at such a young age to malaria.

'Oh the poor woman,' Kate said.

'But don't let her know I told you,' James pleaded, pleased with his deception. 'She made me promise not to say anything.'

They walked on in silence, both engrossed in thought.

'I need to get back to the farm, but I don't want to leave Mama in her current state,' he said after a while.

'Don't worry, James, we will take good care of her. I'll make sure she doesn't get too lost in her memories.' She patted his arm.

'This damned war business is not helping,' he said, but still smiled a thank you to her offer.

'Yes, it has made Mombasa a gloomy place, but I heard this morning that they are expecting troops from India soon. Hopefully that will liven things up a bit and maybe take your mother's mind off her other issues.'

James liked the way his mother's secret had so quickly become 'other issues' as if they were a side show that could easily be overshadowed by the colour, noise and excitement of the main carnival. He could already picture Kate and Hortensia distracting his mother with other things, and he felt some comfort in this. He could now begin to make plans for his return journey.

Before dinner that evening, he bumped into Edward Sinclair who invited him for a drink in a way that made it difficult for him to decline. They sat in the club lounge, Sinclair seeming to fit so naturally into the armchair as if man and seat were long time lovers.

'There are troops arriving soon. From India.' Sinclair did not waste time in getting to talk of the war and there was a sneer in his voice when he said 'India' which James found disrespectful.

'Yes, I had heard that,' he replied.

'It is all well and good bringing that lot here, but what we need is white Englishman fighting for us.'

James wanted to ask what was wrong with the Indian troops, wanted to say that they should be grateful these men from India were coming here to help, but before he could say anything, Sinclair went on.

'These Indian troops are going to give the local Indians ideas above their station. They are going to feel that we owe them something. We don't need them, we are quite capable of defending our colony. Surely they could send British troops from back home and we can raise an army from the settlers here. We have the King's African Rifles and, I hear, that there is a group of volunteers putting together a unit called the East African Mounted Rifles. They are looking for young men who can ride a horse and carry a rifle.

'Personally I would join the King's African Rifles if I were you, James. The other group seem to be a bunch of ragamuffins. Mostly South African

Boers. I wouldn't trust the Boers myself, they never fought fair in South Africa. But at least they are white. Yes, the King's African Rifles are much better for someone of your upbringing. You are planning to join up, aren't you?'

The question took him by surprise. 'Well, I had not actually considered it, to be quite honest. Everything has been happening so quickly. And then there's the farm...'

'Nonsense!' Sinclair interjected, 'You should be doing your duty. As an Englishman. The farm will wait. It will still be there when this war is over. Besides, it won't take you away for very long. I can't imagine the Germans actually being able to hold out, we will have them defeated in no time. Same will happen in Europe.'

James felt uncomfortable. He did he not feel the blind patriotism to Britian that Sinclair just assumed he would have and had no appetite for fighting. It was not in his nature. But Sinclair was making him feel like a traitor because he did not share his enthusiasm.

'I am sure that your father would want you to go and fight.' There was a belligerent tone in Sinclair's voice now and, James suddenly realised, a slight slurring. He recalled seeing Sinclair in the club lounge earlier in the afternoon, drink in hand. And he was already on his third since James had sat down with him. In fact most times he saw the man, he was drinking. And as he realised that Sinclair was a drunk, he also realised that he could not argue with him. But the drinks meant that he could make noises about signing up which would placate the man. Just don't make promises, he thought. You need to stay true to yourself.

'I must admit that, while I had not really thought about it, now that mother is safely here in Mombasa, I have some time to think. I will talk to father when I get home.'

'Attaboy! That's more like it!'

Yes, I will talk to father. I will talk to him about how mother is settling in here, about the harvest, about the weather, about the workers on the farm, but I will not talk to him about joining the King's African Rifles, or that other lot. He grinned to himself at his little act of defiance.

Fortunately, he didn't have to make any further such deceptions as another associate of Sinclair's arrived and he saw his mother with Hortensia heading to the dining room, so took his leave and went to join his party.

※

'Have you thought of joining up with the volunteer regiment?' his father asked. James had hardly had a chance to clean up after his journey home, and seeing Miriam loitering to serve dinner, made him ache to take her in his arms. He had missed her dreadfully and this talk of joining up didn't help.

'Edward Sinclair talked about it,' he said, not answering his father's question. 'He said there was a regiment of volunteers being put together, but they are mostly South African Boers. I wouldn't want to fight with them.' He had never seen a Boer in his life and had no idea what they were like, but thought this may deter his father from pursing the idea of him signing up,

But his father was better informed than he thought. 'No, not with that Boer lot. With the King's African Rifles. A British unit.'

He wanted to lie, to say that he had not heard of the King's African Rifles, but somehow knew that his father would see through this. 'Yes, Sinclair mentioned that unit, but he said that they were based in Nairobi.' He hoped that the distance would put his father off.

'There's the railways nowadays. You can get the train at Voi and it goes all the way to Nairobi. Doesn't take too long from what I have been told.'

James was acutely aware of Miriam standing behind his father, ostensibly waiting to serve or clear away as required, but he knew that she was staying to hear this conversation. It was, however, becoming clear that his father wanted him to enlist and he did not know how he could at least have some time to discuss things with Miriam, try and explain his position to her.

'Can we discuss this in the morning, father? I need to think about my options.'

'I don't know what there is to think about, but I can see that you are tired. McCallum will be here for breakfast, so you can get his views too.' He downed his third whisky of the evening.

As he made his way home, it struck James that his father had not once asked about his mother and how she had settled in Mombasa. In light of his mother's confession, this kind of thing now made sense to him.

He was tired and Miriam had to wake him from a nap when she came in from finishing her chores. They embraced, the recent separation making the moment that much more intimate. Samwelli loitered nearby, his wide eyes watching them, waiting for the moment when he would be allowed to join in.

'I missed you, young man,' James said when he eventually released Miriam. He scooped the boy into his arms, holding him to his chest. The lad snuggled close, putting his head on James' shoulder and looked out across at his mother.

Once Samwelli was settled, James said, 'We need to talk.'

Miriam nodded and they moved into the sitting room.

'You heard father tonight. He wants me to volunteer. To go and fight.'

She nodded slowly.

'But I don't know what to do. It's not just him expecting it. There were others, in Mombasa. They all think I should volunteer.'

'And you don't know what to do,' she said after his pause went on a bit too long.

He nodded. 'I don't really want to go and fight but I do feel a sense of duty to do so.'

Again there was a long pause which Miriam eventually broke. 'You must do what you think is right,' she said, but did not look at him as she spoke. The gesture suggesting that she knew which option she would choose, but it was not her place to say.

This did not help James. He did not want to go but he had a strong sense that not going would cause all sorts of tensions and possibly even adversely affect the farm business. Knowing that Miriam did not want him to go made the decision that much more difficult.

'I suppose I don't have to decide now,' he said at length. 'I can sleep on it.'

Miriam nodded and they smiled resigned smiles at each other.

'Is he asleep?' James inclined his head to Samwelli who still lay on his shoulder.

'Yes. He has been excited all day, waiting to see you again.'

They put the boy to bed, James' heart heavy, knowing that he would have to go away again soon and who knew when ... or if ... he would be back.

☙

Christmas 1914 was a subdued affair. Agnes was still in Mombasa with Hortensia and Kate, so there was no feminine touch to the festivities on the farm. The decorations that James had managed to find, seemed to lack the sparkle Agnes managed to coax from them. Mince pies were conspicuous by their absence as Agnes had never entrusted her secret family recipe to Hannah or Miriam. The roast beef was, however, excellent and the guinea fowl, while tough, made a good gamey substitute for pheasant.

'Have you heard how to cook a guinea fowl so that the meat is tender?' McCallum asked as he chewed on the bird. He had had a little too much sherry and wine and was being over jolly to try and compensate for the lack of female company. 'You put the bird into a big pot of boiling water along with a small rock. When the rock is soft, you know the meat is ready.'

He laughed loudly at his joke while James and Richmond chuckled politely, neither telling the Scot that he told that same joke every year at Christmas.

James had managed to convince his father that the harvest needed to be sorted before he went to Nairobi to join the army. He was hoping that by then it would all be over and he would not need to go. But things continued to escalate and the outlook for a quick resolution was bleak.

Now they had completed the harvest, he was no longer able to put his father off. It had been agreed he would head off in the new year. The allied forces from India who attacked Tanga had been defeated and, as that news came in, they also heard of the losses suffered near Longido, a town not too far from Kilimanjaro. They had also heard talk of South African troops coming to Voi and presumed that they would soon move on the Germans who were still based just inside British territory near Taveta.

With all these defeats so close and the Germans camped not too far away, the idea of heading off to distant Nairobi was both comforting and a little disconcerting. While it felt as if one were running away from the action, he did not savour the idea of being close to the battle front. Oliver was heading to Nairobi too and they had arranged to travel together in early January but this gave him little comfort.

He tried to squeeze in as much time with his wife and son as he could, but it was difficult. The work in the fields left him exhausted at the end of the day and he would struggle to stay awake after dinner. On top of this, his father also wanted a piece of him and even McCallum would detain him after dinner and then give him an apologetic look.

'I'm sorry, laddie,' the Scot said one evening when they had a chance to speak alone. 'I know you want to be with them, but I can't help myself. You are like a son to me and I know I will miss you terribly, and will worry about you.'

He found he could not begrudge McCallum the time. In some respects, the farm manager had been more of a father to him than his own father.

Even time with Samwelli made him restless. He loved his son dearly, but his body would ache for Miriam's touch, and he found himself hoping that the boy would go to sleep early so he could be with her. As if sensing that James was about to disappear, the lad would try and hold on to every moment they had together and, despite his eyelids drooping, he would fight his tiredness and cry out when they tried to carry him to his bed.

But the days melted away in the hot December sun. Each sunset, no matter how beautiful, would bring a knot to James' stomach as if the sinking sun were dragging his heart with it, taking it to the dark other side of the world. He would find himself in the late afternoons, glancing at the sky, willing the white hot light to stay a bit longer, feeling his mood darken as first the light blue took control of the sky from the brightness and then ache as it bruised purple. On nights when the sky burned orange before turning dark, the heat of the colours scalded his being.

But he managed to have some time alone with Miriam, precious moments where the rest of the world would blur to a colourless background. The war, his mother and father, the farm, McCallum, all morphed into indistinguishable blobs in his mind as his wife came into total focus. Her voice, her touch, her warmth caressed him into a place like no other.

He stored every moment like this, saving and savouring, knowing that these memories had to keep him going in the coming months.

New Year came and went without an 'Auld Lang Syne'. None of the three men felt equipped to start the song without Agnes there to lead them. Even Richmond commented that he missed her singing voice, although he was rather in his cups that evening. He had been like that a bit too much of late, but James could not believe it was because he missed his wife. There was something else which he could not put his finger on.

His father was drunk again the night before James was due to leave which cut into the time he hoped to spend with Miriam. When he finally got back to his place, she was already there and Samwelli was fast asleep. They made love then lay together in the darkness, her head resting on his chest. They hardly spoke. There were no words that could satisfy what they wanted to say, but touch and caress filled in and communicated what language could not.

Dawn crept into the room with an apologetic gloom, its dull light embarrassed at being the cause of separating the man and woman who clung to each other. James awoke first and lay for a moment, his hand absent-mindedly stroked Miriam's naked back. Then he heard Samwelli moving around so slipped out of bed, leaving Miriam to sleep, and quickly dressed. He stopped at the door of the room to take one last look at Miriam, knowing this would be their last moment alone for some time.

⚱

'Bad news?' Hortensia asked as Agnes re-read the letter that had arrived that morning. They sat in the club lounge with their morning tea laid out on the table between them. Agnes did not reply for a moment.

'What is it, dear?' Hortensia's voice took on a nervous edge.

'Oh, this is just terrible,' Agnes said, not looking up from the letter.

'What? What is terrible?' Hortensia was not hiding her impatience well.

Agnes kept her waiting a little longer, reading the short letter again, hoping that somehow the words had been playing a nasty joke on her and would now admit to the prank, shamed into its confession by her distress. But the words remained obstinately the same.

'James is going to enlist,' she said at last, her voice now resigned.

'Join up?'

'Yes. He is going to Nairobi to volunteer for the British Army.'

Kate, who had been engrossed in her own letter, looked up.

'Nairobi?' Hortensia said, 'but that's miles away.'

Agnes nodded miserably. 'And he has no time to come to Mombasa to say goodbye to his own mother.' She picked up the letter again to make absolutely sure she had read that bit correctly and then waved it at Hortensia as if the paper itself was offensive.

'His own mother,' she repeated. 'He said nothing about joining up when he was here. Why has he got these silly ideas? This is Richmond's doing. I am sure of it.'

'But, dear, since he was here, the British have suffered defeats. He must have thought he could make a difference.'

'Like your Carl is doing for the Germans!' Agnes regretted the snapped remark as soon as it left her lips.

Hortensia looked as if she had been slapped.

Despite her regretting her words, Agnes could not muster enough feeling to apologise. What she had said was true. Carl had gone off to war long before James had. He had been part of an offensive where at least her James was going to his nation's defence. That was far more noble.

'Will you excuse me please?' Hortensia stood up quickly and left, the tears already beginning to flow as she hurried off.

Agnes tried to call after her, but Kate took her hand gently and squeezed it.

'Let her go,' she said. 'I will talk to her.' There was a slight accusation in her voice, but then she softened and said, 'This is a difficult time for all of us. And particularly difficult for mother. She is completely torn by this war, having a German husband whom she loves very much, yet she herself is British. I have seen the strain it has put on her. She does not know how to take sides, it is not in her nature.'

'I…I…' Agnes struggled to find the words.

'I know,' Kate said and patted her hand. 'I know. I felt the same as you do when Carl went off. I was angry. Not at those around me, but at the situation over which I have no control. I snapped at my father-in-law the way you have just snapped at mother, but my anger was not at him. He is a dear sweet man. No, my anger was at the war and he understood that. Just as mother will understand that you were upset with the war and not her. She will be fine. I only hope to God that James and Carl never have to meet on the battlefield. Now I must go and see mother.'

With that she stood and hurried off, leaving Agnes staring at the two tea cups across the table.

Miriam waited for Wamuhu to leave Mr Richmond's bedroom before taking his morning tea in to him. This had quickly become the norm once James left. She was not sure how she felt about the young girl who was being used by her master. She knew that had Wamuhu shown clear signs of being distressed by the situation, she would have tried to comfort her. But Wamuhu appeared almost untouched by what was going on. She would leave the room as if she had just been in there to make the bed or deliver his tea.

Miriam knew that this was not what had been happening behind the closed door. She had heard the tell-tale noises, the dull syncopated thuds of rhythmic thrusts that caused the bed to dance, the low growls and moans that he emitted. However, she never heard a sound that she could attribute to Wamuhu and she could picture the poor girl lying there impassively taking the ordeal as if it was just a dull kitchen chore. This was compounded by the fact that she never saw a sign in the girl's face that she was in any way affected by this treatment.

She did wonder if Wamuhu was perhaps simple and emotionally incapable of realising what was happening to her, however, they did not interact enough to make a proper assessment. Their different work schedules meant they saw very little of each other. She missed her mother at times like these. Her mother would know if Wamuhu needed some sort of consoling support or whether she just needed to be left alone as she was quite content with the situation, or perhaps even enjoying it. Her mother would know if Wamuhu was simple and that any intervention or hint that what was happening was not right could cause more damage than just letting the poor girl live in her deluded state believing that this was normal and natural.

Miriam fretted about what to do and even more so when, one morning, she found Samwelli standing outside the master's door, listening to the sound coming from inside the room, a puzzled look on his face.

'Come away from there, Samwelli,' she whispered, beckoning him over. She had to keep the urgency and panic out of her voice as that would just feed the boy's interest.

'Mr Richmond is busy doing his morning exercises, he would not want to be disturbed.'

She could see that her son did not believe her, but he nodded as if to say, 'I respect what you are saying. It may not be true, but I understand that I should not stand here listening.' It was so like James that she almost wept but instead drew her son into her arms and hugged him close.

There was a part of her that was grateful to Wamuhu as she could not help but conclude that, had Mr Richmond not taken a liking to this other servant, his attention could well have focused on her. She did not believe she would have been able to cope with that. She would have constantly worried that James would find out. She could not stand next to that thought very long as it distressed her so.

She longed for Mrs Agnes to return, for the old times when Mr Richmond was forced to take his pleasures away from the house and away from her. But the war was not going well for the British, she had heard Mr Richmond talking to Mr McCallum at dinner times, and this meant that Mrs Agnes would not be hurrying back from Mombasa. Her mother would therefore also not be back soon.

The daily chores helped get her through the days which seemed to amble listlessly from dawn to dusk, the sun dragging its heels across the sky. She felt frazzled by heat and repetition and was stretched further by her longing for James' return. Her only hope of news about her husband would be any crumbs she could pick up while serving dinner. But either she missed the vital bits of conversation when Mr McCallum joined for dinner, or the news came in when the farm manager was not there and would have been shared when the men were in the fields.

She kept her room at James' cottage. Mr Richmond never came that way and she liked the privacy it offered her. It also contained the sights and smells that could conjure up James in an instant as if they were an extension of him. Samwelli seemed to sense something in the place too as he showed a kind of reverence for all the things that belonged to the mzungu boss who was his mother's friend.

'Where is Mr James?' he asked one day.

'He has gone dancing with the monkeys,' Miriam answered without really thinking.

'Is he with my father then?' the boy asked.

'Why would you say that?'

'Because you said that my father was dancing with the monkeys.'

Miriam smiled. She had forgotten that she had used that same expression when Samwelli had previously asked about his father.

'I think that Mr James will be very close to your father,' she said.

'How long do the monkeys dance for?' The boy then asked.

Miriam laughed, 'Oh it can be for a long time, or a short time. It depends on how good the people are at dancing.'

'So my father is a very good dancer because they have kept him with them for a long time?' The boy's face was serious.

Miriam nodded.

'And Mr James? Is he a good dancer? Will he be gone a long time?'

'I do not know if he is a good dancer or not,' Miriam answered, although her thoughts turned to those stolen moments when they had stopped beside the road between Voi and the farm and had 'danced with the monkeys'. She hid a smile.

'I hope that Mr James is a bad dancer,' the boy said, 'because if he is, then he will not stay away very long.'

'I hope so too,' Miriam said and drew her son to her, not wanting to continue the conversation, fearing that her emotions would become unexplainable to him.

Fortunately, a tapping at the door distracted them and Samwelli ran to answer it.

'Sorry to bother you so late,' McCallum said, coming in to the room, 'But I have had a letter from James for you. He thought it best to send it via me.' He offered her the letter.

'Is he dancing with the monkeys?' Samwelli asked, clambering to see the letter.

'Dancing with the monkeys?' the farm manager was puzzled.

'Oh yes,' Miriam broke in quickly, 'I told Samwelli that, like his father, Mr James is away dancing with the monkeys.'

'The monkeys? Oh yes, or course, my boy. Mr James is with them. He is a very good dancer,' he said taking the lad onto his knee while Miriam took the letter from him.

'That is not good,' the boy looked crestfallen.

'And why not?' McCallum sensed that he had said the wrong thing and looked to Miriam for help.

'Because if he is a good dancer then the monkeys will keep him a long time. Like they have kept my father.' The boy was almost in tears.

'Ah, but you forget, Mr James is a boss. He is in charge of the monkeys and their dancing. They cannot keep him there. He will return as soon as he has sorted out those dancing monkeys.'

The boy brightened, then became thoughtful. 'If he is the boss, can he bring my father back with him when he is finished with the monkeys?'

Miriam suppressed a smile as she watched McCallum struggle.

'Ah, well laddie, that is a difficult question. Your father, you see, is a good teacher and he is teaching the monkeys to dance. Mr James needs him to be there with the monkeys. I am sure your father will come home one day.'

Samwelli nodded. The master/servant relationship seemed to make sense to him. It was his father's duty to obey Mr James and stay with the monkeys for as long as he was needed. It was clear that he did not like it, but the boy accepted it as a way of life.

'It is time for you to go to bed,' Miriam said. 'Say goodnight to Mr McCallum.'

The boy reluctantly hugged McCallum, then kissed his mother before heading off.

'I don't know how long I can keep telling him that his father is elsewhere,' Miriam said once she was sure Samwelli was in bed.

'Aye, it is tough,' McCallum agreed. 'But soon he will be old enough to understand and able to keep the secret.'

Miriam smiled sadly, 'Yes, he will.'

McCallum stood up. 'Now I must leave you to your letter.'

When he had gone, Miriam sat down and held the letter for a long time before she finally opened it.

Richmond rolled off Wamuhu and grunted. This had been one of her less animated responses. There were days when she just seemed to lie there and take it in a detached way. These were the unsatisfactory times. He preferred it when she was more alive, responding to him and his needs, as if, dare he think it, she was enjoying herself.

In his youth, before Agnes and that fateful party encounter, he had fancied himself as a good lover, even striving to bring pleasure to the woman he was with, eliciting responses in them so that they showed excitement and wanted more. Then came Agnes and that blasted pregnancy. Apart from bringing sexual encounters to a rapid halt for a while, the situation had almost frozen his ego to the point of paralysis. But the warm African sun had thawed that. He found himself attracted to the dark skin of the local women, their 'forbidden fruit' label causing him more excitement.

It did not take him too long after arriving at the farm before he tried his luck with one of the servants. The encounter proved to be exceptionally intense. After nearly a year of abstinence, his pent up frustrations were set free with such a wild roar that he was dubbed Bwana Simba, the lion boss, by the servants. He discovered this by accident, overhearing a conversation between some farm hands who did not realise he was behind a bush relieving himself as they walked by.

Wamahu was a strange one. Not all there in his opinion. There were times when he thought she was actually enjoying herself. She seemed to respond to his thrusts and would giggle when he gave a grunt of satisfaction. But other days she was more reserved and would lie passively, just letting him have his way.

It had been the second day running that she had been like this, unresponsive and turning her head from him when he tried to kiss her. 'If this continues I will have to find another one,' he said to himself. 'A dead fish in bed is no fun.'

He lay staring at the ceiling for a bit, then said, 'Time for you to leave.'

Wamuhu got quietly out of the bed, gathered her clothes, dressed quickly and left without a word.

'No,' he said to himself as he watched her go, 'I need a new one.' He lay a little longer before getting up and attending to his toilet. He had just finished when Miriam knocked at the door to announce his tea. She had an uncanny ability to judge exactly when he would be ready to receive it.

'Come in, Miriam,' he said.

She put the tray on the small table and poured the tea while he sat watching. He wondered if he would be able to find a new, more exciting one but he could not recall having seen any women around the place who took his fancy.

'There must be one somewhere,' he thought. 'I don't get to see all the womenfolk. They hide them away at the servants' village, I am sure. Maybe not hide, but they just don't come out much, so I don't get to see them. Perhaps I should arrange an inspection of the village again. The last one was pretty lucrative. Yes, I think I'll do that.'

He was distracted from his thoughts by Miriam who put his cup of tea in front of him. He looked up and thanked her, then after returning to his thoughts, he looked up again at the servant who had just turned to leave. There was something about her that had crossed her off the list despite her being one of the better looking girls on the farm. Now what was it? He watched her leave the room as he tried to recall why he had never thought of having her. Slowly he remembered that she was Hannah's daughter. He had never had Hannah because she was too close to Agnes, a lady in waiting almost. It had been too risky to have Hannah because of that relationship. Miriam had become 'untouchable' by extension. A daughter may talk to her mother and the mother may talk to her mistress.

He sipped his tea, then a broad grin came over his face. Hannah and Agnes were miles away in Mombasa and would probably be there for a while yet. Miriam was easily accessible. His grin widened.

Miriam heard the commotion well before reaching the servants' village. She had decided to go speak to her aunt about Wamuhu to see if anything could be done. Like her mother, her aunt was wise in the ways of her people. She may have some advice on how Miriam should deal with the master's latest conquest.

The wailing that came from the village was alarming. It suggested tragedy. Samwelli, who had been running on ahead, now came back to her, his little hand seeking hers, the sounds of distress scaring him. Miriam tried not to quicken her step, hoping that if she acted calm, it would ease her son's fears. But as they walked, she got a strange feeling that he was holding her hand to protect her, not because he was nervous.

Arriving at the village, she found the womenfolk together, many of them wailing while others sat nearby, grim expressions on their faces. The men sat in silence further off, watching the women, the air thick with solemnity. Children wondered in a dazed state. Their young lives had been untouched by tragedy before and they were struggling to comprehend this strange atmosphere. They had never seen the adults weeping before, not like this.

As she approached the circle of women, Miriam saw the body lying on the ground and recognised it as Wamuhu. For a moment she felt her soul disconnect from her body, as if her very essence had turned away from the sight while her physical body seemed rooted to the spot, waiting for her senses to return and give the commands to move again.

It was a dizzying moment as her physical and spiritual beings stood side by side, facing in opposite directions, her spirit hoping that if she could not see the body, then it was not there, while the more practical physical being faced the reality with grim reluctance.

She heard a short sharp cry and, realising it had come from her own mouth, forced herself to face the truth. She felt her being and body reconnect like images created by a squint coming back into focus.

Feeling returned to her body and she realised that Samwelli was squeezing her hand tightly. Her eyes took in the fact that Wamuhu's body looked beaten and bloodied. She felt a sickness rising in her which was not stemmed by a blanket arriving to cover the prone body. She turned aside and dry-retched.

'Ma!' Samwelli's concern-drenched voice sounded somewhere far off but drew her back and she reached for him, pulling the boy close to her.

'It is okay, my son.' She caressed the words as she spoke them, hoping that this would go some way to ease the fear in the boy but as she spoke, she realised that the care in her voice was more for her own sake than his.

'It's okay,' she felt the trembling go out of the boy's body. Or was it her own trembling that she had brought under control?

'What has happened to Wamuhu?' the boy asked.

'She is dead,' Miriam held Samwelli away from her, looking into his eyes.

The boy nodded slowly, then said, 'That is not good.'

'No, my son, it is not good.' She forced a sad smile.

Samwelli searched her face, then nodded again before looking back at the covered body. 'She will come back.' It was not a question and Miriam felt proud that her son, despite his mixed heritage, had taken on board some of the cultural beliefs from her side.

'Yes, she will,' Miriam felt comforted by her own words. 'Now go and play with the other children. I need to speak to Aunt Zilpah.'

She watched him go and saw, with some surprise, how he gathered the dazed children around him and brought a calm to that group. He spoke to them in whispers and their confusion seemed to melt away. Those who had wandered further away quickly joined the group and they soon all sat quietly, solemnly watching the adults mourn. None of the other adults seemed to notice this.

Despite wanting to continue watching her son, Miriam tore her gaze away and her eyes sought out her aunt. She was sitting on the other side of the circle around Wamuhu's body and Miriam made her way quietly past the wailing women and found a spot next to her aunt.

'Aunty,' she greeted her mother's sister.

'Miriam, how are you, my child?' The woman's wise eyes were lined with unspilt tears.

'I am well, aunty. How are you?'

'I too am well.'

They sat in silence for a little while, both looking over at the covered body. Miriam waited for her aunt to talk first.

Eventually the other woman sighed and said, 'This is a terrible business.'

'What happened?' Miriam asked.

'She threw herself off the mountain,' her aunt's voice was soft, the words coloured grey with sadness.

Miriam drew in a sharp breath. 'That is terrible.'

They sat in silence again, her aunt giving her space to absorb the shocking news. After the requisite time, Zilpah went on.

'No one is sure why, but some say that she was pregnant. She is not married, so she should not have got pregnant. They are saying it was the shame that made her do it.'

Miriam sat very still. She could feel the blood moving around her body, pulsing to all extremities as if running away from her heart. She had been too late to do anything to help poor Wamuhu. If she had spoken to someone about the way Mr Richmond was using Wamuhu, then there would have been understanding and the girl would have been sent away. She would still have had to live with some shame, but not to the same level.

She allowed herself a few moments to absorb all the news and her thoughts about them, then she drew in a deep breath, sucking the blood back to her heart, feeling the beating again and taking comfort from it.

'Can we speak, aunty?' She leaned towards her aunt as she half whispered the words.

Zilpah searched her face, then nodded slowly. The two stood up and walked quietly away from the mourners, finding a spot just outside the village where a few goats chewed lazily at the low leaves of the shrubs. A lone cow grazed in the nearby grass.

'You know something,' the question was more a statement.

Miriam nodded. 'Mr Richmond...' she started, then wasn't sure how to continue. But her aunt put a hand on hers, the gesture saying that no more was needed.

'I was coming to see you...'

Zilpah stopped her again with a pat on her hand. Everything that she needed to say had been said.

'Come back tomorrow. You can tell Wamuhu's mother then. It will soften the hurt a little. She will not be angry with you. We are all prisoners of the white man's wishes, she will understand.'

Miriam nodded but was unsure. She felt a prisoner of Mr Richmond's will and to some extent Mrs Agnes'. But she had never felt this in her relationship with James.

Realising the implications of what she had said, Zilpah smiled. 'What you have with Mr James is unusual and very special. It is clear that he loves you as a husband should love a wife. He is not like his father.'

The words brought a warmth to Miriam despite the cold air of mourning that permeated the village. She squeezed her aunt's hand.

'Do not blame yourself about Wamuhu,' her aunt said, 'no one saw the problem. Come, you need to get back to the master's house. I will let her mother know that you will come tomorrow.'

The two women made their way back to the village where Miriam beckoned to Samwelli to come over. He said a few last words to the other children and left them still sitting quietly. He took her hand as they began to walk back to the main farmhouse, and she felt a strange calm settle on her as they went. But as they neared the house his grip on her hand tightened and he seemed to want to pull her back.

McCallum picked up on the news of Wamuhu's suicide through an overheard conversation. Some of the farm hands were talking, not realising that the mzungu boss was within earshot.

It took an effort not to confront the men and demand further details. Years of working with the local people had taught him that that way would not work. They would just clam up. The restraint he needed to show in front of Richmond was even greater. Every fibre in him wanted to punch his boss's lights out. But there was an element of shame mixed in with his emotions. He was well aware of Richmond's exploits with the local women but had done nothing. 'What could I do?' felt an inadequate defence.

Walking to the house for dinner that evening, he found Samwelli sitting on a rock, staring out at the fields.

'Well good evening, young man. How are you this evening?'

The boy ran over and hugged him tight. This was not unusual, but when, after a little while, the lad did not loosen his grip, McCallum sensed that things were not right. He put his hand on the boy's head and held him close.

They stood like this for what seemed an age till eventually he felt the boy's grip relax.

He picked him up and sat him back on the rock where Samwelli stared out again at the fields.

'What is it, laddie?' he asked gently.

Samwelli looked back at him, his eyes appearing to search his face. 'Wamuhu is dead.' The boy's voice was soft.

'Yes, I heard.'

There was a long silence as Samwelli once more stared across the fields. He then looked back at the Scot and searched his face again. It seemed he had made a decision.

'Mr Richmond killed her.'

McCallum reeled backwards slightly. 'Why would you say that, laddie?' he struggle to get the words out.

The boy had gained courage now that the accusation was out there. 'He made her do things she did not want to do. In his bedroom. She was not happy with that.'

McCallum nodded slowly. 'How do you know this?'

'I saw her crying. Afterwards. One day. I asked her what was wrong and she told me.'

'What did she say exactly?'

'She said that he made her do things that she did not want to do and then she said that she could not live with it anymore.'

'She said that?'

'Yes,' the boy looked away again and after a short pause continued speaking without looking back.

'I did not know that she would go away and die. They say that she jumped off the mountain. I wish I could have stopped her.'

McCallum saw the boy's eyes well up so took him in his arms and let him cry. He expected this to take a while, but after just a few sobs, the boy pulled away. He wiped the tears with back of his hand.

'So you see. Mr Richmond made her so unhappy that she could not live anymore. That is wrong, isn't it?'

McCallum nodded, 'Yes it is.'

Samwelli took his time again to assess the Scots' response.

'But we can do nothing about it, can we?'

'No laddie, I'm afraid not.' McCallum shook his head sadly.

The field once more took the boy's gaze while McCallum wished he could say more to ease his distress, but no words came.

'He will want a new woman now,' Samwelli continued to gaze out at the field.

McCallum nodded despite the lad not looking in his direction.

'He will want my mother now.'

That shocked McCallum. Richmond had never shown any interest in Miriam so he had never thought there was any danger there. The boy's statement made him suddenly realise that he had never questioned why Richmond seemed to ignore Miriam.

'Why do you say that, laddie?' He felt a need to speak despite his mouth going dry from the shock of this latest thought.

The boy looked back at him now. 'I have seen the way Mr Richmond has been looking at my mother. He has a wanting in his eyes. It has been getting worse lately. And now that Wamuhu is gone, I think he will want my mother.'

McCallum stared at the boy. He was barely five yet had the maturity of someone ten times his age. The way he spoke left McCallum in no doubt that what the lad said was true. His racing mind was slowly catching up with the conversation but, as the consequences of what Samwelli was saying came into focus, so too did a plan.

'We must get you and your mother away from here. Yes, that is it. I will see what we can do. I will make a plan. Now run along. I will make sure that Mr Richmond does not do to your mother what he did to Wamuhu.'

Samwelli smiled and nodded. He climbed down from the rock and began to walk off, then turned and said, 'Thank you Mr McCallum,' before running ahead to the farmhouse.

McCallum stood for a while, details of a plan slowly coming into focus. Eventually he resumed his walk to the house. As he neared it, he saw the horses and vehicles gathered outside.

'Now what can this be?' He wondered out loud. There were uniformed men on the veranda and they had a relaxed, almost confident air about them. Some sat on the stairs down to the garden, others leaned against the railing while some sat on the chairs. They eyed him suspiciously as he approached and one or two picked up their rifles which had been propped against the wall.

'Who are you?' The man who spoke had a heavy accent, his tone was not friendly.

McCallum slowly raised his hands, palms showing. He did not like what he was seeing and felt threatened by the guns.

'My name is McCallum, Malcolm McCallum. I am the manager of the farm,' he gestured to the land around him. 'Mr Aitken can vouch for me.'

The soldier grunted and lowered his rifle. 'Sorry. But we need to be careful. I am Venter, Pieter Venter. We are with the South Africans, 2nd South African Infantry Brigade.'

McCallum nodded. 'I had heard some South Africans were coming this way. You are very welcome.'

Venter gave him an odd look.

'You are a Boer, aren't you?' McCallum said.

Venter smiled slightly and corrected McCallum's pronunciation of the word. 'Ja, we say it like boor not as bo-er.'

'Boor,' McCallum nodded. 'Well no need to worry, I am Scottish not English. We Scots also don't like the English, but please don't let Mr Aitken know I said that.'

Venter laughed and his smile was a lot warmer this time.

'We are heading towards the border. Needed somewhere to stop over. Mr Aitken said we could camp here for the night.'

'I'd better go and see what he wants me to do. Give me a moment and I'll make sure you get the help you need.'

Venter nodded and his men made way for McCallum to climb the stairs.

In a short while McCallum returned and set about helping the soldiers establish camp. Messengers were sent to the servants' village for men to come and help and it wasn't too long before the tents were erected, fires lit and water brought for the men to wash.

Venter and few of his officers were invited to dine with Richmond and McCallum that evening and would sleep in the spare rooms. All of which pleased the Scot as it meant that Richmond would not be able to make any moves on Miriam that evening.

Talk at the dinner table was formal, the ghost of the recent war in South Africa haunted the dining room and Richmond was polite but not overly friendly. Venter was not much warmer and it was left to McCallum to keep the conversation going. It was hard work. All the while he was thinking about how he could help Miriam escape an ordeal with Richmond.

It was while they were drinking some brandies after the meal that a solution came. And it was from an unlikely and unexpected source.

'Do you have any men to spare?' Venter asked in a tone which suggested that the request came from higher powers and this was an order he was reluctantly following. He confirmed this with his next sentence. 'We have orders to request help from the local farmers. We need men to carry supplies, weapons and ammunition. Also, they will be needed to help set up camp and such things.'

Richmond was sceptical. 'I don't like the idea of my men being given weapons.'

'Oh, we are not arming them,' Venter seemed to warm slightly. 'They are just going to be carriers. I would not want them armed either. They are to be labourers. I wouldn't trust them with guns, they may shoot us.' The laughter was superficial but carried a note of understanding. 'You will, of course, be compensated for their time.'

'How long will you need them?' Richmond asked.

'Not long I suspect. We will sort out this German rebellion at Taveta, and then deliver the men back to you when we return this way.'

'I am sure we can spare some of the men, couldn't we, McCallum?'

The Scot nodded. 'Anything to help the war effort,' he said, but his mind was working.

Later he cornered Venter on the veranda while Richmond was talking to some of the others inside. 'I think I can trust you, can't I?' he asked quietly.

Venter looked at him, then nodded slowly.

'I need to get a woman off the farm. She has a young son who needs to go with. They need to go soon. I can't explain why, but it is important. What I need to know is whether they would be safe with you? She is a very good servant and a good cook. She will not be a burden.'

'A native?'

McCallum nodded while Venter searched his face.

'It is really important,' McCallum said again.

'She'll be safe with my men, but I cannot answer for the native labourers,' Venter said at last.

'I'll take that,' McCallum answered.

'Okay. I will send Joubert over to you later to arrange things. I suppose we could do with a good cook, the one we have is useless. She can help him.'

McCallum nodded his thanks. He had done all he could. It was now up to Miriam.

##

'Still no news of James?' Hortensia asked as she sat down for morning tea with Agnes.

Agnes shook her head. 'I can't understand why he has not written.'

'It takes an age for letters to come through,' Kate said. 'The last letter I got from Carl took three weeks.' The look she got from Agnes made her feel like she should not have mentioned her husband. She suddenly realised that she and Agnes were not kindred spirits, bonded together by their loved ones being far away and in peril. Well, not bonded in Agnes' eyes anyway, Kate thought as she sipped her tea. To her, Carl is the enemy who may kill James and I guess I understand that. But then James is the enemy who may kill my Carl. Please God don't let that ever happen. May they both come back alive. In the meantime, it is us women who suffer. Out there they will be busy marching and preparing and fighting. They have things to do. All we have to do is sit here and worry.

It saddened her that what she had hoped would be a helpful comment of support had been taken as something designed to hurt. She made a note to be more discrete about the news she got from Carl. She would, of course, share it with her mother-in-law, but would do so only when Agnes was not around. She would also have to talk to Hortensia and tell her to be frugal with news of Carl around Agnes, explaining her reasons and hoping that Carl's mum would understand.

Her thoughts were interrupted by the arrival of one of the club servants who brought two letters, both for Agnes.

'This one's from James,' she said with glee, snatching up the envelope. She tore it open and began reading, her eyes almost tripping over each other as she rushed to read the news.

'He is fine. He can't say where he is, not because it's a secret, but because he has no idea. Listen here, "I am somewhere in the wilds. We have been marching for many days and I don't know where we are. Nothing looks familiar. So far we have not had to do any fighting." Fancy that, not knowing where you are.'

'It's a big country out there,' Hortensia said.

'Yes, you are right,' Agnes nodded and read on. 'He's made some friends. A chap called Ellis Boyd and another called Seamus O'Brien.' She pronounced the name as See-muss. 'Fancy that, an Irishman all the way out here in Africa with my James.'

Kate suppressed a laugh. There were Englishmen, Irishmen, Germans, Americans, Russians, Scandinavians and many more in Africa. In fact, most white nations had some representation. She knew of at least two Australian men working near the sisal farm she lived on. There was McCallum, a Scot, working on the Aitken's farm for goodness' sakes. She wondered if Agnes had ever found that odd, 'A Scot all the way out here in Africa.' Despite her thoughts, she knew better than to say anything.

'Oh, it's good that he has made friends,' she said instead.

Agnes read on quickly, her lips silently gobbling up the words. She reached the end of the page and turned it over even though Kate could see that it was blank. A slightly puzzled look came over her face.

'It doesn't really say much. He doesn't know where he is, he has made a few friends, he has had to wash his own socks and they shot an impala which they ate. Not much really, is it?' Her voice noted her disappointment and Kate wondered what more she wanted. Did she actually want her son to be involved in combat?

There is no way. I would want my son anywhere near the fighting, she thought to herself. If I got a letter like that, I would thank God that he was alive and that he had not been called on to fight. Again, she did not dare express her thoughts.

'Maybe there is more in the other letter,' Hortensia said, pointing to the one Agnes had left on the table.

'Oh, that is from Richmond. I suppose I had better read it. Maybe James has sent him some more interesting news.'

Kate noticed how less eager Agnes was to read her husband's letter as she took her time opening it and then seemed to read slowly, a look of almost indifference on her face to start with.

'Oh,' she suddenly said, then read on without explaining her surprise. 'Well, that's a bit of a cheek if you ask me.'

'What is it?' Hortensia asked, taking one of the small sandwiches from her plate and stuffing it into her mouth.

'It seems that a contingent of South African soldiers, Boers mostly, stopped over at the farm on their way towards the border. Richmond let them camp round the back of the house, you know round where Rosemary-Jane's grave is. I mean the cheek of those Boers. I'm surprised at Richmond offering hospitality to the enemy. And they have taken some of the farm workers to help carry their guns and things.' She stopped suddenly and looked at Kate. 'Anyway lots happening but no more news of James. She folded the letter quickly and put it back in the envelope, a strange guilty expression on her face.

Kate looked at her and then across at her mother-in-law. Hortensia appeared not to have noticed anything and was concentrating on the small cakes on the table, deciding which one to have next.

Was there news of Carl in the letter, she wondered. But how could that be and why would Agnes withhold it if there was? She was puzzled. Then she realised. Agnes thinks that I am in league with the enemy! She thinks that I will pass this information on to Carl. It was laughable really as, if she were to send it to Carl (which she wouldn't), by the time news got to him, it would be outdated. Despite this, Kate found no humour in the situation, only sadness.

☙

The soldiers were preparing to attack and the camp was abuzz with activity. Miriam helped cook breakfast and received a smile or two from the men. Some had commented at dinner the previous evening that they were glad she was there as the food had improved dramatically. Even the company cook smiled as it eased the pressure on him.

As she washed the dishes and Samwelli helped with the drying, she finally had some time to think. Yesterday had been a whirlwind. McCallum came round late the night before and they had talked until the early hours of the morning. She agreed that she was being lined up to take Wamuhu's place in Mr Richmond's bed but could not think how she could prevent that. However, McCallum had a plan. They were to leave early in the morning with the soldiers. He had arranged it all. With the bustle of the troops packing and leaving, it had been easy to sneak unnoticed into one of the vehicles and hide under a tarpaulin just before they pulled out.

The soldier in charge knew about the plan so they only had to concern themselves with Mr Richmond and whether he would notice. But he had gone to the fields just before the soldiers left so there was no real need to hide. Still Miriam did not feel safe until they had travelled for about twenty minutes and only then did she peer out from under the tarpaulin. They were already well away from the farm and she was amazed at how quickly these new horseless vehicles moved.

Samwelli had been so well behaved. Despite his wide-eyed wonder at the vehicles, he had obediently climbed under the tarpaulin with her and not made a sound, not even when the vehicle began its strange roar and started to bounce along the road. Now he climbed out and stared around as the bushes seemed to whizz by the car.

The soldier in charge, the one they called Venter, had watched as she went about helping with the dinner. There was no emotion on his face and she felt she was being assessed. However, after dinner, he walked past and gave the slightest nod in her direction, although she did get the feeling that he was approving his decision to bring her with rather than acknowledging her or her cooking skills. Right now, she would take that.

She was still shaken by recent events. Wamuhu's suicide, the fear of what Mr Richmond was going to do to her and the hurried escape from the farm all pecked at her nerves like vultures at a carcass. But now, as she washed the dishes, she began to wonder how she would ever find James. These had been McCallum's last words to her. 'Find him and tell him what has happened. Then it is up to you and him. He's a smart lad, he'll figure something out. Now go lassie, and may God go with you.'

She could not be certain but was convinced that there were tears welling in his eyes and she suddenly felt a little choked remembering how helpful he had been in getting her and James together. She would always be grateful to him and wondered if she would ever see him again. The thought brought a tear to her eyes now and she wiped it away with the back of her hand.

'What is it, Ma?' Samwelli looked at her, concern etched on his face.

'Nothing, my son. Just something in my eye,' she said, then seeing that he did not believe her, she said, 'You are too clever. I am just sad because I don't know when we will see Mr McCallum again.'

The boy nodded. 'I am sad too,' he said, 'but we will find Mr James soon, won't we?'

'I hope so, son.'

Just then a loud explosion sounded at the little hill not too far off, followed by a volley of gunfire.

McCallum sat opposite Richmond at the dinner table. 'That's his fourth tonight,' he said to himself as Richmond poured another whisky.

'It's not right those bloody Boers fighting for us,' Richmond's words were starting to slur around the edges and he emphasised the word Boers, deliberately pronouncing it his way, as if making the point that Venter did not know the correct pronunciation of his own peoples' name.

'It is better that they are fighting with us rather than against us. War makes for strange bedfellows,' McCallum countered.

'That it does, but I can think of much better bedfellows to have.' There was a hint of belligerence in his voice. 'Do we really need the Boers' help? We should be making better use of the Indians. And what are the Belgians doing? They have colonies at stake too. Where are they?'

McCallum knew it was useless arguing with him when he was like this so chewed on a tasteless piece of meat, momentarily regretting helping Miriam to escape, then said, 'I just hope these Boers can keep the Germans at bay long enough for us to get the coffee to Mombasa.'

Richmond grunted, but McCallum's tactic worked as his boss began talking about the coffee and how, if he had known that war was coming, he could have arranged to sell the crop for a lot more money. This moved the conversation away from 'those bloody Boers' and soon Richmond was moaning about 'those bloody Arabs who work in Mombasa' and how they couldn't be trusted.

Had Agnes been there, there would have been no 'bloodys' at the table, McCallum mused while Richmond ranted.

Over the next few days after Miriam's departure, McCallum noticed with alarm, a deterioration in Richmond. His whisky intake was increasing at dinner and he had seen him taking the odd nip from a hipflask while out in the fields. He was also neglecting his toilet, appearing unshaven more and more regularly and, at times it was clear that he had not washed.

McCallum was not sure what was causing this. He knew Richmond had been with one or two of the servant women since Wamuhu's death, so he concluded that it was not sexual frustration. Perhaps it is the deterioration in the quality of meals, but he dismissed that idea quickly. It did not hold water. The thought did cross his mind that Richmond had, in fact, had more feelings for Miriam than just lust, but searching through his memories, he could find no signs to back this thought.

The only idea which had any credibility was that Richmond was always that way inclined but having Agnes and James around had somehow held him in check. His relationship with his wife was a queer one, most likely platonic other than the two incidences that produced offspring.

Not knowing who to turn to, McCallum visited Rosemary-Jane's grave that evening. The soldiers' vehicles had churned the ground a bit around it, but they had generally been respectful of the grave itself. He realised, however, that it did need a little tending and made a mental note to get Tobias, the gardener, to do some tidying up.

'Your daddy is in a bad way, lassie, and I don't know what to do. He's drinking too much and he's not taking care of himself. I don't know who to talk to. Your mother is in Mombasa, your brother is off somewhere with this war and Miriam is gone.'

He shook his head. 'But you would not have known James. Or Miriam. You would have liked your brother, I am sure. He was a lively boy and is now a fine young man. And I am sure you would have liked Miriam. She is a native woman, very beautiful and very caring. And then there's little Samwelli. He is your nephew. He is about the same age now as you were when you left us. No, maybe a little older.'

He sighed. 'Look at me. I am an old man now, lassie, and here I am talking to your grave. I do often wonder how you would have grown up. I am sure you would have been a beautiful woman. You had such a lovely nature. I'm convinced you and I would have got on really well. Just like me and your brother. But I fear for him. This war is not good business. I just pray he returns safely to us.'

He paused to slap at a noisy mosquito that had landed on his cheek.

'Well that's about all I have to say. Look down on us poor mortals and if it is in your power, keep your brother safe. Watch over your sister-in-law and nephew, comfort your mother and ... well do what you can with your father.' He stood a moment longer then turned and trudged off.

The following morning the survivors of the battle at Salaita Hill, a bedraggled lot lost in a fog of defeat, arrived. Venter was there, but there was no sign of Miriam and Samwelli. With a sad smile, McCallum heard from Venter how the two had disappeared during the fighting. 'Perhaps Rosemary-Jane is taking care of them after all,' he comforted himself with the thought.

The company cook had answered her questions about the East African Mounted Rifles. He didn't know much, but said that if people had enlisted in Nairobi, then they were probably stationed somewhere inland. They could possibly still even be in Nairobi.

She had lied when he asked why she wanted to know. 'I have had news that my brother was going to be a porter for those soldiers and I wanted to know where he might be.'

The cook had eyed her suspiciously, but a pot had begun to boil over at that point and the conversation was soon forgotten.

When the battle started, she made her move, grabbing her small bag of belongings and, taking Samwelli by the hand, they headed back towards Voi. It was slow progress, but she was pleased with her son who walked quietly beside her without complaint. They stopped often to rest, finding some shade along the way. It was late afternoon when they managed to get a ride on a wagon going all the way to Voi. There, they spent the night at the Smiths. She felt bad lying to Mrs Smith, saying that their lift to the farm had been taken over by the soldiers but someone else was going that way tomorrow and they would travel with them. She did not know if soldiers 'took over' wagons but assumed that if they could 'take over' servants, then why not wagons.

Mrs Smith was sympathetic and arranged a place for them to sleep. That evening she spoke to some of the servants and arranged a lift to Mombasa.

From there, she could get to Nairobi without leaving an easy trail. All the time she was lying and she felt Samwelli's eyes on her as she did so, but there was nothing she could do. If she told the truth, she would be sent back to the farm and who knew what Mr Richmond would do then.

She was glad when she had some time alone with her son later on.

'I do not like to tell lies, my son. And I do not want you to tell lies either. But this is a difficult time. I cannot tell people that we are looking for Mr James. Not just yet. Once we are away from here I can be more honest. But for the moment we need to say as little as possible about what we are doing. Do you understand?'

Samwelli nodded. 'It is not good that you have to lie, Ma. But I understand that if you tell the truth they will send you back to Mr Richmond and that is worse.'

Miriam smiled at her son and nodded. The next day they travelled to Mombasa. Miriam had never been there before and she and Samwelli were wide-eyed at the crowds of people, the broad roads and the number of horseless wagons. Many men dressed as soldiers walked around the streets.

She made enquiries about the railway station and they made their way there. Using some of the money McCallum had given her, she bought tickets to Nairobi. They had two days before the train left, so she got directions to the European Club where she had heard that an uncle of hers worked. She hoped he would have somewhere they could stay until the train left.

The club was in a very beautiful area surrounded by houses bigger than the farmhouse. There was an African man in a smart outfit at the gate who was attending to some wazungu women. As she drew near, Miriam realised with a shock that it was Mrs Agnes with Mr Carl's mother and Miss Kate.

McCallum seldom visited the servants' village, he usually sent messengers if he needed more men, or women, to come and work. The path that led to the village was well worn by countless feet moving back and forth between there and the farm, but it was a narrow one, used to people walking in single file, not one that a man on a horse frequented. The grass grew high on either side and brushed against his legs as he rode. The air out here was somehow fresher and it lacked the rich aroma of roasting coffee that was married to the air around the farm.

He breathed deeply and watched as a grasshopper, disturbed by the horse and rider, flew off in a panic away from the path and into the veldt.

While the ride was pleasant and the solitude of the quiet path was a slight balm to his troubled spirit, his mind was still weighed down by recent events. The dreadful defeat of the South Africans at Salaita Hill was just the latest piece of bad news. The troops had returned to the farm in a bad way. Venter had sustained a minor gunshot wound but a couple of the men who had dined with them a few nights earlier were never coming back. Additional servants had been sent for to help with the wounded and McCallum found walking amongst the soldiers, some of whom would probably not see Mombasa again, a harrowing experience.

Richmond was visually shocked by what he saw and, McCallum noticed, had taken a good few nips from his hip flask. But the farm manger had too many other things to worry about so did not dwell too long on that.

Arriving at the village, he made enquiries about Miriam's aunt and soon sat in the shade of a tree with the pleasant looking woman sitting demurely opposite him. He could see in her a likeness to both Hannah and Miriam.

After the initial pleasantries required by custom, he asked, 'You are Zilpah, sister of Hannah and aunt to Miriam?'

Zilpah nodded, her eyes searching his face, an anxious look in them.

'Do not worry, they are fine. At least I think that they are fine. Miriam asked me to come and see you. She has had to leave the farm. She has gone with Samwelli to find Mr James, her husband.'

Zilpah nodded slowly.

'I am sorry to say this, but she feared that Mr Ait … Mr Richmond would do to her what he did to Wamuhu and I could not let that happen. That is why we arranged for her to go away.'

Zilpah took a moment to digest the news then said, 'You have done a good thing, Mr McCallum. What Mr Richmond does with our women is wrong.' There was some venom in her voice. 'But we know that Mr James is a very good man. He will take care of Miriam.'

'Yes, he is a good man. And he loves Miriam very much,' McCallum said. 'I only hope that she will be able to find him. He has gone away with this war and we don't know where he might be.'

'Miriam is a resourceful woman. I am sure that she will find him,' Zilpah said. 'Thank you for coming here to tell me this news. I am grateful for your time.'

McCallum nodded. He liked this wise woman with the pleasant face and for just a second the thought of trying to woo her crossed his mind, but he brushed it off. He was too old for that and she was probably married. He would be no better than Richmond if he forced himself on her. Had they both been teenagers, then maybe … maybe what? Thoughts of Jana, the servant woman whom he had loved, shot through his mind, barbed with the pain of loss he had suffered.

'Would you like some water?' Zilpah offered.

'Thank you, but I am fine. Before she left, Miriam asked me to come and see you.' The change of subject eased his pain. 'She was going to come and see Wamuhu's mother to explain…' he was not sure how to express this. But Zilpah nodded. 'I will talk to Wamuhu's mother. She will understand why Miriam could not come herself.'

McCallum smiled his thanks and they sat in silence for a while. He tried to study his surrounds, but his gaze kept flitting back to Zilpah. 'Perhaps I will take a little water after all, if it is not too much trouble,' he said eventually.

Zilpah clapped her hands and a young boy appeared who was sent to get the water. Once he had drunk it, McCallum rose to leave.

'Mr McCallum, there is something I need to tell you.' Zilpah put her hand on his forearm. He looked at her and slowly sat down again. She glanced around the village, seeming to need a moment to build up the courage to say what she needed to. At last she looked back at him and, holding his gaze, said, 'Your daughter has grown to be a beautiful woman. We had news last month that she has married. A good man from Kibwezi.'

McCallum stared at her, a thousand questions suddenly damned up in his mind, held at bay by his astonishment.

'She knows who her father is,' Zilpah answered the most important of the unasked questions. 'And she understands.' She let him digest the news, then said, 'I cannot say any more as I do not have more information than that. I do know that her name is Neema.'

'Neema? That means grace doesn't it?' McCallum tasted the name and it felt sweet on his tongue, but it only seemed to make him want more as questions waged war in his mind, each seeking a way to be asked. However, there was one which he knew he had to ask.

'And Jana? What has become of her?'

Zilpah smiled. 'You and Mr James are very alike. He should have been your son, not Mr Richmond's.' Then, realising she had probably said too much, she hurried on. 'The news is that Jana is well. She is living with Neema in Kibwezi.'

'Zilpah,' her name had to climb over the lump in his throat and wiggle past the waterfall of tears that fell from his eyes, 'you have given me a great gift today. I shall never forget your kindness.'

She put her hand gently on his. He was not sure, but through the mist of his tears, he thought he saw a look in her face that echoed his earlier 'what if' sentiments about them being back in their teens. But it was surely the haze his tears brought and the state of his mind that did that.

The ride back to the farm was a strange one as the warmth of the sun matched the glow in his heart. It was, however, at war with a kind of numbing sensation that the news had brought and he felt as if his thoughts did not know where to look.

As he neared the farm, his warm state was shattered when one of the workers, on seeing him approach, came running up. 'Come quick Mr McCallum. It is Mr Richmond.'

Miriam was sure that Mrs Kate had seen them. She had looked straight at them. But Miriam was not sure whether Mrs Kate had just not recognised her, or if it was the desperate shake of her head, pleading with Mr Carl's wife not to say anything, that had bought her silence.

No one called her name as she quickly herded Samwelli away from the club entrance and once they were what she judged to be a safe distance from being recognised, she slowed her pace and breathed deeply, hoping that this would calm the thudding in her chest. She risked turning to see if anyone was following them and was relieved to see that the wazungu women were walking slowly in the opposite direction.

'That was close,' she said to Samwelli who nodded, and it was then that she felt how tightly he was gripping her hand. They waited until the women turned off the road and were out of sight, then hurried back to the club entrance. The uniformed man directed them to the servants' entrance where they found her uncle and after a few hours they had a place to stay.

They did not venture out as they waited for the train, the fear of bumping into Mrs Agnes kept them housebound, but she saw her mother briefly. Hannah nodded as she explained her plans and gave her blessing to the two of them. There was much relief when they boarded the train two days later and Miriam smiled seeing the excitement in Samwelli's face as they pulled out of the station. She too marvelled at this strange method of transportation that the white people had brought to her country.

Nairobi was not as big as Mombasa, but it was busy with soldiers walking everywhere. After a lot of enquiries, she found out where she needed to go to possibly get news of James. There they spent a lot of time wating to be seen. A native woman was not high priority for these important men of the war. They were eventually ushered into a small office where a tall man with yellow hair and a big bushy moustache sat behind a desk. He did not invite her to sit.

'You looking for someone?' He did not look up from the papers on his desk.

'Yes sir, I am looking for Mr James Aitken. He is my … my master.'

'Aitken,' the man said and picked up a pile of papers which he began to look through. 'And what is your business with Mr Aitken?'

'I…I…his father sent me … to look after him … look after Mr James.'

'I see, do you have any papers?'

'No, sir. I am afraid I have lost them.'

He looked up for the first time and studied Miriam in a way that made her feel a little uncomfortable. He then looked back at his papers and continued to page through them.

'He is dancing with the monkeys,' Samwelli's voice floated up from beside her. The man looked up sharply.

'What was that?' His tone was as sharp as his look.

'He is dancing with the monkeys. Mr Aitken's father calls the Germans monkeys.' Samwelli was not intimidated by the man's look or voice.

The man stared for a moment, then suddenly laughed loudly. 'Monkeys! That's a good one, my boy. But they are not monkeys, they are snakes in the grass. They bite and then slither away. But monkeys? I like that one.' He turned to Miriam and pointed to a piece of paper on his desk. 'Private James Aitken is stationed at Kondoa Irangi. That is where you will find him.'

'Thank you, Sir.' Miriam said. She did not know where Kondoa Irangi was but did not think that this soldier would help her with this. She took Samwelli's hand and led him out of the office, hearing the soldier chuckle as they left. 'Monkeys indeed,' he muttered.

They were about halfway down a corridor when she heard the man call after her. 'Can you cook?'

She turned. 'Yes, Sir. I am a good cook.'

He walked down the passage towards them. 'There are some troops heading to Kondoa Irangi tomorrow. I believe they are looking for kitchen help. If you wait here, I will go and check.' He rubbed the top of Samwelli's head, then turned and moved off, chuckling to himself again.

When they were alone, Miriam hugged her son. 'Well done, Samwelli. You made the man laugh and now he likes you, so he is helping us.' The boy smiled back at her. 'But what made you say that Mr Richmond called the Germans monkeys?'

Samwelli shrugged. 'Like you, Ma, I do not like to tell a lie, but I thought it would help us find Mr James. Monkeys can be a nuisance and Mr Richmond did say that the Germans were being nuisance.'

Miriam laughed. 'Well, it worked. We will hopefully find Mr James soon.'

The man returned with news that the troops were heading to Kondoa Irangi the next day and that they would take her along as a cook's assistant.

⚉

The medic with Venter's unit was out of his depth. The casualties the troops had sustained at Salaita were too numerous and he had to prioritise, working with those he thought he could save, prepping them for transport back to Voi where they could hopefully get better attention. Those who were dying he ignored, giving instructions to make them as comfortable as possible. The lightly wounded were looked after by their comrades.

When they brought in Mr Aitken from the field, the medic spent less than a minute with him. The farm owner's head was badly damaged and bloodied on one side.

'He hit a rock when he fell,' had been the report McCallum got from Joseph the farm hand who had been with Richmond at the time.

'He is dead,' the medic said, after trying to find a pulse, then he added as an afterthought, 'I am sorry.' Having done his duty, he moved back to the soldier he was trying to save.

McCallum stared at Richmond's corpse. It seemed quite unbelievable that he was gone. The man had come to Africa with no previous experience of farming, let alone experience of this wild continent. He had survived a snake bite and a few bouts of malaria but had made a success of the farm. And now he lay lifeless on his bed. After a few moments he thought of Agnes and James and, with a sigh, set about instructing the servants.

'Wash the blood from his face,' he said to Penda, the woman who had been working in the house since Miriam's departure. 'Then wash the bed linen.'

'When Penda is done, move Mr Aitken's body to the pantry. It is colder there,' he told Joseph.

He despatched Nathaniel, another worker, to Voi to send the telegram to Agnes and to notify Reverend Smith. Nathaniel would then go to Mombasa to accompany the women back to the farm, picking up Reverend Smith en route to conduct the funeral.

Some of the soldiers volunteered to dig a grave next to Rosemary-Jane's for which McCallum was grateful, although he hoped they would have moved to Voi before the women returned. He also hoped that the smell of whisky would have left Richmond's body by the time Agnes arrived.

Later, after Richmond's body had been wrapped and placed in the coolness of the pantry, he took Joseph to one side and asked for details of what happened. 'And please be absolutely honest with me, Joseph,' he said.

Joseph avoided his look, his eyes fixed on a point on the ground to one side of McCallum. 'Mr Richmond. He was riding very fast by the field over there,' he gestured vaguely. 'Some of the other men said that he had taken much drink from his little metal bottle. He was shouting when he rode, but no one knows what he was shouting. It was maybe English, but we did not understand. The words were,' he looked McCallum in the eye for a second then looked away again. 'The words were broken by their loudness.' He looked back at McCallum to see if he had understood.

McCallum nodded. 'He was drunk.'

Joseph nodded. 'Yes Sir, he was drunk.' Now that McCallum had said the word, it was safe for Joseph to use it. 'He was drunk, Sir, and that is why he fell from the horse.'

'Thank you, Joseph. I appreciate your honesty. But when Mrs Agnes comes, we will tell her that a snake frightened his horse. She does not need to know that Mr Richmond was drunk. Do you understand?'

Joseph nodded, his face showing relief.

McCallum smiled sadly. 'Now go and help with Mr Richmond's body.'

Later, at dinner, Venter expressed his condolences in a formal way, but then moved the conversation on quickly. 'We will be going to Voi tomorrow. I have orders.'

McCallum nodded. 'I understand. Thank you for the help your men have given today. I know things are difficult for you, so I appreciate what you have done. I do have another favour to ask, though. I need to get a message about this to Mr Aitken's son. He joined up with the East African Mounted Rifles in Nairobi. Do you know the best way to pass on the news?'

'I could take a message to the command at Voi and they can send it through to Nairobi,' the Boer responded after a moment's contemplation.

McCallum nodded his thanks. He wondered how James would take the news and whether he would be allowed to return home, given what had happened.

⚲

'It's not James, is it?' Kate could barely ask the question, afraid of what the answer would be.

'No,' Agnes shook her head, her face seemed to be confused about what emotions to show. She looked again at the telegram then back at her companions.

'Well, that's a relief,' Hortensia said, not reading Agnes' expression.

'It's Richmond,' Agnes said flatly. 'He's dead.'

'Dead!' Kate exclaimed and Hortensia gasped. 'What happened?'

Agnes passed the telegram over to her.

'*Richmond* dead. Stop. Fell from horse. Stop. Will arrange your return. Stop. McCallum.' Kate read the news out for Hortensia.

'That's horrific,' Kate said, handing the telegram back.

'Oh, you poor dear,' Hortensia said and put her hand on Agnes' shoulder.

'Why does she not grieve?' Kate wondered as she watched Agnes digest the news. There was certainly some confusion about her demeanour, some shock and a hint of sadness, but Kate failed to see any sign of grief.

'Are you all right? Do you want anything? Water? Tea?' Hortensia fussed.

'No. No, thank you,' Agnes looked around the room as if searching for guidance from it, then said, 'No. I suppose we need to pack. I have a funeral to arrange, and it will take a few days to get back to the farm. Kate, would you be a dear and go and find Hannah? We will need her help.'

Kate nodded and hurried off, wondering how they would get the news to James.

The hurried journey home was not easy, and Agnes was exhausted as she got into bed at the Smiths'. After a night of camping as they had rushed from Mombasa, it was a relief to have a proper bed, although her body still seemed to be bouncing along the road in the wagon as they pushed to get home as quickly as possible.

She had not had much time to think. There had been the packing, organising the wagon and driver, then the rushed departure. Hortensia had spoken continuously throughout the journey and when they had stopped overnight and set up camp, she still blabbered, even when they had climbed into bed. She did not have the energy to ask Hortensia to let her be, understanding that it was just her way of caring. Eventually the talking had faded into a light snore.

Kate had remained in Mombasa and would follow later. They had decided that little Heinrich George was too young to undertake such a hurried journey.

They met with Nathaniel just outside Maungi, a small settlement on the road between Mombasa and Voi. He conveyed the 'snake scaring the horse' story with a servant's usual averted eyes and Agnes had not questioned it. Her mind was numb, beaten into submission by the shock and the onslaught of Hortensia's barrage of advice.

Despite her exhaustion, she could not sleep. The silence of the room screamed at her and her shock-protected mind was beginning to thaw.

What was she going to do without Richmond? How long would the war keep James away? Would the war ever return her son? Who would run the farm in the interim?

Even trivial things played on her mind. How long would Hannah and Kate take to follow them back to the farm? Was there enough food there for them, or did they need to get supplies en route? Who did they need to invite to the funeral?

The whining of a mosquito just outside the net brought her back from these thoughts and tiredness washed over her. She allowed herself to submit and fell into a deep dreamless sleep.

The following day, the Smiths received a visitor while they were having breakfast. It was a soldier with a strange accent who introduced himself as Venter.

'I am here to pass on my condolences to Mrs Aitken. I heard that she was staying here,' Agnes heard him say at the door. Mrs Smith ushered him in, and he stood at the far end of the room, passing the brim of his hat through his fingers.

'Mrs Aitken, I am very sorry about Mr Aitken. He was a great help to us, he provided us with food, men and a place to sleep when we were heading up to Taveta.'

Agnes nodded.

'I am afraid there is not much I can offer by way of help. I need all my men. But I have left all the farm hands for you. My orders were to recruit as many as I could, but I have managed to get permission to send those from your farm back there today.'

'Thank you,' was all that she could manage.

The soldier bowed slightly then added, 'I have sent a message from Mr McCallum on to Nairobi. They will ensure that your son gets the news.'

Again, Agnes could just manage a 'Thank you.'

The man looked around the room, bowed slightly again and then took his leave.

'The cheek of those Boers,' Hortensia said after the door closed.

'He meant well,' Mrs Smith said, and her husband nodded.

'They have been very polite to everyone in town,' he said.

'I don't think I have ever seen a Boer before,' Agnes said. She had been quite taken by the man. He looked very handsome in his uniform and his polite, somewhat shy manner appealed to her. 'Maybe,' she thought, 'I will find a handsome Boer and re-marry.' Then, shocked at this, she added hastily, 'After a suitable period of mourning, of course.'

'Are you all right, dear. Did that nasty Boer upset you?' Hortensia asked.

Agnes realised that she had been blushing and was flustered by Hortensia's attention.

'No. I am fine. I just haven't got used to the idea that Richmond is gone, and Mr Venter just reminded me. I will be all right in a moment. It was good of him to make the effort to come. He must be very busy with war business.'

'I suppose it was,' Hortensia conceded, somewhat reluctantly. 'He was a rather dashing young man, wasn't he?' She looked at the others, then added quickly, 'For a Boer.'

'And polite,' Mrs Smith added, trying to conceal a smile.

Reverend Smith, who had just finished his breakfast, took his leave, wishing them a good onward journey and saying that he would be at the farm early the next day to conduct the funeral.

The word 'funeral' had a sobering effect on the women.

The telegram telling of Richmond's death landed on the desk of the 'yellow-haired' soldier who had dealt with Miriam a few days earlier. Before he got a chance to read it, he was called to the Major's office to discuss another mater. He placed the telegram inside James' file and left it on his desk to deal with later.

While away from his desk, a new delivery of files was dumped on top of James' and when the clerk returned to his office, he looked briefly at the new files, then told his assistant to wrap them all up and send them off to London.

It was quite a large unit that Miriam had been attached to. There were white soldiers, askari from Nigeria and a good contingent of native men and women whom she soon found out were called 'porters' and 'camp followers'. She was regarded as one of the latter.

The white soldiers took an immediate liking to her as she impressed with her cooking skills. The Nigerians kept to themselves while one or two of the porters paid more attention to her than she would have liked, but, due to the large number of people in the contingent, they never had any opportunity to attempt anything untoward.

Samwelli was the only child in the group and was loved by all. The white soldiers who had horses would take turns in letting him ride with them while the Nigerians would teach him words in Yoruba, their native tongue. The boy would help out with the tasks assigned to the camp followers and his dedication to the jobs endeared him to his fellow countrymen.

Progress was initially good, and the men were in fine spirits. They joked and sang as they marched. In the evenings they would play football or sit around talking, writing letters home, or playing cards.

But after a week or so, the monotony began to chip away at their morale. Then they hit an area infested by tsetse fly. Their horses and cattle began to die from the fatal bites of the insect and the men broke out in horrid and painful sores on their unprotected arms, legs and faces. It felt as if a plague had been sent amongst them.

A few men were lost to wild animals, snake bites, the occasional attack by lion. Two were lost when they attempted to kill a buffalo for meat but got gored for their efforts.

And just when they thought things could not get worse, the rains came, bogging them down in sticky black cotton soil and rendering the few vehicles they had, useless. The more senior men, who had commandeered Miriam as their own cook once they discovered her skills, were concerned about the forces already at Kondoa Irangi where supplies were running low. The loss of horses and cattle meant that the relief column would arrive with insufficient supplies to make a real difference. And intelligence reports were warning that the Germans were gearing up for an attack on the town. The column was put on rations.

As Miriam moved in and out of their mess tent, an unseen and therefore harmless servant, she gathered her own intelligence, which distressed her and she fretted about James' well-being.

'What is it, Ma?' Samwelli asked one day when he found her sitting head in hands outside a tent.

'I am worried about your … Mr James,' she said. 'I hear the important men talk and they are saying that things are not good where he is.'

The boy nodded, a serious look on his face. 'Is he still dancing with the monkeys, like my father?'

Miriam gave a sad smile. 'No, my son. I do not think he is still dancing with the monkeys. I do not think that the war allows people to dance anymore.'

The boy thought for a moment, then said, 'I do not like this war thing. I do not like something that will not let people dance.'

'I do not like it either,' Miriam said and hugged her son, who let her do so for a short while, then wriggled free.

'Ma, come let us dance now. We cannot let this war stop people. Dance with me. You sing and we can dance.'

Miriam looked at her son. Slowly the heaviness that weighed her down began to lift as his bright-eyed expectancy melted it. She giggled and nodded, then stood and started to sway, beginning to clap and sing. Samwelli joined in, dancing and clapping with her. They did not notice the crowd that started to gather around them, nor were they aware of others who began to dance too. They were in their own world, drawing on their rhythm, the beauty of Miriam's voice and the innocence of the words of her song.

The journey from Voi to the farm was a strange one for Agnes. She sat upfront in the wagon as it swayed and bumped along the road and stared out at the bush and long grass that lined the route, trying to grasp at a word, any word, which would explain to her how she felt. There was a kind of emptiness mixed with numbness, but there was also a strange sense of relief. The latter giving birth to feelings of guilt. And as if all this wasn't enough, there was the fear to deal with. What would become of her? All she had left in this world was James and his future would be decided by the randomness of war.

The columns of soldiers moving in the opposite direction, dragging their wounded with them, only served to heighten her concern for James while making Hortensia more nervous as they approached what she kept calling 'The Battle Front'.

McCallum was at the house to meet them. 'How are you doing, Mrs Aitken?' he asked, helping her down from the wagon and then leading her up the stairs to the veranda.

'I am fine' she said. Her voice sounded flat and hollow, as if all emotion had been sucked from it. She hated its dullness, so tried again. 'I am fine, really. Thank you.' That sounded better. It was a voice that was not happy, yet at the same time did not give the impression that she was totally distraught.

McCallum nodded and she realised in that gesture that he understood. She should not have been surprised. The farm manager had been around them for many years. He must have observed the strange relationship she and

Richmond had. And yet she found herself wondering how he could have known.

Her shoes made a dull clunk on the floor as she moved through the house and she marvelled at how her footsteps could sound so heavy when she could not feel the ground beneath her. It was as if the sound were echoing outside a cocoon that she floated in, just above the floor.

There was a strangeness about the house. Everything was so familiar, yet it seemed she was seeing it for the first time. She felt as if she had been given a new lease on life.

She asked questions of McCallum in order to free herself of these strange feelings and to put some distance between the part of her that felt relieved that Richmond was gone and placed her closer to where she knew she was expected to be emotionally. That part of her must remain hidden, especially from Hortensia. It would not be good form and Hortensia was the kind of woman who would not be able to keep from gossiping.

She touched a few of Richmond's things – his hat hanging by a door, a photograph of him as a young man which they had brought from England all those years ago – giving each item a light caress, hoping that this behaviour would seem appropriate to those watching.

'Come, my dear. Come and have some tea.' Hortensia's voice told her that she had made the right impression.

They sat on the veranda and McCallum filled in the details of what had happened, repeating, almost word for word, the snake story that Nathaniel had told them earlier. Agnes watched as he spoke and she could see that he was holding something back, but she could not work out what it was.

She did not want to see the body. She had already decided on that before McCallum gently broached the subject along with a sympathetic recommendation that she should not.

'The wound to his head was...' he searched for the right word, '...disfiguring. And he has been gone a few days now. We have kept the body as cool as we can, but this African heat...'

She nodded, noting the impersonal reference to 'the body' rather than a more humanising 'his body' and again she wondered what he was not telling her. But with Hortensia there, she had no opportunity to press him for details.

Later however, when Hortensia had retired for a nap, she got her chance. 'Tell me the truth, Mr McCallum. Tell me exactly what happened. It wasn't a snake that scared his horse, was it?'

McCallum shifted uneasily in his chair. They were in the sitting room, the heat of the afternoon sun thickened the air around them and Agnes' fan fluttered uselessly against it. Despite her confidence in demanding the truth, Agnes kept her voice low, not wanting any uninvited ears to hear.

'No,' McCallum also spoke softly. 'He took to the bottle, Mrs Aitken. Not too badly, but enough. He was a little…' he saw her look, shook his head sadly, then with a resigned sigh, went on. 'He was pretty drunk when he fell. From what the men are saying he was probably blind drunk. He may have survived had he not hit his head on a rock.'

Agnes nodded. 'Thank you for telling me the truth. I appreciate you protecting his reputation and when the time comes, we will tell the story of the snake to James. He does not need to know what really happened to his father.'

McCallum nodded. 'Yes, that would be for the best.'

Agnes fanned herself some more. 'Do you have any idea why he started drinking? He rarely over indulged, just odd occasions.'

McCallum shook his head. 'I do not know for sure, but I think that it was a combination of James having gone off, your being away and the war. The wounded coming back from Taveta affected us all. It was quite traumatic, I must say.'

Agnes nodded. There was no accusation in the Scot's voice when he said, 'your being away'. Neither of them could have predicted that it would have had such an effect on Richmond. The phrase did, however, bring a lump to her throat. The thought that her absence could have affected him so made the guilt twinges she had been feeling earlier now more acute. And, although she had not consciously released them, she felt the tears trickle down her cheeks.

The boost to morale that their dance had created was short lived. It was a brief moment of hope stuck awkwardly like a diamond in the mud of reality. Everyone seemed to know that it had been a one off and that to try it again would not have the same effect. It would feel forced.

But the uplifting of spirits had helped the troops through the next day as they trudged further into unknown lands, battling with the claustrophobic humidity, fighting off the madness induced by the whine of mosquitoes and scratching away at the tsetse bites. They watched as their friends fell ill with malaria, hellish fevers descending on them. All watched for and dreaded seeing someone's water turn black. That invariably meant they were not long for this world.

Miriam became a nurse in addition to her kitchen duties, tending to the sick. She mopped brows, took the white man's medicines around to those who needed it and cleaned up where necessary. She would be exhausted by evening and sleep came quickly and was deep. She was vaguely aware of dreams that visited her during the night. But they were fuzzy and unclear, distorted as if in a heat haze. Yet she clung to them, feeling a presence of her husband somewhere inside the mumbled colours. She would wake each morning and drag herself to her feet to begin a new day, taking with her the leftover dream fragments of James wrapped tightly in her heart.

Samwelli kept her going too. He would flash a smile at her, give her a hug or even come and hold her hand just at the moment she felt despair descending.

But as time went on and the column's progress faltered, she felt James calling to her, urging her to hurry. Dreams became urgent tug-of-wars, fighting between the protection the column offered and the hinderance to progress it threw in their path. She fretted about what to do.

One evening, too tired to get up and go to bed, she sat staring into the flames of a fire that was dancing its last. Samwelli sidled up to her. 'Ma, you are troubled.'

'Yes, my son,' she answered. It was an effort to speak.

Samwelli waited for her to explain.

'I do not know what to do. I feel Mr James is calling us to come quickly to him, but I do not know if we can survive in this land without the soldiers. We need the food and water they provide. I do not know what other soldiers are out there and what they may do to us if we head off on our own. And there are animals to think about too.'

Samwelli nodded slowly, then after some thought he said, 'Do you love Mr James, Ma?'

Miriam's gaze jerked up from the fire, a flash of surprise and sharpness burned in her eyes for just a second, then it softened. 'Yes, my son, I do.'

Samwelli's face seemed to tell her that he already knew the answer before he had asked the question. He took her hand in his and they sat together quietly for a while, listening to the soft murmurs of the soldiers, their voices dulled by the darkness of night. The last flames of the fire faltered and collapsed into the brightly glowing embers, occasionally spitting out firefly sparks.

Samwelli squeezed her hand. 'Ma, is Mr James my father?'

She did not look up from the fire and was unmoved for a few seconds before she began to nod slowly. 'Yes, he is.'

The boy was quiet for a while, but just as Miriam began to worry that the news had adversely affected him, he said, 'Then I have a good father.'

She smiled at him, nodding slowly.

'I have a good father,' he repeated, 'and if he is calling us, then we must go to him.'

It was Miriam's turn to squeeze hands. She turned to her son and said, 'Yes, you are right, we must go to him.'

The funeral was a strange affair. The Reverend and Mrs Smith were joined by a few of the neighbouring farm families to form a small contingent of settlers. Agnes struggled to put names to them as they had dealt almost exclusively with Richmond. She recognised the faces of a few. She had seen them in Voi, or they had come to the farm to sort out some deal or other.

The farm staff made up a large contingent, standing silently on the opposite side of the grave to the European settlers. However, Agnes could not shake the feeling that the large turnout was because they were there to ensure that her husband was really dead, that they were glad to be rid of him. She tried to console herself with the thought that perhaps McCallum had commanded them to be there and the undertone of feeling was just resentment at being forced to attend.

She caught the eye of a woman whom, she thought, looked quite a lot like Hannah. The woman bowed slightly to show her respects, but then her eyes moved back to the grave and a kind of anger flashed across her face which Agnes could not fathom.

As she watched the hastily constructed wooden coffin being lowered into the grave, she suddenly recalled her younger brother's words many years earlier when they had held a funeral for a dead bird they found in the garden. 'In the name of the father, and of the son, and into the hole he goes.' She had made fun of her brother then for his misheard words and had to smother a giggle that rose in her at the memory, covering it up by turning it into a sob. Hortensia put her hand on her shoulder.

Afterwards, they had some sandwiches and cakes on the veranda and she made a point of getting to know the other settlers, realising that she would have to deal with them to keep the farm going until James returned. They were a polite group, all offering condolences and promises to help wherever they could.

It was late afternoon by the time the last of the attendees (they could hardly be called mourners) had left and the servants tidied up. She sat on the veranda, letting Hortensia's babbled words melt around her as the sun began to merge with the mountains, turning the sky orange, then pink, then inky blue.

After a light dinner, they sat outside again with McCallum. Hortensia was concerned about the war being so close, but he answered that the Germans were moving out of the Kilimanjaro area and the immediate threat was over.

'We must do everything necessary to keep things here going for James,' Agnes said, then added, 'Still no word from him?'

McCallum shook his head. 'I don't understand it. I thought we would have had a telegram by now. And I was sure the army would release him from service. I will send another message when I am next in Voi, perhaps the first one never got through.'

They began to talk about the details of work that was needed and what she could do to help. This eventually drove Hortensia to bed with the words, 'Agnes, dear, you should not be worrying about all this today. You must be worn out.'

She smiled at Hortensia and replied, 'Thank you. I am fine. But I must. It helps me to take my mind off everything else that has happened.'

Hortensia nodded and bid them goodnight. McCallum made to leave too, but Agnes said, 'Mr McCallum, sit with me a little longer, will you? Perhaps we could have a sherry?'

He nodded and went inside to pour the drink. On his return, he found her sitting staring into the dark beyond the house. There was no moon to speak of and the stars flickered on and off as the vast areas of blackness caused by the clouds stalked across the sky. He handed her the drink and they fell silent after her 'thanks'.

Eventually, still sitting staring into the darkness, she said, 'What must I do? I do not know how to run the farm, but I must keep it going. For James.'

'Aye,' he answered, 'the lad would want that. But never you mind, Mrs Aitken, we can keep things going. It will only be for a short while before he comes back. They can't keep him in the army with his father gone now. He'll come back soon, I'm sure.'

'And if he doesn't?' Agnes asked. 'I have a horrible feeling that something has happened to him.'

'Ach, you're emotional with all that has happened. I am sure the lad is fine.' Even he could hear the uncertainty in his voice.

Agnes looked over at him, her eyes searching his face. Then she nodded. McCallum had the same concerns as her and somehow that was a comfort.

'I shall have to start helping with the farm business tomorrow. There are bridges to be built with the servants. I need to repair the damage Richmond has done.'

They left quietly the next day, disappearing into the bushes before the column began to slowly wake. Miriam had managed to hide away a little food and water, but they could not take much. They needed to travel light so they could move quickly and get ahead of the soldiers.

Their absence would not be noticed until the men broke for lunch. By then they needed to be well ahead. Miriam hoped that the soldiers would not waste their time and resources searching for a lost native woman. They had more important things to be doing. But if they were to send men to search for her, she hoped they would assume she was heading back to Nairobi and not guess that she was pushing on in the same direction.

When she felt they were well enough ahead, they re-joined the road and progress was quicker as they did not have to contend with the long grass and bushes. They stopped briefly for a small lunch and a few sips of water, then pressed on. By nightfall they had put some distance between themselves and the column.

Samwelli was exhausted and quickly fell asleep but, despite her tiredness, Miriam lay awake for a good while, staring at the sky. Unseen clouds blotted out patches of stars and the lack of a moon gave extra brightness to those that remained visible. She had never embraced the white man's god, the one that Reverend Smith and Elizabeth had spoken of, but as she stared at the heavens, she called on this unseen spirit, pleading with him to keep James safe.

Eventually she slept, a light alert sleep, her ears keeping watch as she floated just inches above consciousness. They were up and walking again as the darkness softened into daylight. The road was deserted except for a few wild animals – impalas, wildebeest, warthog and some elephant – that paused in their grazing to watch the humans go by. Unhindered by the column, they made good progress but always there was the nagging doubt that she had gone wrong somewhere, that she had taken a wrong turn and they were heading away from, rather than towards, James. However, there was no other road, so she kept going.

Their meagre supplies dwindled and hunger twisted their stomachs. Samwelli did not complain but she could feel his strength leaving him as his pace slowed and his usual smile turned by degrees into a grimace. Despite this he continued on, determined to find his father.

Then, just as she was beginning to give up hope, they came across a small village. The neat huts a little off the roadside felt unreal, a mirage thrown up in her exhausted mind. But they did not disappear as the weary travellers approached. In fact, they lost their hazy edges and began to crystalise into hope.

A toddler was the first to notice them. The child stared wide-eyed at the newcomers, watching them approach. Then its young mother looked up. At first she started, preparing to flee, then stood and waited for the two strangers to approach.

Miriam greeted her and asked politely for the village chief. The woman directed them to the chief's hut and then followed a few paces behind as they trudged along. The chief's first wife sat outside, surrounded by some of the other wives. They chatted and sang as they worked, grinding maize, threading beads or softening impala hides.

Miriam greeted the first wife and then the others. Once the necessary protocols had been observed, the first wife, who had not let go of her suspicious look, asked Miriam her business.

'I have been sent to look after my master's son. He is a soldier. I have been told that he is at a place called Kondoa Irangi, but I fear I am lost. We have not had much food for days and very little to drink.'

The first wife looked from her to Samwelli and then commanded a young girl to get some food and water.

While they waited, the first wife quizzed Miriam further, asking where she was from, how she got here and why she was travelling with her son.

Miriam was as truthful as she could be but had to build all her answers around the lie that she had been sent to look after her master's son. The first wife watched her closely as she answered, eyes moving between Miriam and Samwelli who had fallen asleep next to his mother.

Eventually the first wife said, 'Is your master's son the father of your child?'

This took Miriam by surprise and she put a protective arm over Samwelli. The gaze of the first wife was severe and Miriam knew she could not lie.

'Yes, he is.' It was almost a whisper.

'And you are ashamed.' It was a statement, not a question.

Miriam looked up sharply. 'My shame is for the lie I have told. I have no shame about my son, nor for his father.' She controlled her anger, knowing it would not do to let it show.

The first wife nodded slowly.

'The soldier is my husband. We were married with the blessing of my tribe's elders. He is a very good man. I was not sent to look after him, but left my master's farm because...' She stopped, not feeling she should give the real reason. But then she saw the way the first wife was studying her and knew that she could not lie again.

'My husband's father is not like him. His father has his way with the African women on the farm. His parents do not know that we are married. They do not know that Samwelli is his son. I had to leave the farm as I was going to be the next woman my master took.' She held Samwelli close as she made her confession.

The first wife surveyed her face for a moment, then she asked, 'Do you love your husband?'

Miriam nodded. 'Very much. I have travelled many days to try and find him.'

'And he loves you?'

'Yes.'

The first wife's features softened. 'Eat something. Regain your strength and then we will take you to Salimu. He is a man from the village. He knows the soldiers. He will be able to help you.'

Miriam lowered her gaze. 'We thank you, Bibi.'

The food arrived and the first wife shared it out. 'We do not have much,' she said. 'The solders came one day. They had been walking for a long time and had little food. They wanted bananas. "Banana, banana" was what they kept saying. They were like the monkeys who come into the village and steal the fruit.'

The group laughed at this and some of the young boys who had come to see the strangers began to imitate the soldiers, turning to each other demanding 'banana, banana.'

Miriam smiled and Samwelli, who had perked up having had a little to eat and drink, laughed. There was further hilarity when someone arrived with a small bunch of bananas.

Miriam ate sparingly, not wanting to take advantage of the hospitality and aware that the village could ill afford to feed another two mouths. The first wife nodded her approval when Miriam turned down the offer of more food. In days of plenty it would be rude not to have a second helping, but these were not those times.

The food and water revived them and when they were finished, the first wife said, 'Now, we will take you to Salimu. He will help you.'

♛

Kate and Heinrich George arrived a few days after the funeral along with Hannah. Agnes was relieved to have Hannah back. The housekeeping had been neglected in her absence, particularly since the mysterious disappearance of Miriam.

She had a suspicion that the Scot had something to do with Miriam's departure. He was cagey whenever the subject was raised and the thought crossed her mind that McCallum may have got Miriam pregnant. However, she quickly dismissed the idea. He was too old for such shenanigans.

There was still no word from James despite a second message being sent and Agnes began to fret. 'Why is it taking so long? Surely they could have got a message to him by now.'

Hortensia shook her head. 'There must be some explanation. Perhaps he is on a secret mission and is incommunicado by necessity.'

It was not a helpful answer. A secret mission implied additional danger.

Agnes thought that Kate might have a better answer, but there was a gap between them. The young woman had become more withdrawn while they were in Mombasa. She didn't share news about Carl like she had in the early days of the war and said very little whenever the topic was raised.

Agnes watched her playing with Heinrich George and felt a slight twinge as she recalled James' early days. How quickly youth passes, she thought. It does not feel that long ago that James and Carl were running around the place, playing soldiers. 'Boer versus Brit' they called it. It was a game back then, but now they fought on different sides in a real war. She tried hard to push aside the images of the soldiers in Voi, the bandaged and maimed young men. She could not let those sights near any thoughts of her son.

The farm business helped. It was a distraction as she had a lot to learn. McCallum was brilliant. He did most of the work and she found the natives to be helpful and friendly. They respected McCallum and, she liked to think, were giving her a chance. She had started to learn their language and had begun to ride the horses but was yet to venture too far on one.

Each day someone was sent to Voi to check for post, but no news came of James. A letter from Carl arrived for Kate, forwarded from Mombasa.

'What is his news?' Agnes asked when Kate did not offer any comment.

'Oh, he is doing all right,' was the only response she got and she noticed the furtive glances between Kate and her mother-in-law. Later, she saw the two of them at the far end of the garden and it appeared to Agnes that they were obviously discussing the latest letter from Carl. She felt a bleak loneliness creep over her.

Then an official letter from the army arrived. Agnes could not bear to open it, yet she was desperate to know its contents. McCallum, who had brought it back from Voi, volunteered to read it for her, although she noticed a slight tremble in his hands as she handed him the letter. He opened it, read it slowly, then looked up. 'It is not the worst news, but it is not good either,' he said, trying to prepare her. 'They have been unable to get a message through to James. He is alive but has been taken prisoner by the Germans.'

'Oh dear God,' Agnes said, her hands going to her face. Then she reached out to take the letter back. The words could not be true until she had seen them for herself. She read and re-read the letter then put it down on the table.

'Are you all right, Mrs Aitken?' McCallum asked. 'Shall I ask Hannah to get you something? Some tea? Water?'

Agnes stared out across the lawn to where Kate was playing with Heinrich George. She shook her head slowly. 'No. Thanks. I am fine.' She touched the letter lightly, an unconscious gesture.

⚜

'Shh! Stand completely still.' The man waved an impatient arm at them as he crouched near a small stream. Their guide, a young girl, put out an arm to stop their progress. They watched the man move slowly. He had a bottle in one hand which he held over the water for a few seconds, becoming as still as a rock. Then in a seamless movement, he scooped some water into the jar and quickly screwed the lid on. He held the bottle to the light and peered at the contents intently, twirling it slowly round. Then he nodded and smiled. 'Mr Loveridge will like this one,' he said to himself.

He stood, still staring at whatever was in his bottle, then eventually became aware of his audience.

'Dada, sister,' he greeted Miriam with a slight smile.

He was not a tall man, about her height with skin a few shades darker than hers. He was roughly her age and had a friendly face. The smile that danced in his eyes hadn't yet touched his lips.

'Kaka, brother,' Miriam returned the greeting and bowed slightly.

The man looked from her to Samwelli and the smile now touched his lips. 'Greetings, young man,' he said.

Samwelli moved closer to Miriam but, she was pleased to hear, still gave the respectful greeting, 'Shikamoo,' in a strong voice.

'Marahaba,' the man gave the required reply.

'We are looking for Mr Salimu,' Miriam said despite being sure that they had just found him.

'I am Salimu,' the man replied, and Miriam gave another slight bow to acknowledge this.

'The first wife from the village,' she indicated somewhere 'back there', 'said that you could help us.'

Salimu nodded. 'Come, let us go and sit and you can tell me your troubles. I will help if I can.' He gestured for them to walk further along the path they had just come along.

A short way on, they came across a tent beside the stream. It was like one the soldiers used. A small table sat outside. It was covered with an array of bottles and, as they got closer, they saw that a number contained frogs and some had small coiled up snakes in them.

Samwelli stared at the bottle, a puzzled and somewhat disturbed expression on his face.

Salimu laughed, a pleasant sound. 'No, kijana, young man, those are not for medicines. They are for Mr Loveridge.'

'Mr Loveridge?' Miriam asked.

'A mzungu. A white man. He is a soldier, but he is a man who studies frogs and snakes. They call him Bwana Chura, Mr Frog.'

'Why does he study them?' Samwelli's curiosity overrode his shyness.

Salimu laughed again. 'I am not totally sure. He says that the frogs and snakes we have here, they do not have in Europe. He says that understanding all the different types of frogs and snakes helps people understand the world.'

Samwelli nodded slowly, as if he understood this.

'And, I think Bwana Chura will be excited about this one.' He held up the bottle he had recently filled. Inside it they could just make out a tiny frog. 'I have never seen one like this before. Mr Loveridge gets very excited when he sees a frog he has not seen before.' He stared at the bottle for a moment.

He is not the only one who gets excited, Miriam thought.

After studying the jar for a moment longer, Salimu reluctantly put it on the table with the others and looked back at her.

'Please, sit. How can I help you?'

They sat on the rough stools that stood outside the tent and Miriam started to tell him her problems. She was honest about her relationship with James, feeling that Salimu would understand.

He nodded as she spoke and even smiled gently when she revealed that James was her husband and that Samwelli was their son.

When she was finished, he sat and clicked his tongue. 'That is quite a story, dada. You have made a long journey for this mzungu husband of yours, I can see.'

Miriam nodded.

'I cannot help you. I don't know the soldiers that well. But Mr Loveridge, he is a soldier. He will help. He is a good man. He may be able to find out where your Mr James is.' He smiled, then a sad look crossed his face. 'I must warn you though, dada, many mzungu soldiers have died. From fighting, from sickness. Some have been taken by the German soldiers. I hope that your Mr James is not amongst them.'

Miriam nodded her thanks.

'Also, dada, I would not tell Mr Loveridge that Mr James is your husband. The mzungu don't always approve of such things.'

Miriam nodded. 'I have told the story that he is my master's son and that I have come to serve him,' she said.

Salimu grinned, then said, 'Ah, here comes Bwana Chura. I am sure he will be able to help.'

Dinner was a strained affair. Although no mention of James' plight had been made since the news was passed on to Hortensia and Kate at tea, the fact that Carl was fighting on the German side sat like an invisible wall between them. They skittered around the topic, all searching for something to say that would either only touch lightly on James or Carl, or preferably would not come near them. The war was out of bounds.

But talk of the farm and the work needed to be done was beyond Kate and Hortensia and would also be a reminder to Agnes of her departed husband as it highlighted the void he had left. Even the mystery of Miriam's disappearance, while a trivial matter in the grand scheme of things, was thought to somehow be linked to the war, or perhaps Richmond, so was avoided too. The weather was hot and sunny, as it had been every day for the past month, so it offered little by way of conversation material.

Kate and Hortensia retired early and McCallum took his leave at that time too. Hortensia was just getting ready for bed when a gentle knock came at the door and Kate entered.

'Sorry to disturb you, mother, but we need to talk.'

Hortensia nodded. She knew what her daughter-in-law was going to say.

'I have already started a letter home,' she spoke softly indicating the papers on the little desk in the room. 'I think we will be better off back in Mombasa. I hate to leave Agnes at a time like this, but I fear we are just a reminder to her of the Germans.'

Kate nodded. 'You have read my mind. But how do we break the news to Mrs Aitken? While it is clear our presence here is making her uncomfortable, I also think that our leaving will be seen as a betrayal.'

Hortensia nodded. 'You are right, my dear. But what if we arrange for a letter to come saying that the fighting has move on and we are safe to come home. She could not begrudge us that. Someone can come from Pangani to collect us and rather than taking us there we can go back to Mombasa. Agnes will be more accepting if she thinks we are going home and will be none the wiser if we headed north instead of south.'

Kate nodded slowly. 'It is a little deceitful, but a good plan. It will cause the least offence.'

'I was going to speak to you about it tomorrow before sending the letter, but now I will finish it in the morning and get it sent.'

'Yes, do that mother,' Kate smiled, then kissed Hortensia's cheek. 'Goodnight then. Sleep well.' She left the room quietly.

Things did not improve over the next few days, the uneasy atmosphere lingered like an unwanted guest. Kate and Hortensia kept to themselves during the day and Agnes busied herself with farm work. They only crossed paths at meal times where the talk was superficial and touched on harmless things like the roses in the garden, Heinrich George's teething issues and the horse that Agnes was taking a liking to.

It was three days after the letter had gone off to the farm down south that McCallum came to the house during the day. This was unusual as he was normally out supervising the workers. Agnes had gone for a ride into the fields so only Kate, Hortensia and Heinrich George were at home.

'Here is a letter from Carl,' he said, handing it over to Kate. 'I did not want to give it to you in front of Agnes. She is a bit sensitive about things at the moment.' He waved his hand as he said the word 'things' to indicate that he thought she would understand.

Kate nodded, both as a thank you and to indicate that yes, she understood.

Once McCallum had taken his leave, she tore open the envelope, hungry for news from her husband. She read quickly, devouring the words. She would always do this, an initial speed through, then she would re-read it to digest the news and then again to savour the link between her and the one she loved. But she suddenly stumbled as she raced through the first read.

She re-read the paragraph that had tripped her up. Then she read it again to make absolutely sure she had understood.

She was at the far end of the garden, but now walked quickly back to the house. Hortensia was sitting on the veranda doing some needlework.

'A letter from Carl,' Kate said as she climbed the stairs.

'Oh, may I read it?' Hortensia said quickly setting her needlework to one side, then a puzzled look came over her face as Kate seemed reluctant to hand over the letter. 'Is something wrong?' a note of panic crept into her voice.

'No. All is fine with Carl. He is well, it's just…'

'What? What is it?'

'It's James. I think. No, I am sure.'

'What is it, Kate? Please tell me and stop being vague. Please, you are frightening me.'

'Oh, I did not mean to frighten you, mother. It's just that Carl's letter is a bit cryptic. Here I will read you the strange part. "I came across J., an old school friend today. He was in the camp when I got back. You might remember him, not a very good dancer. Sadly, he is not well. I don't think he will be going anywhere in a hurry".'

Hortensia looked at Kate, still puzzled.

'J. An old school friend. Not a very good dancer. It has to be James. Carl is at the camp where James is being held as a prisoner of war,' Kate explained.

Hortensia took a moment to process this, then said, 'But why doesn't Carl just say that?'

'Well, I think he was worried that the army may censor his letter.'

'They would do that?'

Kate nodded while Hortensia shook her head in disbelief.

'That is good news then, isn't it?' Hortensia went on. 'Carl will make sure that they look after him, won't he?' she smiled, but Kate shook her head sadly.

'It's good that Carl is there for him, but I worry about the other bit where says "he is not well. I don't think he will be going anywhere in a hurry." I fear that James may be seriously wounded or ill or something.'

Hortensia's smile faded. 'Oh dear God! What on earth are we going to tell Agnes?' she said.

🐰

Bwana Chura was a tall, slim man. He had neatly combed hair, a sharp nose and alert, serious eyes. He wore the green-brown uniform of the soldiers, but where a lot of the men wore trousers that cut off at the knees, his were long, full-length ones. He strode with some purpose into the small camp, taking in Miriam and Samwelli in a quick jerky movement of his head before looking across at the table with the bottles on.

'Anything new, Salimu?'

'Yes, Bwana, I have found this one,' Salimu picked up the latest bottle and handed it to the frog man.

The mzungu took the jar and carefully peered at it as he held it up to the light. His eyes studying the contents intently as he slowly turned it round.

'Amazing. What a beauty.' He said, not taking his eyes off the bottle. 'I don't believe we have ever seen one like this before.'

'No, Bwana.' Salimu agreed.

'Yes, yes. This is a new one. A rare find indeed. Well done, Salimu. We must catalogue it straight away.' There was excitement in his voice.

'Yes, Bwana,' Salimu said and then gave an apologetic glance over to Miriam. The look said, 'I am sorry, you will have to wait.' He followed the mzungu into the tent, leaving Miriam and Samwelli sitting outside.

It took a long time before the two men emerged. Samwelli waited patiently at first but then got restless. 'May I go for a little walk, Ma?' he asked.

Miriam nodded. 'Don't go too far,' she said and watched her son walk slowly away, her heart ached for him. He had suffered much on this journey, but never once complained.

Eventually Bwana Chura stepped out of the tent and took a deep breath. 'Some coffee, perhaps? Salimu, would you?' He stared at the table with the bottles for a moment before looking at Miriam as if seeing her for the first time, then he gave a slight shake of his head.

'I am frightfully sorry. Salimu mentioned that you wished to speak to me. I completely forgot. I got so caught up in all this,' he gestured at the bottles. 'And the one Salimu caught today was a special one. A very exciting find. Very rare. But I am babbling again. I am sure you are not here to discuss frogs.'

'No, Sir,' Miriam said.

'Of course not,' he smiled kindly. 'A pity. Your country is rich with wildlife. Some fascinating frogs.'

'I am afraid I would not know,' Miriam lowered her eyes.

'No. No, of course not.' Bwana Chura said with some sadness. Then he perked up. 'Never mind. What is it you wish to ask me?'

Miriam began to explain her quest, taking Salimu's advice and not revealing her true relationship to James. The words of her story felt worn from overuse and, despite trying hard not to, she could not help the story from sounding weary. She had not given up hope, but her words seemed to have.

Bwana Chura nodded slowly as she spoke, then when she mentioned James, he lifted his eyebrows and repeated the name, 'James Aitken?'

'Yes, Sir,' Miriam said. 'Do you know him?'

'Yes. Fine lad.' Then he shook his head sadly. 'Got captured by the Hun about three, maybe four weeks back.'

'The Hun?'

'The Germans. Terrible business that. But, I have been told, they treat their prisoners fairly.'

Miriam nodded, although her heart sank at the news.

'Do you know where the Germans are?' she asked.

He shrugged. 'They move around a lot. I am not sure I can help you further.'

'Thank you, Sir. I am grateful for your time.' She looked around for Samwelli. He had not yet returned. 'May I wait here until my son returns. I am sure he won't be long.'

Bwana Chura nodded kindly. 'Again, I am sorry. I wish I could help you, but this blasted war…' He stood. 'I wish you good luck. I hope you find him,' he said and took his leave, taking her hopes with him.

'We will be heading home in a few days,' Hortensia had left it to Kate to break the news to Agnes. She had not felt she would be able to carry off the deceit.

Kate was not comfortable doing this but knew she would be better at it than her mother-in-law.

'We've had a letter saying that things have calmed down enough for us to go home. The war has moved past Kilimanjaro.'

Agnes nodded. She was taking the news better than they expected. She appeared almost relieved but tried to cover her feelings with some rather poorly acted and clearly insincere protestations.

'Are you sure?', 'It will be sad to see you go', 'Won't the journey be dangerous?', 'You should really stay till it's all over.'

It was a bit of a relief that the tone and their delivery were clearly in conflict with the meaning.

Kate and Hortensia had agreed they would not mention the news of James. They had debated long and hard about what to do, eventually deciding that the fact Carl was worried about James' health, coupled with the fact that Carl was essentially James' captor would be too much for Agnes to bear. Especially as she had just lost Richmond.

Kate thought they could, in collaboration with Carl, deny knowledge at a later date if needed. He could claim that he could not say anything in a letter for security reasons. This was partly true. Carl had only managed to smuggle out the news by wrapping it in cryptic words.

All they could do was hope and pray that James' condition improved and that he could escape, or be exchanged for German prisoners or, even better, the war would come to an end and everyone could return home.

'Well, if you really must go, I cannot stop you,' Agnes tried hard to get some reluctance to show through.

'We shall be sorry to leave you. I have enjoyed spending time getting to know you in person. It has all been through letters and what the boys have said before now.' Kate was a little surprised at how genuine Hortensia sounded, but then, when she thought about it, she echoed the sentiment. Until their visit, Agnes had been a name signed to the bottom of a letter or had been hidden behind the words 'my mother' spoken by James with affection. Now they knew her and, had the circumstances been different, they would have got on very well, she was sure of that.

It was with some sadness that they said their goodbyes to Agnes and Mr McCallum and with some relief that they swayed with the wagon as it trundled down the long road from the farmhouse toward the Voi-Taveta road. They exchanged guilty looks as they turned towards Voi rather than Taveta. On reaching Voi they found it necessary to hurry through the town, not wanting to encounter the Smiths and only began to relax once they were well clear and heading to Mombasa.

'Bwana Chura,' Samwelli's voice caused the tall Englishman to turn around.

The boy had returned just as Mr Loveridge was about to leave Miriam to her disappointment.

'Bwana Chura, I have found a frog for you,' Samwelli held out his hands which gently clasped something.

'How very kind,' the man smiled the indulgent smile that adults give children to humour them.

'Salimu, get the boy a specimen jar.'

Salimu hurried off and returned moments later with the bottle, holding it for Samwelli to guide his captive into the open neck.

Loveridge watched the process, still smiling his patronising smile. 'Thank you very much,' he said again as Salimu secured the lid on the jar and then turned to leave.

'Bwana!' Salimu's voice made him turn sharply. 'Bwana, I think that you should look at this.' He held out the jar.

Loveridge took the bottle and held it to the light, squinting slightly as he studied the contents.

'Well, I'll be,' he said. 'Surely not.' He moved the jar around. 'I can't be sure, but I think … I will have to compare it…' There was a note of excitement in his voice. 'Where is the other one, the one you found earlier, Salimu. I am sure this is the female of the same species.'

Salimu hurried to bring the other jar and the two men disappeared into the tent. Miriam took Samwelli's hand and they walked slowly back to the main road.

'He is unable to help us, my son. We will have to keep walking on. But now we need to find the German soldiers. Your father is with them. Bwana Chura at least could tell me that.'

Samwelli nodded. 'We will find him, Ma,' he said.

'Yes, we will,' Miriam took strength from her son's determination and they walked on with purpose. 'I think if we continue on this road, we will get to Kondoa Irangi. If the Germans took your father they cannot be too far away from there. Maybe we can get some information at the town. Hopefully it is not too far. I do not know if we will find food on the journey.'

'That is fine, Ma,' Samwelli said, 'I had plenty to eat at the village.'

Miriam smiled sadly as she knew how he had held back on eating too much. Without her telling him, he too had realised the need to show constraint.

'Come on then,' she said, 'a journey that is never started can never reach its end.'

They reached the main road and started in the direction of Kondoa Irangi. It was getting late in the afternoon and they watched the shadows that walked alongside them grow taller.

It was about an hour into their journey when they heard one of the horseless vehicles approaching from behind, so they moved to the side of the road to let it pass. The car drew level, stopped and they watched as Bwana Chura stepped out.

'I am so glad I caught up with you. You really must pardon my manners. The frog your son brought me was indeed the female of the one Salimu found earlier and, well, I got so excited I forgot my manners and did not thank you properly.'

Miriam nodded an acknowledgement but was puzzled. Surely this mzungu did not come after them just to say, 'thank you'.

'I would like to offer you a lift to Kondoa,' he said. 'As a proper thank you. It was quite some find the young lad made. I am incredibly grateful.'

'We would very much like a lift if it is not too much trouble, Sir,' Miriam said.

'No trouble at all,' Bwana Chura smiled. 'Please do get in.' He gestured to the back door of the car. Miriam looked at Samwelli then at the car, unsure what to make of all this. She felt a gentle tug on her hand and Samwelli led her to the vehicle.

Salimu sat in the front passenger seat with a big smile on his face and Bwana Chura got into the driver's seat.

'You hungry?' he asked as he eased the vehicle back into motion. 'Salimu, give them some food,' he added without waiting for their response.

Salimu produced two boiled eggs, bananas and biscuits which he handed over as the car gained speed.

They had barely finished eating when Bwana Chura announced, 'Kondoa Irangi, just up ahead.'

The car was stopped by some soldiers with guns a short way up the road and Bwana Chura exchanged some words. He explained the presence of Miriam and Samwelli and the car was soon waved on. Not too long after, they pulled up outside a mzungu building that had been painted white.

He took them inside where the evening light had settled and a kind of gloom filled the corridors. At the end of the passage he opened a door and ushered them in. A small desk sat in one corner of the room, surrounded by a number of filing cabinets similar to those Mr Richmond had in his study back at the farm.

'Salimu, get Ezekiel to bring some lamps will you please.'

He indicated for them to sit and a few moments later a young African boy came in with two hurricane lamps which spread a lazy light around the room.

'Ezekiel, this is Miriam and her son, Samwelli. Samwelli helped me make a very important scientific discovery today. They have come looking for Mr Aitken. Do you remember Mr James?'

The youngster nodded, then turned and smiled at Miriam and Samwelli.

'I want you to find them a place to sleep tonight, then tomorrow, we will see what we can do to help. Is that understood?'

'Yes, Bwana.' Ezekiel bowed. 'Please,' he said to Miriam and indicated the door.

The following morning, after a good night's sleep and a sizeable breakfast, Ezekiel showed them back into Bwana Chura's office.

'Ah, good morning, Miriam, good morning, Samwelli,' he smiled warmly. 'Did you sleep well?' The two guests nodded. 'I have some good news. There is a soldier here who may know where the Germans are camped. His name is Ellis Boyd. He is a friend of Mr Aitken. I have arranged for you to meet with him at 10 o'clock.'

The house felt empty. Agnes tried to keep her mind off this feeling by throwing herself into the business of the farm. It was challenging work, both physically and mentally as she had to ride out each morning to check on things, then pore over ledgers full of numbers in the afternoon and sometimes well into the evening.

Despite the demands of the work, she found it strangely satisfying and wondered how she had managed for so many years to be content sitting around doing comparatively little. She was spurred on by the thought that she had to keep things going for James. But as each day passed, she felt more and more that she was doing this for herself. The lack of news about James began to invoke a mix of feelings in her. She fretted about his well-being and yet she now worried that his return would mean she would have to go back to being a meek and mild housewife.

Every night as she went to bed, her muscles ached from the physical exhaustion of the day, or her mind buzzed with numbers from the accounts or words from contracts. But she always made time to fire off a prayer for her son's safety before falling into a fitful sleep.

She would visit Richmond's grave most evenings before dinner and update him on the day's production figures, the height of the crops, which machines needed servicing and such details. Occasionally her eye would stray over to Rosemary-Jane's grave and she would wonder what help her daughter would have been had she lived.

McCallum joined her for dinner most nights. They grew friendlier by degrees, but as far as she could see, it would never bubble over into anything more. They were both alone in this world, but there was no spark between them that could ignite a more intimate relationship. And she felt comfortable with that. She just hoped that he felt the same way.

One evening, when he couldn't make dinner, Agnes watched Hannah go about her work and suddenly remembered Miriam.

'Hannah.'

'Yes, Mrs Agnes.'

'Have you had any news of Miriam?'

'No, Mrs Agnes.'

'You must be very worried,' Agnes said, suddenly realising that her servant was in a very similar situation to her. They both had a child out there somewhere but had no news of them.

'I am sure she is all right, Mrs Agnes,' Hannah replied politely, although her face told a different story. There was concern in her eyes and a slight furrowing of the brow.

Agnes smiled gently. 'Maybe she has gone to find Mr James and look after him, she always took such good care of him.' She gave a laugh to indicate that it was a little joke, designed to help Hannah feel better. But she quickly stopped as a strange look, almost one of alarm flittered across Hannah's face before she regained control and flattened her expression. Then she gave a forced smile.

'Maybe that it is, Mam. She had always been very dedicated to her work. Should I bring in the dessert now?'

'Yes, please.'

Agnes watched her leave the room, then puzzled over the reaction she had just witnessed. What was that look of alarm? What could it possibly be? She had a strange sense that Hannah knew more about Miriam's disappearance than anyone was letting on. She had a similar sense that McCallum knew something about this too, but neither had reacted in this way until now, when James' name was mentioned in the same breath.

Her mind went back to the two of them as children. The way James, even as a toddler, had been drawn to the little black girl and how they had played as kids. There was certainly a bond there that went back to those days.

'Dessert, Mam.' Hannah interrupted her thoughts as she placed a bowl of stewed fruits on the table. 'And would you like coffee this evening?'

'Oh, no thank you, Hannah. Perhaps some tea.'

'Very good, Mam. And will you have some sherry afterwards?'

'Yes, I think I will.'

The interruption distracted her from her thoughts and she struggled to return to them as she ate her fruit. She did, however, resolve to mention James in relation to Miriam when next the opportunity arose with McCallum. She would be interested to see how he reacted.

🙎

Ellis Boyd met them in the courtyard of Bwana Chura's building. He was a short young man, about James' age with the rich brown skin that wazungu who spend lots of time in the sun acquire. His eyes were light brown with a hint of green and a touch of grey. He had an alert look to him and a face that always seemed to smile even if his mouth didn't.

'Good morning. You must be Miriam. And you, young man, must be Samwelli, the famous frog finder. Mr Loveridge could not stop singing your praises.' His voice was as smart as his uniform.

Samwelli moved a little behind his mother but smiled at the compliment.

'So, you are looking for James?' his voice became serious.

'Yes, Sir. I have been instructed…'

'Instructed nothing.' Boyd stopped her with a wave of his hand. Then he looked around the courtyard. 'I know you are his wife,' he lowered his voice.

Miriam started.

'We are good friends and he confided in me. I will do everything I can to ensure that the two of you are reunited.' He smiled. 'But we will have to keep up the pretence that you are here as a servant. I am sorry. Those further up the chain of command would not approve.'

Miriam nodded slowly.

'Right, I have some idea where the Germans are. I am not sure if James is with them, but it is very likely he is there. The best I can do is give you directions, then you are on your own. There is something I would like you to do for me if you can.'

Miriam wondered what it could be.

'Take note of everything you see. As a native woman you will be able to move around more easily than most. The Germans are not likely to question you, especially if Samwelli is with you. But can you note how many German soldiers and askari there are. What sort of defences … how is their camp guarded, what kind of weapons they have. Do they have big guns like that one?' He pointed at a cannon. 'Those sort of things. Oh, and most importantly, we need to know the layout of their camp, especially where James and the other prisoners are kept. The more we know, the better chance we have of launching a successful attack and freeing James and the others.'

Miriam nodded. She did not like the idea of helping plan an attack, but if it freed James…

'Good,' Boyd smiled. 'Right, this is where we think the Germans are camped.'

He explained in detail then, after giving them some supplies for their journey, he saw them to the door of the building where Bwana Chura and Salimu were waiting to wish them well.

'God speed, Miriam,' Bwana Chura said. 'And take good care of Samwelli. He will make a fine biologist one day.'

Miriam had no idea what a biologist was, but she smiled and nodded.

'Go well, dada,' Salimu said.

They moved off, Samwelli clinging to her hand as they walked.

The place where Mr Ellis said the Germans were was a day and a half's walk and Miriam wanted to get as far as she could before the heat of the day slowed them down.

🐰

'Tell me the truth about James and Miriam, Mr McCallum.' Agnes' voice was stern. 'What is going on there?'

McCallum shifted nervously in his chair. It was not the first time that evening he had shifted like that. The whole of dinner had been pretty uncomfortable from the moment Agnes said she had been wondering what had happened to Miriam and did he have any news.

He had managed to answer without too much problem.

'I have no idea where she is.' This was technically not a lie, so he felt comfortable with that. But when Agnes made the comment about Miriam going off to look after James, he saw through the laugh and realised that she knew, or at least suspected. He could tell by the way she watched him carefully as she laughed.

He stumbled as he said, 'I really don't think she would do that.'

'Really?' Agnes said, her laugh dried up and she looked sharply at him.

'I...I ... wouldn't know. Maybe. What makes you think...?'

Agnes did not answer but continued to stare at him.

'What possible reason...?'

She suddenly shook her head, as if dismissing a thought.

'Oh, no particular reason. It was just a thought. A joke really. Hannah is there more gravy?'

He relaxed. And that was a mistake because after serving herself more gravy, she hit him with 'Tell me the truth.' His guard had been lowered and now he had no chance to re-establish it.

He tried, without success, to rebuild his defences, but failed as he stammered and stuttered a denial of any knowledge.

'I am not a fool, Mr McCallum. Please do not treat me as one. I want you to tell me the truth now,' Agnes interjected.

He took a deep breath, realising defeat and that the time had come for him to tell all. Knowing this brought with it a calm and he knew that he had to take the story slowly, building up to the fact that the two had married and that Agnes had a grandson she knew nothing about.

'Could I have some more wine please, Hannah,' he said, giving her a resigned look.

Mr Ellis' directions were good and they came to the German camp about a day and a half later, just as he had said. The camp consisted of neat rows of tents, separated by dusty paths with a main path for the horseless vehicles to drive down. Tall wire fences surrounded the compound and, as they got closer, Miriam noticed a smaller wired off section within the main camp.

They had been passed by a few vehicles and one or two soldiers on horseback but, as Mr Ellis had predicted, they paid no attention to a native woman walking with a young boy. However, as they neared the camp, the two soldiers who stood at the gate began to take notice of them.

They seemed very young to Miriam, maybe the same age as James was when he finished at the school in Mombasa.

'What do you want?' The man who spoke had a funny accent and held his gun menacingly while the other one looked Miriam up and down in a way she did not like.

'I am looking for my husband,' she said holding Samwelli's hand tightly. Mr Ellis had suggested that she say this.

'While it is true, they will hardly think it is one of the British prisoners,' he said with a laugh. 'They will assume it is one of the askari or camp followers.'

It worked. The man with the menacing gun used it to gesture her through. He seemed to assume that Miriam knew where to go so she walked on with Samwelli in tow, hoping that they would not make a wrong turn and get into trouble.

While her impulse was to head towards the smaller wired section, she resisted and headed to the far end of the camp where she could see the native askari milling around. They could blend in there, then work out how to get to see the prisoners.

Her heart was pounding as she walked, and it felt to her as if she were dragging Samwelli along. She turned to look at her son to reassure him, thinking he was just scared, but he was looking around at everything and smiling at the German soldiers as he walked, even waving back to those who waved at him.

'Samwelli!' She gave a tug at his arm and walked straight into a soldier who was crossing the path in front of them.

'I'm so sorry...' She stopped and stared. 'Mr Carl!' she exclaimed, then quickly tried to swallow her outburst when she saw his expression.

Agnes sat on the veranda looking across the fields. A light breeze brought some relief from the growing heat of the day. In the distant sky a couple of vultures circled lazily while some small colourful birds chattered away in the nearby bushes.

She had not slept all night and the brightness and freshness of the new day was sharpened by the way it contrasted with the ethereal blur of her tiredness. She had spent the night searching for the right emotion to match her mood. But her mood was a mishmash of bitter and sweet which swirled, collided, merged, separated and merged again. 'A gallimaufry,' she said to herself, recalling a word she had read somewhere. It meant a ragout or stew or something. And that was how her thoughts felt. Numerous different ingredients bubbling in a pot, hoping to draw on each other's diverse tastes to create a new dish that was kind to the palate.

She knew there was anger in there. A lot of it. Anger at James, at Miriam, at McCallum. There was even some directed at Richmond. It was his responsibility to guide their son in these matters, steer him clear of such pitfalls. The worst though, was the anger at herself. There had been signs, but she chose to ignore them. She was being unfair on herself, she knew, and resented the self-accusation. How can defence and prosecution live in the same consciousness?

The anger sat at the opposite end of her mind to a sentimentality born out of her love of romance novels and her own loveless marriage. From McCallum's description, James had found true love. If one could neutralise the skin tones of the hero and heroine, it would make for a good story. But this went deeper than pigmentation. Miriam was from 'below stairs' and Agnes had never read a novel where the lovers met on the landing.

And then there was the child. Samuel, was it? She couldn't quite remember the name that McCallum had dropped into the maelstrom of information. She could not, for the life of her, picture the child she must have seen so often, clinging to Miriam as she worked. The child did not even feature as a faceless being or as a sort of presence in her memories. It was only Miriam who featured and even then, she realised, she did not have a proper picture of the girl in her mind anymore. There was a kind of image, but its focus had been dulled by servanthood.

'She is your daughter-in-law and their child is your grandson,' she said the words out loud as if somehow this would bring their faces into focus. But they had no effect.

She let her words disperse with the breeze while she gazed over her garden. Her tiredness felt metallic, as if the bitterness of the coffee beans that grew in the surrounding fields was running through her veins. She closed her eyes and relaxed her body. She needed to drain her mind of thoughts, deconstruct all her emotions and then rebuild them from the start and try and find a new path through all this.

She must have dozed off as the next thing she knew was becoming aware of someone standing near her.

'Will madam be wanting some lunch?' Hannah asked when she opened her eyes.

She took a moment to orientate herself, then looked blankly at her servant before the question reached the processing part of her brain.

'Yes. Please, Hannah.' Her voice sounded defeated but as Hannah moved off and the grimy remnants of her nap melted, she felt a clarity growing inside her. Despite the sense of betrayal she felt at the moment, she knew that her son was all she had left in this world. If she truly loved him, she would have to work through all the issues she had with this marriage. It may take time, but she had to get herself to a position where she not just appeared to be, but was actually fully at ease with it. It was either that or become an embittered old woman, alone and friendless.

As she stood to go inside for her lunch, she glanced again at the farm and saw McCallum riding out to the fields. 'It's not just James I have to forgive,' she said to herself as she turned and went inside.

ё

'Miriam?' Carl, after his initial annoyance at having someone bump into him, suddenly recognised her.

'Mr Carl,' she said meekly, unsure what he was doing here and even more unsure how he would react to her presence.

'What are you doing here?' he asked then, realising the reason, he nodded. 'I can't believe that mother sent you. Actually, I can believe it.' He looked at her in a way that told her she needed to play along.

She gave the slightest nod and said, quite loudly, 'Yes, Mr Carl. Your mother said I must come. And I have brought Samwelli,' she added, hoping that her son would realise the need to continue the lie.

'Hello Samwelli,' Carl said and smiled.

'Hello, Mr Carl,' Samwelli's voice was shy. 'It is good to see you again, Sir.'

Carl took a quick look round the camp and Miriam followed his glance. None of the other soldiers seemed to be taking much notice of them.

'You must be exhausted. Do you need food? Something to drink?' His voice was quieter now.

'Some water, and a little to eat, if you have to spare.'

'I'll take you to the servants' area and sort you out, then we can talk in my tent.'

He took them to the far end of the camp where the natives were and instructed one of them to see to their needs.

'Bring her to me when they are finished,' he commanded as he walked off.

Once they had eaten, the man who had been told to look after them motioned for her to follow. She felt ill at ease leaving Samwelli, but he had already made friends with the askari and was busy helping one of them shine his boots as she was led off to Mr Carl's tent. It was one of the bigger ones which told her that Mr Carl must be quite important. There was a desk and a cot with a small trunk at its foot. Clothes were strewn around the place and a mess of papers covered the desk that Carl sat behind.

'Ah, Miriam. I am glad that you are here,' he said looking up. 'This tent is in desperate need of cleaning.'

Miriam knew that he was saying this for show, but still set about tidying the tent.

'You don't have to do that,' Carl said after her escort had left them.

'It is fine, Mr Carl,' she smiled. 'I want to do this. Also, it will be good in case someone comes by.'

Carl nodded, then a shadow came over his face. 'James is here. He is in with the prisoners. But it is not good.'

Miriam stopped her work and looked at him. 'Has he been shot?'

'No. He is not wounded, but he is very ill.'

'Ill?'

Carl shook his head sadly. 'His water has turned black.'

'Black?' Miriam did not understand.

'It is what they call Black Water Fever. It is some form of malaria or something like that.'

Miriam nodded. 'Can they give him medicine for it?'

Carl sighed. 'There is medicine, but it doesn't always work. And there is not enough for everyone. Germans get it first.'

Miriam stared at him. Her heart felt as if it had been tied into a tight knot. She could see from his face that things were not good.

'Is he going to die?' The question seemed to float into the tent from an unseen source.

Carl shook his head. 'I do not know, Miriam. I do not know.'

'Can I see him?' It was her voice this time.

'It will not be easy to see him alone, but I will try and arrange things.'

Miriam nodded. 'Thank you, Mr Carl,' she said and wiped the tears off her cheeks.

A week later Ellis Boyd and a regiment of King's African Rifles walked into the camp. The Germans had been chased off, Carl narrowly escaping death as a bullet passed within inches of his head as he galloped away.

The prisoners were left behind. Ellis found Miriam at James' bedside, almost oblivious to the commotion of the battle, her husband's hand in hers. Samwelli sat quietly on the floor nearby, a serious look on his face.

'Get the medic,' Ellis instructed an underling. 'Quickly!'

The medic came and checked James' temperature, looked for a pulse, then pulled one of James' eyelids up. He shook his head. 'I am sorry, Sir.' he said, giving Miriam a quizzical look.

'Thank you. Leave us, please.' Ellis said.

When they were alone, he stood for a moment, then gently touched Miriam's shoulder. 'Miriam,' his voice was soft.

She seemed startled by his presence, as if she had not heard him come in nor seen the medic examine James.

'Come. There is nothing you can do now.' He helped her to her feet, but her legs buckled and he had to grab her to stop her falling.

Samwelli gave a slight gasp and moved to stand, but then sank back as Ellis eased his mother onto an adjacent cot where she sat with her head in her hands.

'Have you had food? Water?' Ellis asked her.

'We have had a little, not much, Sir,' Samwelli answered as Miriam remained unmoved.

Ellis nodded. 'I will be back shortly,' he said, turning and headed out the tent. He returned a short while later along with a young native man who carried a tray with two plates of food and some water.

'Make sure she eats,' he said to Samwelli. 'I have to go and sort some things out but will be back soon.'

The other man put the tray down and left.

Samwelli moved to his mother's side. 'Ma, you must eat. Please.' He picked up a plate and handed it to her. She took a few moments before finally taking it from him and then began to eat, chewing slowly. The food seemed to melt her dazed state and as she ate, she gained some strength. Seeing the improvement in her, Samwelli began to eat his own food.

When Ellis returned, the plates were empty and Miriam was busy tidying them onto the tray.

'He died this morning, not long before the fighting came,' Miriam said, then added, 'Blackwater.'

Ellis nodded. 'A dreadful thing, blackwater. We have lost many men to it.'

They were silent for a bit, then Ellis said, 'We will arrange a burial and get word to his parents.'

Miriam nodded.

'What will you do?' he asked after another pause.

Miriam shook her head. 'I do not know. I can't go back to the farm. Not until the fighting has stopped.'

'Why not?' Ellis asked.

Miriam looked at him. 'I...I just can't,' she said then, feeling that she owed Ellis some more, said, 'There is someone there that would, I do not know the right English words. They would want me?'

She looked at Ellis who nodded slowly.

'While James was around, that person would not touch me, but...' She left it there.

'I see,' Ellis said, 'But you said you may return after the war?'

'Mrs Aitken, James' mother, would also protect me by being there. But she is in Mombasa because of the war.'

'I understand,' Ellis said, nodding. 'Okay. Let me talk to a few people and I will see if you can stay with us until the war is done. Can you cook?'

'My mother is the best cook, Mr Ellis,' Samwelli said before Miriam had a chance to answer.

'Then I am sure I will have no problems getting my superiors to agree to you staying with us.'

The Reverend Smith rode out to the farm along with his wife to deliver the news to Agnes. She took it better than they expected.

'A mother knows,' she said as they sat on the veranda drinking tea. 'The day he died, I felt something. I don't quite know how to describe it, but it was like a sharp pain in my soul. And I knew then that something had happened.' She stopped to sob quietly while Mrs Smith put an arm around her.

They stayed late into the afternoon, waiting for McCallum to return from the field and his work. The Scot did not notice the Smiths until he was starting to climb the stairs to the veranda. He stopped on the lower steps as he saw Agnes' face.

'James?' It was barely audible.

The Reverend Smith nodded as he came down to greet McCallum and caught him just as his legs buckled. He then helped the Scot up the stairs and guided him into a chair.

'Ach, not James.' He shook his head, then reached out and took Agnes' hand. 'I am so sorry, Mrs Aitken.'

Agnes gave a sad smile. 'He loved his Uncle Malcolm dearly. You were like a second father to him in many ways.'

The two of them stared out across the lawn, lost in their memories of James.

'Will you be all right, Agnes? Or do you want me to stay the night,' Judith Smith asked when Agnes finally stirred and gently took her hand back from McCallum.

'Thank you, Judith. I think I will be fine.'

Judith nodded, then turned to her husband. 'We had better be going if we are to get back to Voi before it gets dark.'

The Reverend Smith agreed. 'We will arrange a memorial service for James,' he said as they took their leave.

Agnes thanked them for everything they had done, then watched as their wagon trundled off down the long road. As she and McCallum walked back to the house, she said, 'Will you sleep in the main house tonight, Mr McCallum. My life feels very empty right now. I don't want an empty house to add to that feeling. Hannah can make up the guest bedroom.'

'Of course,' McCallum replied. 'I am grateful for the offer, as I am not sure I want to spend a night in my own empty house.'

Agnes took his arm in hers and they walked back up to the veranda together.

Over the next few weeks, Agnes threw herself into the work of the farm, battering the pain she felt into submission by tiring her body and mind so that she could not think about her situation. She would fall asleep at the dinner table and McCallum would carry her to her room where Hannah would prepare her for bed.

The guest room became McCallum's new home as he looked after the bruised soul of his employer. In the evenings, after having put Agnes to bed, he would sit out on the veranda. He would not light the lanterns, preferring the softness of the dark, letting it smooth the rough edges of his daylight thoughts.

He worried about Agnes but knew that he could do nothing but support her. He was sure, given time, she would pull through this, but the ragged uncertainty of what she would do once she recovered, gnawed at his mind. Would she keep the farm, or sell up and move to Voi, Mombasa, or even back to England? Where would that leave him?

He also thought about Miriam and Samwelli, wondering where they were. Had they found James before he died. Were they even alive? There was a war on out there, anything could have happened.

Then at times, when he could not face the thoughts of Agnes or Miriam, his mind would go back to Zilpah and the news she had given him about his daughter. Perhaps, he thought, if Agnes did decide to sell up, he would go in search of his daughter and maybe even try and find Jana, her mother.

The days merged, the heat melting one into another. Despite their best efforts, the farm suffered, but this was more a consequence of the war than from anything lacking in their work. The farm produced a bumper crop which they ended up having to destroy most of as the local market was small and the ships that would have taken it to Europe, were either carrying troops or the owners did not want to risk them on trips around the tip of Africa,

McCallum arranged for a portion of the fields to be given over to subsistence farming where he planted some corn and vegetables for the table. They also managed to get some chickens and goats which provided milk, eggs and the occasional treat of a roast.

To them the war had become a murmur in the background, taking place on the other side of the country and in far off Europe. Its long tentacles touched them via headlines that reached out but were so stretched that they could not curl around them to fully grip their attention.

Then one evening, McCallum got a message from Zilpah, asking him to come and see her. The next morning, he saddled up and rode out to the servants' village. Zilpah sat outside her hut surrounded by a few women who chatted away as they set about their various daily tasks. Some young children played nearby but, on seeing McCallum approach, they stopped to watch the mzungu.

He greeted Zilpah who invited him to sit on a small bench and offered him some water which he gratefully accepted. They spoke generally, as was the custom, asking about each other's family and friends, commenting on how generous the land had been this year and even touched on the white man's war.

Zilpah gave condolences for the passing of James and noted that one of the young men from the village who had gone off to be an askari would also never be coming back.

All the time McCallum wondered why he had been invited here. But he knew that he could not rush things. Africa had its own way of keeping time. It was not something you tried to stetch or shorten. Here time was born a certain length and it was not for you to try and change it.

Eventually, once time was ready for them, Zilpah got around to the reason for her invite.

'Someone has come to the village who would like to meet you,' she said. There was a hint of a smile in her eyes as she gave him the news, but the rest of her face remained impassive.

McCallum's heart jumped in his chest. 'My daughter?' he barely heard his own question as the blood thundered in his ears and emotion tried to throttle the words as they escaped.

Zilpah shook her head, then called out, 'Jana.'

McCallum felt a trembling start inside him that he could not control. He tried to rise to his feet as he watched a woman emerge from the hut. There was a shyness to her, yet she held herself proudly. She was dressed in the colourful attire reserved for special occasions.

Her body was older than the one he held in his memory, but the face, and in particular the eyes, did not seem to have aged. There was still the gentleness about them that had first attracted him to her and that was unchanged.

He searched for her name while struggling to his feet but found that it was hidden under the rubble of shock and emotion. He wanted to rush over and take her in his arms yet was held back by some unseen force.

He cleared his throat and at last managed to speak, her name coming out in a hoarse whisper. 'Jana, dear God, it is really you?'

Agnes re-looked at the page of numbers. They did not tell a good story. The farm was keeping its head above water, but only just. They would have to make further sacrifices to stay that way, but she was hard pressed to see what else they could forego.

She pushed the accounts away from her and sat back, rubbing her eyes. Then she noticed the photograph of James on the desk.

'Oh, my son,' she said, 'you would have been proud of how I have kept the farm going. But I am getting to my wits' end. I need to continue as I have nowhere else to go.' She pushed a strand of hair out of her face. The air in the office was close and she felt the sticky sweat breaking out on her brow. She needed some air.

Closing the books, she made her way onto the veranda where a slight breeze cooled her face. She breathed deeply, taking some of the breeze into her lungs.

It was then that she noticed the dust trail of the wagon coming up the long road. She had not expected McCallum back from Voi so soon and he would never travel that fast. Her heart caught in her chest. Who was this coming to the farm and why were they in such a hurry? For a second, she thought something had happened to McCallum, but the wagon was already beginning to come into focus and she recognised the Scot's hat.

'Why is he in such a rush?' she muttered under her breath. 'The fool, he will do himself an injury.'

The wagon was much closer now and McCallum was waving his hat and shouting something, but she could not quite make out what. However, the excitement was clear in his voice. It was good news, whatever it was.

'It's over!' she could hear the words now. 'The war is over!'

She gripped the railing of the veranda. Could this be true? Was the war really over?

'It's over, Mrs Aitken!' the cry came again as the wagon reached the edge of the garden. McCallum slowed as he guided the horses along the driveway and stopped on the gravel just at the bottom of the stairs. He was flushed from the exertion of his race home, but his eyes were alight with joy and a huge smile split his face.

'Is it true?' Agnes asked. She dared not believe it even though it was as obvious as the joy on his face.

'Yes, it's true. All over. Here and in Europe. The Germans surrendered somewhere in Northern Rhodesia, a place called Abercorn.'

'That is wonderful news,' Agnes exclaimed, the reality finally sinking in. The farm could flourish again, the markets, both domestic and in Europe, would start to open up. She could stay.

'That is wonderful news,' she repeated.

'Yes, it is. Now, if you will excuse me, I must go and tell Jana.'

'Yes, yes of course.' Agnes nodded and watched him expertly guide the wagon round and head off, thoughts swirling and crashing inside her head.

The war, that faceless beast that had taken her son from her, had finally been defeated. This conflict which had slowly strangled the farm, had now released its grip on her livelihood. She felt she was floating as she processed all that the news meant. But while she was floating, something was rooting her to where she stood. She looked down and saw her hands still gripping the railing tightly. With a small smile, she slowly released her grip, enjoying the sensation of freedom as she did so.

She turned and went inside, 'Hannah! Hannah!' she called. 'The war is over, Hannah,' she said as the servant appeared.

Hannah nodded but showed no excitement. 'That is good, Mam,' she said. 'Would you like some tea?'

Agnes took a moment, her thoughts knocked sideways by Hannah's lack of joy.

'Are you not happy, Hannah?' she asked. 'The war. It is finished.'

'I am happy for you, Mam,' then in a rare moment of confidence she added, 'This was a wazungu war, Mam. I am happy for the wazungu. But the African people have suffered greatly because of it.' She stopped suddenly as if reminding herself of her station. Then she repeated, 'Would you like some tea, Mam?'

Agnes was a little shaken by the boldness of Hannah's statement and thought to rebuke her servant, but then stopped herself.

'Yes, please, Hannah. On the veranda.'

As she sat waiting for the tea, she replayed Hannah's words over in her head. She could not deny the truth in them. It had been a white man's war. A European conflict that had torn a strip across this vast continent, thousands of miles from the epicentre of its cause. She wondered what other natives felt about the war. Was Hannah's view widely held amongst them?

She thought of McCallum and Jana and their against the odds and against all traditions love. Her sensible British upbringing told her that she should not be allowing this affair to carry on so openly on the farm. The other settlers would not approve of it. But then she thought of James and Miriam and how her son had been deprived of happiness because of the views of others. She knew that Richmond, the man who, for a few moments of pleasure, denied her the life she had dreamed of as a young woman. How much of James' secrecy about Miriam was because of his fear of Richmond's reaction and how much did he fear his mother's views.

She like to think that it was all Richmond but knew that she was just as guilty. James would have worried about Richmond's anger but just as much worried about her disappointment.

She sighed. 'You should be feeling happy, the war is over,' she told herself. She looked out at the coffee fields then at the gentle hills beyond them and finally her eyes took in the brilliant blue sky. She breathed in the air which mixed dust, coffee, woodsmoke and earthy wildlife smells into an intoxicating scent made clear-edged by the light of the sun. It smelt of home.

'You are happy,' she said this out loud. 'This land has slowly saturated your soul. It has crawled under your skin, and you are comfortable with that.' She stood and walked over to the two gravestones around the back of the house.

'I am going to stay, Richmond. This land has taken you, Rosemary-Jane and now James. But I have come to love this place. I now understand how you loved your work farming here. I have touched the soil with my own hands. I have checked on the coffee beans as they grow and have watched as they are roasted. I have also seen the beauty of this land. The clarity of the light, the rich browns and reds of the soil, and the grace of the strange animals that wander around here.

'And the people, Richmond. I don't think that you could ever look beyond the prejudices we brought with us from England and see the beauty of the people here. There are many gentle souls who we never got to know because we could not see beyond the skin colour and our preconceived ideas. But I have now spent some time with Jana, Mr McCallum's ... his love interest. She has been living on the farm these last few months.

'She came back because she heard about James and Miriam and hoped that she could be reunited with McCallum. I don't think that you could ever understand that kind of love, Richmond. You cared for me, but never loved me as a husband should love a wife. And the feeling was mutual. I cared for you but never loved you as a wife should love a husband. In fact, I hated you for dragging me here, but now I would not have it any other way.'

She looked from Richmond's grave to Rosemary-Jane's. Then slowly nodded to herself. 'I don't know why I am telling you all this. Maybe now you can understand.'

She turned to go, then stopped and looked back at the gravestones. 'My only wish now is that I could see Miriam again and meet my grandson properly. I need to make things right for James. You can haunt me if you don't like it, but I will welcome them into my home if they ever come back.'

She stood a moment, waiting to see if Richmond responded then smiled and walked back to the house. There was a lightness in her step.

It was two months after the war ended that they came. Agnes was in the fields with McCallum discussing the preparations for next year's crop and whether they should consider extending the field a little or if it was too soon to know how markets would recover post-war.

There was a light breeze which brought some relief to the heat of the day. Agnes had taken to wearing culottes, something that she would never have dreamed of doing earlier. But now found that, not only was it becoming more fashionable for women, but they were also extremely practical for horse riding and other farm work.

It was McCallum who first noticed the visitors arrive.

'Hello, who can this be?' he said shading his eyes to get a better look.

Agnes wiped the sweat from her brow with the back of her hand and pushed a loose strand of hair behind her ears before shading her eyes too.

As the wagon got closer, McCallum stared and then said, 'My goodness, I do believe that is Carl Muller.'

'Carl?' Agnes peered at the new arrivals and then said, 'I think you may be right. But who is he with?'

McCallum shrugged. 'We'd better get ready to meet them, whoever they are.'

They hurriedly splashed water on their faces and Agnes patted her hair into place as best she could as they mounted their horses and rode out to meet the wagon.

'It is Carl,' Agnes said as they drew nearer and she waved.

Carl waved back and spurred the horses on a little.

'Is that Miriam in the back?' McCallum suddenly asked, his voice catching.

Agnes stared, suddenly aware that, what she had taken to be just another servant, may just be her son's widow. She found that she could not respond to McCallum, her voice suddenly damned up with emotion.

As if by some sort of unspoken signal, they both stopped. There seemed to be an invisible barrier that had sprung up between them and the approaching wagon. Carl continued to wave and they could hear his hollered greeting wafting over the field.

Agnes felt a whirlpool of emotions hurtling around in her head, making her dizzy. Her hands tightened on the horn of her saddle to steady herself.

'Is the boy with them?' her voice was barely a whisper.

'I cannae see the laddie,' McCallum replied as he strained his eyes to try and find Samwelli.

A horrible fear gripped Agnes. She felt as if a strong hand was strangling her heart, slowly squeezing it. She shook her head, 'No, I will not let it be,' she said. 'I cannot lose my grandson before I get to know him. This land has taken too much from me, it owes me this one life.' She dug her heels into the flanks of her horse and began to gallop towards the wagon.

Miriam felt uncomfortable sitting on the veranda. Even more so when her aunt Zilpah appeared carrying the tray with the tea. She looked nervously across at Agnes who smiled back and nodded as if to say, 'It's all right.' Zilpah also gave her a reassuring smile.

'He was already quite ill when we captured his unit,' Carl was telling Agnes about James' last days. 'But we made him as comfortable as we could. Of course when Miriam came he perked up tremendously. He knew he was dying, but I'll never forget the look on his face when he saw her and Samwelli.' He glanced across at Miriam and smiled. 'And then when Samwelli called him father for the first time, there were tears in his eyes. Tell Mrs Aitken what you said, Samwelli.'

The young lad moved closer to his mother, his head bowed with shyness at the sudden attention.

'Go on, Samwelli. You can tell me.' Agnes prompted gently.

'I asked him if he had been dancing with the monkeys.'

'Why did you ask that?' Agnes probed.

'Because...' he looked at Miriam who nodded, '...because my mother always told me that my father was dancing with the monkeys.'

Carl laughed and Agnes smiled.

'And what did your father say?' Carl asked.

'He said that he and my mother had been dancing with the monkeys when they made me.'

Agnes' hand went to her mouth to stifle the giggle that arose in her.

Samwelli looked at her and grinned, but his face said that he did not really understand exactly what was so funny about it.

'I am glad that you, both of you,' Agnes took in Miriam and Samwelli with her look, 'were there with him. And you too, Carl.'

Carl nodded, then looked sad. 'I am afraid I had to abandon him at the very end. Ellis and his crew were too strong for us. We had to leave in a hurry. But I knew that Miriam would take care of him.'

Agnes turned to Ellis who had been sitting quietly to one side, an outsider to this reunion.

'Thank you too, Mr Boyd. At least he did not die a prisoner.' There was no accusation towards Carl in her voice.

Ellis nodded.

The sky was beginning to turn bruise purple as dusk approached.

'I will be going on south tomorrow,' Carl said. 'I am so anxious to see Kate and Heinrich.'

Agnes nodded. 'We'll be sad to see you go, but your family needs you.' She thought for a moment then added, 'Tell Kate...' she searched for the right words. 'Tell her I am sorry I was not the best hostess. I was so worried about James that I forgot she would just as worried about you.'

Carl smiled. 'Thank you, Mrs Aitken. Kate will appreciate that. I think that she would want you to know that she understood. She wrote to me saying that she wished her presence here did not have to remind you so much of the enemy and she hoped that you could be friends once the war was over.'

'I would like that very much,' Agnes said. 'Mr Boyd, what are your plans,' she asked after a moment's silence.

'I am not sure, Mam. My father died just before the war and my mother died giving birth to me, so I have no family. My father was a dentist in Mombasa, but I have no training in that profession.'

'We could always use some help on the farm, laddie, if you are interested,'

McCallum said. He looked across at Agnes who nodded her support of the idea.

Ellis thought for a moment, then said, 'Yes, I think I might enjoy that.'

Miriam opened the door to the small house where she and James had lived as secret man and wife. Much to her surprise, Mrs Aitken had said that she and Samwelli could continue to live there. She felt trapped. Not quite European enough to sit comfortably on the veranda sipping tea, but now not native enough to return to the village.

Samwelli busied himself with unpacking their meagre belongings and sorted out the bedrooms, seeming to be unaware of his mother's inner turmoil.

There was a soft tapping at the door and Miriam found her mother there. They embraced warmly, the first time they had been able to do so since her return. Samwelli made them some tea and they sat out on the little bench at the back of the house.

'It will be difficult now, my daughter. You are in a half world. Partly in the world where you grew up and partly in the wazungu world. One world is a foreign land to you and the other is one you know so well. The two worlds will pull at you from either side.'

They were quiet for a while, then Hannah continued, 'But you are a strong woman. Stronger than any I have ever known. You travelled across this land, a land at war, to be with your husband. The new half world will be a different journey, but you will find a way through it.'

Miriam's smile was part sad at the prospect of the struggles that lay ahead, but part of it saw the truth in her mother's words. What lay ahead was another journey.

Samwelli came out to join them. He cuddled up to his mother and she hugged him close. He looked up at her and in that moment she realised that she would not be on the journey on her own.